Gone

Anna Bloom

Dear Camnnie

Thank you for your inspiring words!

Much love

Anna Bloom

Copyright © 2014 Anna Bloom
All rights reserved.

ISBN-13: 978-1499712148
ISBN-10: 1499712146

DEDICATION

For my sister and best friend.

CONTENTS

Acknowledgments	i
Fourteen Days to Go	4
Thirteen Days to Go	12
Twelve Days to Go	46
Eleven Days to Go	78
Ten Days to Go	111
Nine Days to Go	133
Eight Days to Go	170
Seven Days to Go	195
Six Days to Go	229
Five Days to Go	252
Four Days to Go	293
Three Days to Go	329
Two Days to Go	353
One Day to Go	372
Gone	383

ACKNOWLEDGMENTS

This book started out as what should have been an easy write. A tale about two weeks on the beach. It turned into something so much more. I ended covering many sensitive subjects that mean a lot to me. I rewrote the manuscript three times in a bid to get it right.

We live in such a small world these days you would think something as vile as bullying could no longer take place. But it does. Worse perhaps because of the technology we all use in our daily lives. Whether it be by Social Media, email or in the classroom and playground like in days past, bullying is wrong.
My hope is that books like this will inspire young people to take control of their lives and come out from under the shadow that being bullied creates.
This book is for all who have been affected by bullying.
Thank you to all the amazing people who helped this book become what it is. You know who you are.

Gone

LONDON

London

1st August 2013

Dear E,

Remember how you always said that one day I would push Dad too far. Remember how you said that I would always need you about to make sure it didn't happen, to keep me on the straight and narrow.

It finally happened. I'm in two minds about whether you should have been there. You would have gone mental. I would even have shocked you. But in a way I'm glad you weren't around to see my lowest moment. I've got another new name. Facebook went crazy. Dad shut it down in the end. I didn't even know he knew how to do that. He said he didn't want me seeing it, but what I think he meant was that he didn't want Emily to see it. I don't either.

Mum's been crying non-stop. It's killing me to hear it. Death by a million teardrops. I wish I could cry. I haven't shed a tear since the night you left. I haven't really done anything since you left. I've barely even left my room. Well you know that. I've written you every day. Yesterday I decided to venture out and it ended in disaster. Bad. Bad disaster.

Now we're moving. I don't have the address yet. I don't even know where we are going. No one is really telling me anything but as soon as I know, I will write you and let you know. It's probably going to be the Outer Hebrides or something. Oh God, Mum and Dad are going to make me live in the Highlands to try and keep me out of trouble.

I've promised them I'm going to do it. For two weeks I am going to prove to them that I'm not always going to justify the names people call me. Dad says if I manage it he will pay my Uni fees. I need that money, E. I need to escape.

It's just two weeks. I can do that can't I? What do you think?

Miss you.
B.
x

FOURTEEN DAYS TO GO

Rebecca

"Josh, come on! Don't be such a girl."

I grind an elbow into warm sand as I lean up to find out who Josh is, and why he is a girl.

Instantly I feel on edge. There are six guys running down the beach, surf boards under their arms.

I don't want to talk to anyone, or even be seen by anyone. I was just looking for some peace and quiet.

I should have stayed in my room. That way I can't hurt anyone and no one can hurt me.

I breathe a sigh of relief as five of the guys dive straight into the sea, completely ignoring my exposed spot on the sand. Then I offer myself a rueful laugh as I realise that these people are used to seeing strangers on a beach. I won't hold any interest for them, yet. Not until they realise who I am and the rumour mill starts up again. I will be long gone by then.

It's the bastard thing about Social Media. It's impossible for people not to find out who you are.

No matter how much you might want them not to.

Facebook is the bane of my life. I know I've made mistakes. I don't need status updates about it.

I wonder which label will attach itself to me first?

I'm a girl with lots of labels and I'm not talking about current fashion trends.

Allowing myself a slow exhalation of air I repeat the words that are currently keeping me going. *I will be gone soon.* Soon enough.

I watch as the six guys, splash through the waves keeping their wetsuits rolled down, giving me what would be an arresting eyeful of toned abs, if my eyes weren't distracted by something else. The sixth one.

Josh, the girl.

He doesn't look that girly to me. He looks broad-shouldered and golden. More than that, he has long thick dreadlocks loosely tied in a band at the base of his neck. There is something totally mesmerising about them.

I don't want to be interested, because I don't do the whole drooling over guys thing, but I can't prevent myself from shifting onto both my elbows, to get a closer look. While his friends all circle the water like sharks on their boards, his focus is only on the sand. He snatches up a stick and starts to doodle.

I watch him for an age. He never takes his eyes off the sand, which he scores with purposeful and graceful strokes. I completely forget that I am even sitting on a beach, surrounded by strange men. I slide my glasses up onto the top of my head so I can see him clearly without an orange tint.

What is he drawing?

For the first time in two weeks I find myself interested in something, anything, other than the bad stuff I have in my head. I edge up off the sand, ready to move down the beach to try and find out what he is creating. Before I can come up with a reason to walk down by the water's edge, he jumps up and throws down the stick, sliding one foot across the drawing. As he turns to pick up his wetsuit, his eyes flick over in my direction. He gazes at me for a long moment, his face motionless, before slowly lifting one half of his mouth at me.

Damn it. My glasses are still on my head and he can clearly see me, open mouthed and fixated. I wouldn't exactly say I am drooling over him. More intrigued by the doodling, and maybe the dreadlocks.

I can't help it. Even though I know he knows I am watching him, my eyes stay focused on him as he slides his feet into his wetsuit and stretches it up his thighs. He is just about to start zipping his suit when I see a flash of a tattoo on his hip, just under the waist band of his board shorts.

I want to know what that tattoo is, almost as much as I want to know what he was drawing in the sand. But I know I'm not going to find out.

What would I say to him?

"Hi. My name is Rebecca. My parents brought me here because I'm a very bad girl and need to be kept from temptation..."

Yeah, that's just never going to happen.

I hang about for another couple of minutes and

watch him run out into the sea, he quickly paddles past his friends, which makes them jeer as he starts looking for a wave to ride.

With a sigh I start to put my boots on and gather my stuff. I brush the sand from my skin, watching it fly into the air like miniscule beads of glass catching the light. I keep my eyes firmly away from the sea and its occupants as I turn and head back up the path to the beach car park. It's time to head back to the cottage for my daily bollocking. I may as well get it over with.

In two weeks I will be leaving this town, just as quickly as I arrived. I'm going to go somewhere where no one knows me, where no one will ever know me, and I'm going to leave my family to live their lives in peace without me. My only hope is that I manage to make it through the two weeks without anyone asking me why I am here, and just why it is that I have to leave again so soon.

Joshua

Doodling in the Sand

It's one of my favourite past times. Doodling in the sand. You can draw anything, and then a few minutes later it will be completely erased. No record of it to be found anywhere. I sometimes wonder what life would be like if we had that ability with our memories. Wash and erase.

Today I have drawn butterflies. Ironic really; beautiful sweeping butterflies with their freedom to fly and me unable to deal with my broken heart and set myself free.

Dan and others are larging it about in the sea. There is a girl on the beach by herself, so they have gone into a masculine over drive of flexing to try and impress her. I didn't bother looking at her that closely as we walked to our rock, the rock we have sat by for five years as we all learnt to surf and drink sea water. I could see a bikini clad body flat against the sand but that is all I registered. I really dislike holiday makers and try to avoid them at all costs.

Dan declared that she was an easy 7.5 with the possibility of an eight, if she stood up and they could confirm her body was as hot as they assumed it would be.

My friends are such charmers. It is a complete miracle that they don't have girlfriends. Out of the six of us I'm the only one that really ever has, but she is gone now and I am still dealing with losing her. Dan along with the others, and even Andrew to a degree make use of the holiday makers. That's not really my style. They have a six week shag fest, where they hike it out to Newquay every night to mingle with the wasted teenagers all enjoying a 'surfing' holiday. A surfing holiday that normally only involves one type of exercise on the sand. Sex.

I did one summer, and I'm still trying to forget about it. Now, I sit back and laugh waiting for one of the gang to panic because he may have caught an STD, or worse, got a girl pregnant because the sandy condom ripped. Or because they were too drunk to even use one.

This morning I had to do a shift at Aunt May's shop. So let's just rephrase that to, 'this morning I had to spend three hours counting pencils.' It never used to be like that. I started working there two years ago to earn some money, but really I spent all my time using up Aunt May's stock, as I painted my way through a wall full of canvasses. She stopped paying me in the end. I can't really blame her. Oil paints are really expensive.

I don't paint anymore though, so I guess I should ask for some form of financial reimbursement for my pencil counting.

I'm supposed to be going to Art College in a few

weeks, but I can't see the point of it. Does an artist who can't draw anymore, unless it is doodles in the sand, deserve a place at an Art College? I don't think so. I'm never going to be a huge success. I'm gonna have to come up with something else to do.

Even thinking about it is enough to make a guy depressed. I throw my stick in the sand and jump up, brushing the sand from my legs as I turn to get my wet suit.

The holiday maker is leaning up on her elbows staring at me. Her gaze is steady and intent like she may be contemplating something, and it makes me hesitate. The moment of hesitation allows me to inspect her closer. Her colour is like none I have ever seen. All gold like the sun.

For a split-second I get caught off guard and my brain goes into some crazy free-fall where I find myself thinking of what oil colours I would need to blend to get that depth of gold. But then I remember that it really doesn't matter because I don't paint anymore. Even if I did, holiday makers just come and go, leaving a carnage of destruction in their wake. I won't need to worry about not being able to blend the perfect oils to make that iridescent gold, because I won't see her again. And if I had to be honest I don't want to see her again. Anyone or anything that makes me think about painting is not welcome on my beach, or my village for that matter. Technically I know it's not mine, it's probably the opposite. The village owns me, and that's why I will never leave. I can't leave the ghosts that haunt me behind. I know I have to stay here and live my life with them.

It's only as I'm sitting on my board out on the waves that I see her get up from her spot on the sand. After struggling into a pair of what look from the distance like biker boots, she stretches up, and curves her back into a graceful arc, her long limbs stretching for the heavens. The sun glints off her hair and I find myself momentarily side tracked. A massive wave smacks into me, nearly wiping me out. I can hear Dan laughing in the distance. "Josh, you are such a dick," but I concentrate on keeping the board straight and not going over. I have just righted myself and stabilised the board when I find her on the beach again. Relaxing her pose, she runs her fingertips under the string of her bikini, removing some grains of sand. Something about the actions makes a flicker of recognition spark to life inside me. *What is that?*

Dan has completely underrated her. She is at least a nine. I watch the sun bounce off her red hair as she stomps back off towards the car park. She oozes attitude. I find myself smiling a little, I kind of like it. Although it's just as well she is a holiday maker. That attitude shit does not go down well around here. Believe me I should know.

THIRTEEN DAYS TO GO

Bridge Cottage
St Agnes
Cornwall

14th August 2014

Dear E,

Please note the address! Not Scotland! The absolute other end of the country. It's the smallest village I've ever seen. No joke. You know when I promised Mum and Dad that I would behave for two weeks. I think basically they decided to limit the chances of me getting into trouble by moving two hundred and fifty miles to nowhere. I've been allocated the room in the attic – the furthest room from the rest of the family. . . No !

You'd love it! I've got my own shower, although the pipes make the whole place vibrate when you turn the taps and the hot water only lasts ten minutes.

While everyone else unpacked I snuck off to the beach. I'm not going to lie, it was very pretty, but that just made me hate it even more. I didn't want anyone to see me, or *know that we had moved here. I'm pretty sure it won't take long for the rumours to follow me. Things were pretty bad back at home before we left. I'm not worried about what people think about me. I just want Emily to have a fresh start here. Mum and Dad should have left me behind when they moved, that way they would never have to be associated with me in their new home. I tried to tell them, but they weren't having it.*

We are still having 'Family Healing Time' like that mental Counsellor told us to do, you know, after you left. It still results in a full out screaming match. Last night they asked me if I couldn't leave my bangles at the old home! How rude! I just screamed that they should have left me behind instead. Mum's worried my clothes are going to offend the locals. Personally I think my outfit is the last thing they are going to be interested in.

I also told Mum and Dad that Emily would end up a crack whore in a town this small. I'm sure someone once told us that drugs were rifer in seaside towns than in London. Maybe I made that up. It had an effect anyway. I got sent to my room!

Anyway! Oh God, that's what I was trying to tell you . . . when I was at the beach, there was a whole gang of surfers. You would have screamed the place down if you'd seen them. Remember that summer you decided to learn at the pool because you fancied the lifeguard? I thought of that yesterday. It still made me laugh.

One of the "Surfer Dudes," had dreadlocks. Can you believe it?! How cliché is that?! What a loser. They didn't look too bad though. And he had a tattoo. I couldn't get close enough to see, well not without it being really obvious.

Gone

I would have had to crawl down there on my tummy trying to hide behind the sand dunes. Ha! Can you imagine that?
  Anyway, gotta go.
  I'll write tomorrow.
  Miss you
  B.
  xx

Rebecca

A Breakfast of Kissing Arse

It has to be done. I'm bloody starving.

Last night I was plagued by the nightmares. I woke screaming to the usual voice in my head.

"Rebecca, will you just learn to behave and get in the damn car."

I took a moment to lock the voice back deep inside me and waited for the sweat to cool on my skin. No one came up to check on me. Actually, no one has been up to the naughty area of the house to see me at all. Even Emily hasn't been up to see me. This has made me realise that my crack-whore comment may have been unnecessary. I don't know why my family is surprised at my outspoken outburst last night. It's not like I'm not known to do really stupid things at really stupid times. But the truth is I feel kind of bad. It's not Emily's fault that she is perfect and all things a daughter should be and I, well, I'm not. Not even close.

Emily is thirteen, with silver blonde hair that bounces around like a halo. She is small and petite, and one of those girls that always gets chosen to be the Arch Angel in the Christmas Nativity – the one whose head strangers pat as they pass by saying "Isn't she a beautiful girl."

Emily is also the sort of girl who will be relentlessly bullied at school by the other children who look at her, see a perfection that they don't understand, and therefore want to destroy it.

It's how all my troubles began. Two years ago when she started High School. That's when I effectively stopped being Rebecca Walters and instead became Bad Rebecca Walters. That's when I first flipped the switch and let the rage inside me take control. It led to the first of my many labels.

Rebecca Walters the dangerous girl.

It was during the emergence of Bad Rebecca that our fractious sibling relationship started. I would protect her from anything and anyone at any cost, but at the same time I began to resent her for it. I used to be normal, okay, tall, freckly with bright red hair, but relatively normal. But everything changed for me. I became known as the girl that would kick the shit out of anyone. I got invited out with the wrong crowd and sometimes even now I look in the mirror and wonder just where the girl with freckles and the red haystack went. All I see is labels.

Deep down inside me I know the only way I can truly protect Emily is to leave and let her live a normal life. A life without drama, a life without emergency visits to the A&E, a life without the police knocking on doors telling my family that terrible things have happened. A life without people hurting her because of who her sister is.

Her sister the dangerous girl.

I wander down the stairs, trying very hard not to stomp my feet, and find my family all sitting around the table. I should call them the Munch Bunch.

No one looks at me or speaks. They just sit there eating in silence as the clock on the wall behind me ticks at a deafening level.

"Hey," I say.

They all look at me.

"Is there any food?"

They all look at me.

"I'm sorry about yesterday," I sigh. "I know I shouldn't have walked off for all those hours. I realise you'd have been worried. I also know I shouldn't have said those things, I'm just, you know, trying to ... adjust?" I end with a questioning lilt to my voice, because to be honest I am just trying to find the words to stop them glaring at me. Mum and I stopped communicating about six months ago when my second label affixed itself to me. Dad and I about two weeks ago when the third and final label stuck itself to my soul with superglue. Now we don't talk at all, we just shout during "Family Healing" time.

Mum is watching me. It looks like she wants to say something. Silently I will her to speak. "Come on, Mum, talk to me, I'm your daughter, I'm standing right here in front of you. Hello! Tell me what to do to make all this better!"

She doesn't say anything, her eyes slip away from me and the moment passes. Just like it always does.

I turn my head towards Emily who is watching me

with her big sparkly blue eyes. "Emily, I'm really sorry about yesterday. Would you like to do something with me today?"

She offers me a tentative smile. "Sure."

That's Em – always so quick to forgive me. Even two years ago when this nightmare started, she was the one who crept into my bed in our shared bedroom and slung her skinny arms around me. She always made me feel like it didn't matter what I did, that I would never scare her. She still looks at me with the same frank blue gaze, despite everything that's happened.

Dad offers an interrupting cough. It's one of those annoying grown up interruptions telling me he hasn't finished with me. "So we won't hear you speak like that again Rebecca?"

I frown at his tone. Did he not just hear my apology? *Come on!*

"No, Dad. I mean yes, Dad. Uh no, Dad." *Smooth*.

"Bex?" Emily is the only person in the world allowed to call me that. Anyone else gets a black eye. She slides a plate toward me and I grab a pancake off a stack in the centre of the table. Mum is still eying me cautiously. Her worry lined face scrunches ever so slightly as she sweeps her eyes over my outfit. I notice Mum glance over at Dad. The look is normal. It's the worried parental glance they share when I go out dressed all in black looking like I may harm small kittens. I never would. I'm rather fond of cats.

It's my armour. I hardly ever go out, it's kind of hard when people shout at you in the street. A few months back I burnt all my old clothes and decided to give people what they want. They all think I am fucked up. So be it.

It's that switch. I can't control it.

Today, I've got my usual fifty-three bangled statement of guilt on my wrists and I'm wearing fishnet tights, my extra short cut-offs and a vest top that is too large and showing rather a lot of bra. I figured if we ended up going into town I may as well give the locals a show. I also put all my make-up on, this was after I spent some time staring at myself in the mirror looking for the old me, the one before the labels. She wasn't there.

Ignoring Mum's worried glance I turn my attention to Emily.

"Shall we go town?" she asks.

Like I hadn't guessed that was coming. "That will take two minutes. What shall we do with the rest of the day?" I can already confirm there is nothing to do in this town.

"Paint?" Emily offers optimistically.

I pull a face. *Boring*. As well as being blessed with angelic looks Emily can also paint. It's damn annoying. I can read. It just doesn't have the same ring to it. I did use to have other talents, but what's the point of having a talent if you haven't got anyone to show it too?

"Okay you paint. I will find something else to do." I shove a whole pancake in my mouth.

"No drinking," Dad warns.

Mum just frowns further. My mouth is still full but

it doesn't stop me from answering. "No drinking, I promised. It sounds more like, "Oo unking why omished." *Yep, that clears that up.*

I push back from the table and swallow my mouthful. "Ready, Shrimp?"

"Ready, Amazonian?"

We are walking for the door when Mum calls me back. "Rebecca, there is a key on the dresser."

The sound of her voice calling my name stops me abruptly, it's rare for her to address me directly. I turn to face her as I register her words. *The evil daughter is allowed a key?* I'm not going to risk saying anything other than, "Thanks Mum."

"You're welcome, Rebecca." Then she does something I haven't seen in about six months. She smiles at me. For a moment I just stop and stare, did she really just smile at me? I just don't know what to do with that, so I sort of shrug instead and give a little wave.

"Oh, Rebecca," she calls again.

There is going to be a catch to the key. A curfew or something equally ridiculous. Like I need one? Then I remember the events two weeks ago and wonder if my parents had given me a curfew a year ago I would be in the position I am in now.

No. I am to blame, not them.

"Take a tenner so you girls can get something while you're out."

Emily has her mouth open. So do I. My Mum hasn't given me any cash since she found out I was spending it on fags and vodka.

"Uh, thanks." It's not the most gracious thanks I have ever given, but right now I'm in too much shock to say much at all.

Outside we walk down the path to the gate which is covered in insect attracting flowers. Once we are out on the sunlit path I stop and look at Emily. She also looks a little confused.

"Did Mum just give me money?"

Em sniggers a little. "Just be grateful they didn't give you fifty pence to spend on sweeties instead."

Joshua

Death by a Million Degrees of Boredom

I've walked to the graveyard and stood there in silence as normal. I've jogged to the beach, with my board. No mean feat by any man's standard. I've surfed. I've lied to Dan, telling him that I can't possibly go out tonight because my Aunt is having a root canal. Aunt May no longer has any roots left to canal. I have jogged back from the beach, with said board and now . . . well now I am staring out of the window of the shop.

This is my day:
Graveyard
Surf
Lie
Stare
Surf
Sleep
Every single day is exactly the same.

My days never used to be so monotonous. My life used to be in colour. I used to see colour everywhere I went. And I used to want to paint it all. Now I see nothing. It's not so much that I don't see it, but rather that I don't want to. So I never look too closely. My friends ask me out every single day and every single day I think of an excuse, not necessarily a believable one to say no. Before I never had to think of an excuse. The conversation used to go something like this:

"Hey, Josh, fancy coming for a pint later?"
"No."
"Okay then, maybe tomorrow."
And that was it.
Now it goes like this:
"Hey, Josh, fancy coming for a pint later?"
"No."
"Why?"
"Because. . ." And then I have to think of some excuse why I don't. Some excuse other than, "Why don't you all just fuck off and leave me to brood in peace. Then one day, probably in a very, very long time, I may decide to come for a pint. Don't worry though, I will make sure the story runs on the front page of the local paper when I change my mind so you all know."

It's not that I am moody or anything, but you know. I'm dealing with shit. My girlfriend is dead. If that's not shit and a reason to be left in peace then I don't know what is. I just wish everyone would go do one and stop asking me stuff. When you going to paint again, Josh? When you going to go to Art College, Josh? When you next going to go to Newquay, Josh? When you gonna date again, Josh? When do you think you will ever be back to normal, Josh? When you? When you? When you?

I'll tell them when. Bloody never. And that's it.

Faye will be in shortly to make sure I haven't topped myself by sniffing all the paints. I wish. They are all chemical free. I've checked.

Talking of paints, I could waste half an hour mixing up all the tubes again. Every time Aunt May comes in she puts them into perfectly blended rows of colour. I don't like things perfect anymore, so I mix them all back up again, making sure to put the black somewhere in with the yellows and the pinks in with the greens.

Fuck that's the highlight of my day, every day.

Even I realise how pathetic that sounds. I just can't be arsed to do anything about it.

Rebecca

Town

There is a huge problem.
The town planner forgot to actually plan a town. I think someone should contact the authorities and let them know.

It has taken us two whole minutes to walk the 'high street.' A pub, a newsagents and a few tourist friendly shops does not make a town. Well not in my opinion anyway.

"Was that it?" I exclaim in despair as I turn on my heel and look back down the path we have just walked. The sun is glaring off the glass pane windows of the limited shops and I'm raising my hand to protect my eyes, causing my bangles to jingle and slide along my arm.

"I think it might have been." Em confirms as she also glances up and down the non-existent high-street.

"For fuck's sake," I mumble under my breath.

"Um, I'm telling, Mum said you weren't allowed to swear in front of me."

I glare at Emily but her attention has turned towards the shop behind us. Great it's a bloody art shop.

I am beginning to realise this town has been created to destroy what little will to live I still have. One of the two shops is a Budgens selling stale bread and overpriced milk to the holiday makers. The other is an art shop, the kind of place my sister would happily spend three hours perusing the shelves without actually buying anything. *Bloody great.*

"Can we go in?" She bounces on the spot and grabs my hand all eager enthusiasm.

I glance up and down the street again, well aware of the interested glances we, or rather I, am getting.

I'd like to think a village used to holiday makers would be slightly more accepting than most, but you can never be too sure. I might get shouted at sooner than I would wish.

"Okay, but you only get a fiver." Anything has got to be better than standing on the high street for another moment with a growing audience of grannies staring at my shorts and boots combo.

Emily gives a little squeal and bounds into the shop. It is one of those ridiculous twee shops where the door rings a bell as you enter. Just in case you plan to dash in and steal a lifetime supply of 2B pencils.

To be fair, whoever owns this shop is not that bothered about anyone stealing. The music is pounding, and I can't see anyone obviously serving. Saying that, this shop is clearly run by a lunatic. The paints are all over the place. I know nothing about art, but as I scan my eyes along the shelves, even I can see that there is something wrong with the displays.

Emily glances at me and I shrug in response turning to look at the stock, my fingers itch to put the colours in the right place. Emily starts to rifle through the paints her head nodding in approval when she sees the colour clash on display. Weird. I turn my attention to the pictures on the wall. I may not be artistic myself but I do enjoy looking at the work of others. I might ask Emily to paint me something to take back up to London. Maybe she could paint the beach I sat on yesterday.

"Can I help you?" calls a voice from behind me.

"Nah," I shout back, not bothering to turn around.

I watch as Emily turns to look at the voice and notice her eyes widen fractionally. I refuse to turn around and look. I point blank refuse to be interested in anything this rubbish excuse of a town has to offer. Instead I continue to stare at the art work. All the pieces are abstract, all of them separate from each other and all in varying styles, but there is something that links them all together. I take a step back, nearly knocking over a revolving stand of tubes of oil paint. Correcting myself and ignoring the sarcastic sounding snigger from behind me, I continue to stare at the paintings.

They are all of the same object. The object being the same person, you just wouldn't know it because they are only fractured glances of the subject. At a first glance you wouldn't see it, but stare at them long enough and you can see that the angles and shapes of the limbs are all the same, and all the eyes are all exact same shade of deepest brown.

Together they are like a complete book of poetry

where every line has been written with just one person in mind. A never ending love sonnet.

Something about it makes my eyes sting a little and my throat thicken in a way I am not used to. I swallow around it hoping the strange sensation will go away.

"Bex, what are you staring at?" Emily pulls me from my reverie with her words and I come back out of my zone. Giving my head a sharp shake I glance again at the paintings.

"Would you like to buy one?" the voice asks from behind me. This time the voice sounds bored, like it's already over serving the public.

"Yes please, which one costs a fiver?" I turn around to see who the bored voice belongs too.

It's the doodle guy from the beach. I feel my mouth fall open slightly, and for the life of me I can't make myself shut it. Even though I didn't see him clearly yesterday across the beach I know it is him straight away. The dreadlocks give it away, but my eyes are quick to scan over the rest of him. Low board shorts, snug vivid green T-shirt, and eyes of the deepest green I have ever seen. Contacts, he must be wearing contacts. I don't even know why I am thinking this. Who gives a shit if he is wearing contacts? Doodle guy is obviously waiting for me to stop staring because he has one eyebrow cocked a little, an eyebrow ring glints in the light through the shop window, and I stare a little more, completely fixated. He doesn't look amused though. He looks pissed off.

"So do you?" I push.

"Do I what?" Doodle guy, places his hands on his slim hips and appraises me with a bored look.

What a tosser. He's not going to win any prizes for customer service. "Have any paintings for a fiver?"

He makes a snorting noise. "No."

"Okay then." I am glaring back. Jesus this guy doesn't even know me and he is being rude. Normally people at least give me half an hour before they realise I am not worth knowing.

"So are you buying anything?" He creases his eyebrows into a full on frown, his wide lips turned down at the edges.

"Well how much are the paintings?" Not that I really want an abstract picture of someone's elbow, but I can't back down now.

The green gaze slides over me again before clearly finding me unappealing and glancing off to the side.

"More then you could afford."

Prick.

"Emily, have you got what you want?" I call out as I tear my gaze away to find my sister. I don't have to look far. She is standing at my right elbow grinning at me.

"Yeah, I think so."

Scrunching my hand into my shorts pocket I thrust the crumpled money at her, and turn for the door.

I am just pulling the door, making the bell ring when I turn back and catch him frowning at me some more. "You're completely shit at customer service," I shout as I step out onto the sunlit pavement, before he can point his death stare in my direction again.

Rude much. I want to make a complaint.

God I hate this town.

"He said you walk like a percussion instrument." Emily grabs my elbow with an impish grin as she catches up with my pacing.

"What?"

"He said you'd give anyone a headache."

"Who does?"

"That guy in the shop, you know the sexy one who made you blush." She nods her head back to the art store.

"Shut up! He did not!"

"Did not what? Say you sound like jingle bells or make you blush?"

I stomp away from her down the street, after a few paces I screech to a halt and wait for her to catch up.

Mum would kill me if I lost her on our second day here. Hell I would kill me if I lost her on our second day here.

The whole way back to the cottage I stew on what I could write in a customer complaint letter. The loud music for one. The terrible organization, for two. Thirdly, very rudest sales assistant ever.

Joshua

The Curse of Holiday Makers

Five pounds for five hours stuck in a shop, and the only two customers who come in are holiday makers. That's just painful on any level. On all levels.

My dislike for holiday makers is widely known. Why I work in a shop where I have to try and be nice to them is one of the many ironies of my life.

The customer today was Dan's grade nine from the beach. Oh that girl's got attitude alright, just like I guessed yesterday. My mood wasn't actually that bad, for once, but she's completely fucked me right off offering me five quid for one of my pictures. I tried to give her the intimidating stare I give to all annoying customers, but she just stood there and stared right back. *What the fuck?* She wasn't intimidated at all. A good couple of minutes passed with us just watching one another and the whole time I found myself noticing things about her. Her outfit was some crazy statement, asking for, no not asking, begging, for attention. I found myself wondering who she wanted attention from but shook it away. There was a pulse in the base of her neck, right in the dip where her collarbones meet. The hair on her arms is so fair it glimmered in the sunlight. Her skin was covered in a thick layer of make-up, and her wrists were adorned by more bangles then I could count.

Obviously I didn't want to notice anything about some shitty holiday maker, so it just pissed me off even more. Then I got even more annoyed when she was stomping towards the door in her boots and turned to catch me watching her legs stride away. The glare she shot me was a killer, but if she didn't want guys staring at her legs what the fuck was she wearing those fishnets for? She may have some serious attitude problems but those legs are fine, long, slender and never ending. But that is the only good thing about her.

Bex. That's what the other girl called her. Bex with the attitude.

I've been so bored the rest of the day I've actually given in and blended some paints, nothing major, just a dib of this colour and a dab of that. The music has been pumping and I've been maintaining a steady out of tune singing session all day which I quickly stop when I hear the doorbell chime again.

"Heard you outside," calls a voice I have known since I was five.

"Kiss my arse, Faye, you love my singing." I turn and face my oldest friend, a grin on my face. There is only one person who has singing skills worse than mine and she is standing right in front of me. I quickly notice she is not looking at me but at the board behind the counter.

"Josh, when did you start painting again?" She sounds surprised, but then I guess she would be. Six months ago I swore I was never going to paint another stroke.

"What you talking about, dumbass, I haven't."

She raises her eyebrow and I turn and follow her glance to the board. It's covered in a rainbow streak of palest yellow to deepest gold.

Oh.

"Nice palette," she says. "What's it for?"

I stare at the huge stripe of gold and yellow. "I have no idea, I don't remember doing it."

"Have you been drinking again?" She laughs.

"Very funny." I don't drink. I haven't for six months, not since the last time I picked up a paint brush.

Saying that I could do with a cider.

Hold on. Stop the press.

"Do you fancy a cider?" I ask.

Faye leans forward, her dark hair swinging over her shoulder and places her hand against my forehead. I recoil slightly at her touch. I don't like people touching me, even Faye, sometimes especially Faye. "Are you sick, shall I call Aunt May and tell her you need some of her special tonic?"

I elbow her in the ribs. "You should do stand up."

"You should shut the fuck up."

"So do you fancy going for a drink?" I tuck her hair behind her ear as I ask again. It's an automatic motion for me.

Her eyes flicker over mine as my hand comes to a

rest back on the counter. "Really, you want to go for a drink? I thought you were never going to drink again? Not ever?"

That's true, I did say that. More than once. "Maybe I changed my mind. Do you fancy one or not?"

"Shall we call the others?"

I glance at the clock on the wall. It's five in the afternoon. They'll be preening and smothering themselves in aftershave getting ready to shag some holiday makers. "Nah, just us."

She raises her eyebrow again. "Okay then, but Dan is going to be pissed when he finds out you have broken your dry spell and he wasn't there to gloat."

"And that's why we are not calling them. Come on lets go."

The air is warm and dry as we march up the lane to the local pub; August is reigning supreme and supplying the British Isles with a scorching summer. Shame for me this means more holiday makers are arriving every day instead of ripping up Spain or Ibiza.

We walk in silence to the pub. As we walk through the door the whole place which is packed with local's, stops and stares at me as we walk in. Then they stare at Faye, and then they glance between us 'that' look on their faces.

I haven't been in here for six months. I would imagine Faye hasn't been in here since yesterday, but that's not what's causing the strange looks. Whenever Faye and I go anywhere together we get these sympathetic glances. I learnt to ignore them a while back. People can't help feeling sorry for us. The expression we are normally met with is part sympathy, part hopeful optimism that one day we might get together. Which we won't. Not that she isn't beautiful but it would be like shagging a sister if I had one. And I hear that's frowned upon.

The village adopted me fifteen years ago when I arrived in town as a five year old orphan. My parents were killed in a car crash, yeah it sucks, but the truth is I only have the faintest memories of my life before that day. Aunt May has been my only real family since then, with the local community acting like an extended unit of well-wishing Aunts and Uncles. I met Faye on my first day. I was getting out of the car, and there was this skinny girl hiding behind a hedge, watching me with over large dark eyes. She ran down the lane, and I chased after her leaving Aunt May calling in my wake.

"Alright, Josh? Pint of the usual is it?" Eric the barman starts to pull me a pint of the local Scrumpy just like I have never been away. Just like he doesn't know the reason why I haven't been in the pub for six months. All the locals spin back around in their seats and also pretend that they don't know why Joshua Adams has been M.I.A for six months. And for once I am pleased that they choose to ignore me. It's almost like I can hear them breathing a sigh of relief. "It's okay Josh hasn't totally flipped. He can still drink cider. All is not lost."

"Thanks, Eric." I take the pint he offers me, allowing the cool liquid to slosh over my fingers from the over filled glass just like it did in days past. There used to be times when we all used to wear more cider than drink it.

By the time we have our cloudy pints our table has mysteriously become free. I'm being treated like royalty!

I should have a psychotic break more often.

"So, have you seen the new family?" Faye asks after taking a deep sip of her pint.

"Nope. The only people I've seen are some fucking rude holiday makers."

Faye rolls her eyes as I take a sip of my drink. It tastes good. Cool and sweet, and easier going down then I would have expected. "What new family?" I ask when I have finished.

"A couple from London and their two girls, they've moved into Bridge Cottage." Our eyes instantly meet, and her words create a tightening in my stomach. She waits for me to say something, anything. She wants me to show some emotion. But I can't, and I won't. I knew that this was going to happen. I knew Bridge Cottage wouldn't stand empty forever, so I lock any emotion I feel away inside me.

I choose not to comment and instead think about the new family. I did spend a generous amount of time staring out of the window of the shop today but I don't remember seeing a new family.

"Nope," I take a sip of my drink. "Let's hope they are prepared for a life of seasonal boredom and weathered skin syndrome."

"Grump."

I flip her the finger. "So why aren't you out in Newquay tonight?" She would normally be. Getting ready to tease lots of guys on a local dance floor, before telling them all to bugger off at the end of the night. Faye has been in love with our friend Andrew for as long as I can remember. Not that she has ever bothered to tell him. He has also been in love with her for almost as long. This makes for highly amusing nights out as they edge around each other on the dance floor trying to make each other jealous. At least that used to be what it was like, it may have changed now. Hell, Faye and Andrew could be at it like rabbits together every night and I wouldn't know about it. Not because I don't care, I just can't talk about that stuff anymore. It's not that I don't want Faye and Andrew to get together and be happy, that's all I ever wanted for them. I'm just jealous that they still have the option to do that when I know I probably won't ever be happy again. Not properly happy. Not in laughing and crying together, sharing a life together. My only chance of getting those things died six months ago careering around a bend on a back road from Newquay. Call me bitter but I know I won't get to do those things again and I don't want to know about those who do.

Faye is watching me closely, her dark eyes intent and scrutinizing. "I spoke to Mum and Dad yesterday."

She is still watching me so I make it look like I am breathing. Which I'm not. "Yeah?"

"Yeah. They wanted to know if you had thought any more about Ai—"

I hold my hand up instantly. "No." One word. The

only word. No one is allowed to say my girlfriends name near me. And yes I know I am being a bastard.

Sorry I mean old girlfriend.

Faye shifts a little in her seat and frowns at me. "Okay, okay, Josh. So anyway I heard you fell off your board yesterday so I thought I'd better check on you."

"I did not!"

"From sitting down," she clarifies.

"Who told you that?"

"Everyone."

Crap.

"It was a wobble."

Faye sniggers into her drink so I let her have her moment of glory. It's not often I have a wobble on my board. There has never been any photographic evidence. She changes the subject straight away, and I instantly see she was trying to distract me. "So you're painting again?"

I watch her over the rim of my glass. The cider tastes surprisingly good after not having any for so long. "No. I don't think making yellow stripes constitutes painting."

"It's okay if you do. Everyone wants you to."

I glare at her. This is getting too close to the mark. There is a line, and no one, not even Faye is allowed to step over it. "I'm not painting again."

"Okay, okay." She gives a little sigh and settles back into her chair. "Fancy coming to Newquay tomorrow?"

"No."

"Why?"

"Because I am getting my knob removed and a fanny inserted."

"Okay. Fancy another drink?"

"Yeah, sure one more."

It is only one more. By the time I have sucked down the second pint, acidity is burning in my stomach and I just want to have some fresh air. All of Faye's words are swirling in my mind and I can't shut them out. They are battling with the din the regulars in the pub are creating and it's making my head feel like it's going to explode. I need air.

"I'm going to go." I lean over and whisper in Faye's ear. She is chatting to Sandra Didds, the crazy lady who owns the post office, and that is a conversation I could do without.

Faye, throws her arms around my neck. She has had four pints to my two. "Okay, Joshy baby."

And that, is my cue to leave. "Will you get home safe?" I start to laugh. Faye only has to walk upstairs, this is her home. Her parents decided to return to their youth and go travelling three months ago. She has been renting above the pub ever since.

"Hands and knees, baby, all the way."

"You are so classy, that's why I love you." I don't wait around for her answer. I make a quick exit into the cool evening air outside.

Walking down the lane from the pub I decide to take a detour to the beach. The light is fading but the glimmer of light from the sun setting on the horizon is just enough that I can make my way down the path without landing on my face.

I spend a lot of time on the beach at night. This isn't like the beach in Newquay which is filled with drunks attempting to get it on under the cover of darkness. Our quiet beach in St Agnes is perfect for a solitary ten minutes. If I go home now I know Aunt May will be twitching around me like she has the last half a year, ever since my life ended at the end of one drunken night. She doesn't know what to say to help my get out of the 'phase' I'm going through. Six months in, I think we can rule out the chance of it being a phase. This is just me. I'm a guy without a plan. Aunt May tries, but having her wandering around wringing her hands, asking me every three minutes if I'm hungry and need some food is not a relaxing way to spend an evening.

I don't know what people want. Do they expect that one day I will wake up and suddenly be over the fact that I carelessly lost my girlfriend one night?

As I walk down onto the beach I keep thinking of Faye's words. "Bridge Cottage." "Painting." "Mum and Dad." They hammer inside my head.

I know everyone is waiting for me, for some resolution. They want to know that I've let go of the past, and that if I can do it, they all can too. But I can't. I want them to, but I can't do it myself. I can't even acknowledge to myself what happened. I can't even think about it or let the thought enter my mind.

Small steps, that's what a counselor told me a few months ago. "Just take small steps, Josh, and everything will work out." Today I have picked up a paint brush and drunk a pint of cider. That's got to be two small steps in the right direction. I'm not sure what direction those things are taking me in, but it's heading somewhere at least.

As I tread over the dark sand I can see someone sitting on my rock. That's just plain rude. Everyone knows it's mine.

Edging myself closer, I slip off my flip flops and sink my toes into the cool sand as I walk down the beach and try to get close enough to investigate without being seen.

It's *her*.

My feet come to a grinding halt.

I want to move in the opposite direction but my damn legs won't listen. Instead I stand there, looming behind her on the sand, like an axe murderer.

"I can see your silhouette in the sand."

Busted.

"What are you doing?" *On my rock?*

"Thinking. What are you doing?"

"Thinking too."

"That's nice."

"Yes it is."

I stand there like an idiot working out what to say next. "Nice bangles."

"Thanks. They make me walk like a percusssion instrument."

"Why so many?"

"None of your business, dreadlock boy."

"Well you're a charmer aren't you?"

"I was sitting here first. You're the one with the stalking, stealth-like sand walk."

"It's my rock." *It's my rock? It's my rock? Really. . .?*

She does not say anything. Let's be realistic there is not much to say to that comment. She just sits there looking out to the sea, and I stand there my feet sunk into the cool sand.

"I like your dreadlocks," she says after an age has passed.

"Thanks. They're a lifestyle choice."

She turns to look at me and for a moment, just one brief moment my mind swirls with colours. The make-up is gone and the waning sun illuminates her skin. She look different. So different. A better different.

I should walk away. I don't talk to holiday makers unless I'm taking their money in the shop.

I don't.

Instead I fold my legs and sit on the sand. My fingers automatically pick up a splinter of driftwood, as I cast my eyes up at the sun and start to draw.

"So do you have a name girl with the bangles?" I'm trying to remember what the young girl who was with her in the shop called her yesterday. Becca? Something like that?"

Turning to me with a frown on her face she bites her lower lip. Jeez, I only asked her name.

The frown and the angry glare instantly make me recall her name. "Bex." I answer for her. The frown deepens.

"No one calls me that, only my sister."

"Well I don't know what else to call you?" I prompt. Her feistiness is rather amusing, it's actually doing a good job of distracting me from the usual shit I try to keep out of my head.

Her top lip curls a little in distaste at my goading. She really doesn't want to tell me her name. Who doesn't want people to know their name? My eyes flick over her with a little more interest. She is rather pretty. Hot, Dan would call it. But I would go with pretty. Pretty is a more delicate sounding word, easy to pair with the freckles and flame hair.

Oh good god. I've realized what I am doing? I'm looking at another girl. I try and turn myself away from her a little. She must register the motion because she speaks, her voice low like she is sharing a secret.

"Rebecca." She clears her throat. "My name is Rebecca."

Something about her low tone makes me cast my eyes back over her. Well not exactly willingly, my eyes just won't damn behave themselves and head straight back to the smooth sunlit skin.

She looks nervous, her fingers brushing over her overload of bangles.

"Does Rebecca have a second name?" My feet do this bizarre thing where they scoot over the sand towards her toes.

"No."

"What no surname? So you are Rebecca No Name?"

She scowls further. "Yes. I am Rebecca No Name."

Her tone and the death stare she lays on me make me do something I am not expecting in the least. I laugh. Fucking loud. I laugh like I never stopped.

"Well Rebecca No Name. I am Joshua Adams, it's

a pleasure to meet you and your bangles."

I lean forward and shake her hand my fingers grazing against hers, sand rolls between our connected skin.

Rebecca No Name digs her toes into the sand, burying them deep. "Walters. It's Rebecca Walters."

"Bex Walters, now that has a nice ring to it."

"It's Rebecca Walters." She spits her name out like it burns her lips to say it.

"Okay, okay."

"So Rebecca Walters where are you on holiday from?"

"Nowhere."

Seriously. It's like talking to a wall. I don't even know why I am still sitting here. This makes an evening with Aunt May look like a social highlight.

I get up and start to brush the sand from my legs.

The girl with attitude stares up at me from the ground and I hesitate. "London. I come from London, and I'm not on holiday. My family have moved into Bridge Cottage."

Just like that the air gushes out of my lungs. The girl with the attitude and the wrong clothes and the frown lives in the house that I was fully expecting to move into one day. The cottage I expected to grow old in.

I sit back on the sand with a bump.

"I am leaving though, in two weeks." Her gaze is on the sea as she speaks. "Two weeks. I've just got to get through two weeks." She repeats almost to herself.

Two weeks of what?

"Who are you running from?"

Rebecca, Bex, the girl with the attitude turns to me, her eyes hidden in the shadows of the dipping sun. "Myself."

And that I just don't know how to answer, so I don't. I pick my stick back up and start to draw some more.

TWELVE DAYS TO GO

Bridge Cottage
St Agnes
Cornwall

15th August 2014

Dear E,

Yesterday I had to suffer the pain of taking Em around the shops. Painful. Everyone stared at me. I mean I knew they would, but the whole damn street practically came to a halt to look at me. Haven't they seen fishnets before? Em was completely oblivious, but the experience only reaffirmed what I already knew. I need to leave ASAP. I don't know what Mum and Dad were thinking bringing me to a place this small. If I stood out like a sore thumb in London, what the hell am I going to do here? I was expecting someone to shout "Tramp" at me. I even regretted burning all my normal clothes after you left. I do still have my skinny jeans but it was way too hot for them. I would have melted into a puddle.

We went to the art shop, Em's idea of course. Guess who was in there? The dreadlock guy! Oh my god he was so rude!

You would have had a few sarky comments to make back to him. I just stood there bright red under his death stare before running away. I've never met anyone quite that rude before, which is saying something!

I had another row with Mum and Dad during, 'Family Healing Time'. Apparently it's not acceptable for me to accuse the locals of being inbreds. I tried to explain about the obnoxious guy at the shop but they just looked at me like I must have started it in the first place. Which for once I didn't. I promise.

Dad wanted to talk about you. He seemed to think that the change of scene should help me let go. Wait for this! He suggested that I should try and leave a few bangles off ... just to see if it helps me forget. Like I could forget you. Like I would even want to.

So I stormed out again. It was either that or go and sit in the naughty corner in the attic by myself.

I went back to the beach and sat there willing the next thirteen days to speed up. Then the rude guy with the dreads just rocked up and sat down on the sand next to me! Uh hello? Who does that? According to him it's his rock. I think I may not be the only crazy in this town! Somehow he managed to wrangle my name out of me. I didn't want to tell him. But I did.

He actually seemed quite nice. Weird but nice. I won't be telling him anything else about myself though. It's enough that he knows my name.

Miss you as always.

B.

xx

Rebecca

Kissing Arse

I stare in the mirror and perform my daily label attachment as I slide on my bangles. For every one I remember I have fifty-three reasons why I need to go.

Glancing at the black shadows under my eyes I can't help but think of my deep slumber last night. The deepest sleep I've had in weeks. Last night when the nightmares came it felt different. I wasn't dragged into the black hole of my self-conscious. Instead I lingered in a shady area of grey and silver and the voice shouting in my head was kinder, more reproachful than cross.

"Rebecca, will you just learn to behave and get in the damn car."

It must be the sea air making me get all soft. Sitting on the beach last night must have re-wired the nightmare programme in my brain.

It's making it very tempting to sit on the beach all night every night, regardless of whether I have company or not.

I make my way down from the naughty corner and head into the kitchen. "Hey."

The Munch Bunch are sitting around the table.

Instead of pancakes like yesterday, today we have healthy muesli and berries. I cast my mind back and try to remember Mum having breakfast like this on the table in London. I don't remember it once. But then we rarely all used to be together. Dad always worked and Mum spent her time running around making sure that Emily got to the right places on time and in one piece. I, well I used to spend my time hanging out in the wrong places with people who I was assured were wrong for me too. I realise that after the situation I found myself in the other week, the one that necessitated our move to the country, that Mum and Dad may have been right. Maybe I was hanging out with the wrong people all the time. But I guess I always felt that it was best to hang with anyone then no one. I was wrong.

Now after our speedy move to the country Dad is freelancing his design work and the Munch Bunch get to sit around having breakfast together.

"What time did you get home?" Mum pours me a coffee and manages to avoid all eye contact with me as she slides it across the table towards me. *Look at me.*

"Not late." I shrug. No one has mentioned me being grounded yet, or having my tuition fees taken away. Maybe I will be forgiven for slamming out of the front door last night after "Family Healing." I hope so. I have plans today.

"Well I stayed up until ten thirty waiting for you," she says.

Of course you did. "I got home at ten thirty five."

"Did you find your way home okay in the dark?" Emily looks at me with big frightened eyes. Emily is not a huge fan of the dark.

"Uh, yeah I guess."

I am not disposed to tell them I was escorted home in the dark by a dreadlock swinging surfer.

I did clearly state that I didn't need help getting home. I got the help regardless. I start to smile a little thinking about the, "I don't need help getting home," "But you are getting help walking home," conversation but quickly wipe the smile off my face when I catch Mum frowning at me.

"We are going into Newquay today, would you like to come? I believe that town will be big enough for you." Dad rustles the paper he is hiding behind. Dad has not made eye contact with me in two weeks.

I'm about to answer when I hear a car rumbling outside the open kitchen window. I glance up at the flowery clock on the wall. This makes me stop for a moment. We have been here two days and I have not yet noticed how incredibly kitch the kitchen is. It's all sky blue walls and yellow cupboards. Seriously, what were my parents thinking? *Oh yeah. I remember what they were thinking.*

My moment of hesitation checking out the kitchen décor has delayed me from dashing out the door before the owner of the car knocks on it.

Too late.

Dad sighs and puts his paper down. "I'll get it."

Shit.

I take a sip of my coffee and wait for the arrival of

my new 'reason to be given a bollocking.'

I can hear him chatting at the door but Emily distracts me from earwigging by asking, "Bex. Are you wearing flip flops?"

I glance at my feet. Yes I am. I don't get a chance to answer.

"Bex needs them surfing, you can't surf in big boots," a voice calls from the door. I turn to face the door and bite down on my lip to stop from smiling.

It's Joshua. Joshua who managed to coax my name out of me in the first five minutes of sitting next to me on the sand, even though it was the one thing I never wanted to tell anyone here. It's Joshua whose skin shines in the dark like he is made from the moon.

Joshua. The worst sales person in the world. His name sounds funny in my head. Joshua. Joshua.

"Joshua," he says when he walks into the room and shakes my mum's hand. He stops and glances around the kitchen, his eyes flicking over the cupboards like he knows the things that are kept behind the doors. Even I don't know what's kept behind them. His shoulders which I can't help but notice are raised and tight start to relax as he looks at all our belongings scattered about. Finally he rests his eyes on me and for the moment I am rooted to the spot as I scan over his face trying to read what he sees when he looks at me. *What is there to see?*

Joshua, is wearing a dark green T-shirt paired with black board shorts and flip flops. I have my mouth open.

"We haven't got around to decorating yet," Mum explains waving her hands at the clutter and general living debris around the room. I kind of thought Mum would be a bit hostile to the dreadlocked stranger.

Joshua offers a half smile. "It's cool, you haven't been here long. I didn't realise the place had been sold."

Dad gives one of his coughs as he walks back into the kitchen "Well it was a bit of a rush."

"I see." Josh turns his appraising glance towards me again and I stand rooted to the spot. Does he see? Does he realise I am the reason we had to move with just a few days notice? Does he realise I am the reason my family had to move two hundred and fifty miles? Does he see the labels?

"Hey Bex." Joshua doesn't smile at me. In fact it feels like he is not even sure why he is here.

"Rebecca."

"Bex."

"So are we going surfing or not?" I ask with a resigned sigh.

A grin switches on, flickering to life and it's as if his whole face lights up. It's beautiful and I know I definitely have my mouth open. Then he ruins it by speaking again. "Yes, Bex we are."

I let a deep sigh burst from my lips before turning to my parents catching them watching me with a strange look on their face. What is that? Worry? Concern? Shock?

"Nice to meet you," Joshua leans forward and

shakes both of my parent's hands again. "I'll have her back this afternoon if that's okay?"

I automatically tut out loud and scrunch my face into a scowl. It gives me the raving hump when people talk about me like I am a piece of property that needs to be cared for or returned after use. Call me over sensitive. I don't know why he's asking anyway. We may have spoken for hours last night, but I didn't in any way tell him anything important about myself. Admittedly we did have a weird conversation where I decided to blurt out that he shouldn't try and look for me on Facebook or Twitter. He absolutely wet himself laughing and then turned to me, his arms spread wide, and said "Do I look like the type of guy on Facebook or Twitter?"

I had to admit he didn't, which amused him even more for some reason.

"Would you like to stay for a BBQ when you come back?" Mum glances between myself and Joshua as she asks. She has an expression on her face which I would describe as confused but optimistic.

My own expression must be downright shocked.

Is she joking? In two years she has never willingly invited a friend of mine into our house. A risky game to play with your teenage daughter. She may have kept unsavoury characters out of her house and away from Emily, but at the same time she opened up more opportunities for me to loiter down alleyways and get thrown out of pubs for under-aged drinking. It's a game she lost.

Maybe the sea air has gone to her head and she has

decided to change tactics. Or maybe she has finally given up caring. *Who knows?*

I am shaking my head at both her and Joshua. A BBQ with my family sounds like a dead boring idea — just for me.

"A BBQ sounds great." Joshua gives another one of his breathtaking smiles that make his cheeks look like they are going to split.

I am thinking up a reason for why the BBQ does not sound like a great idea at all, but the only one I can come up with is, "I wouldn't bother, it's going to be dull." I roll my eyes in their sockets just to reaffirm my point.

This makes Joshua laugh, a noise he looks quite surprised at as he places a hand on my elbow and turns me for the door.

"Shall we go for your surf lesson, Bex?"

"Rebecca."

"Bex."

Rebecca."

Joshua starts to tow me towards the door, my elbow still firmly in his grip. It's the closest thing I have come to physical contact in I don't know how long.

Once we are safely outside I screech my feet to a halt, removing my elbow from his grasp.

"One more time, and let me say it slow so you understand. My name is Rebecca."

He leans right in towards me, until he is close enough that I can see three freckles along the bridge of his nose.

"One more time and let me say it slow so you understand. Your name is Rebecca, but you look like a Bex."

I have no idea what to say. What are you supposed to say to that? So I don't. Turning my attention away from the taunting green eyes I scrutinize the rust bucket parked haphazardly in the lane by the cottage. Its nose is buried in the honeysuckle creeping along the garden wall and it has a wheel precariously balanced half on the curb.

"What is this?"

"Daisy."

"You named your car?"

Technically it is not a car, despite the covering of honeysuckle debris I can clearly make out it's a Volkswagen camper. A Volkswagen camper that has seen far better days.

"Daisy meet Bex. Bex meet Daisy."

Pulling open the passenger door I slide myself in, glancing at the mountain of mess littering the interior. There are crisp packets and empty coke bottles everywhere.

"I refuse to shake hands."

"You just did."

I roll my eyes but can't prevent the lip twitch that hints at my smile. I bite my lip to stop the foreign sensation of a lip twitch extending into a full smile.

Joshua cranks the engine and the 'thing' shudders to life. Music blares at a deafening level and I put my hands over my ears.

"No Beach Boys?" I shout over the thundering

noise.

Joshua twirls the stereo dial and lowers the music. "Sure it's in here." Leaning right over to my side he tugs hard on the door to the glove box which falls open onto my knees, causing thirty cassette tapes to clatter to the ground.

Surely they stopped making those things a decade or so ago? I laugh, I can't help myself. Then I stop. I haven't made that noise in, I don't know how long. It feels strange and unnatural bursting from my lips like that.

Easing myself back into the seat, I strap up my belt and attempt some small talk with the complete stranger taking me out for the day. "Leather seats?" Yep. Small talk is another talent I lack.

"100 % PVC."

"Classy."

"It will be in a minute."

"What do you mean?"

"Don't worry you'll find out shortly."

If small talk is not a skill, then understanding cryptic conversation is pretty much like understanding French – a subject I got thrown out of at school. I change the subject in the vain hope of creating some form of verbal rapport. "Where are we going?"

This whole situation is starting to strike me as being a bit odd. I understand that odd is normal for me. But, it's my second day in a new town and I am trapped in a camper van, with a stranger, heading somewhere that I don't know. Even odder is the fact my parents willingly let me go, no shouting, no arguing, no slamming of doors. No resistance at all.

I mean, I know I am known for doing silly, sometimes dangerous things, but to be honest I don't fancy being murdered down a Cornish country lane by a strange, dreadlocked surfer today.

It's weird, and I don't believe in any of that instant connection crap. That's bollocks made up by people who have no sense of reality. I have a healthy respect for reality, largely brought about by the crap situations I normally find myself in. But the guy with the green eyes, dreadlocks and eyebrow ring does not feel like that much of a stranger. This leads me to believe that my own grasp on reality may finally be slipping.

Last night after we had sat talking on the beach about everything and also absolutely nothing for two hours straight he walked me up the lane to the cottage in the dark. As we got to the cottage gate he leant right in towards me, his body stopping a couple of millimetres from mine and asked if I fancied a surfing lesson. I quickly weighed up the option of walking around the two shops in the village and then mooching about the house for the day by myself, or, a lesson with the boy whose skin shines like silver and decided the lesson sounded a far better option. I believe this was the moment that my grasp of reality loosened.

Spontaneity is not one of my strong points. It normally ends in disaster. Actually it always ends in disaster. As Daisy starts to head away from town I hope that I don't end up regretting my choice. Or, for that matter end up in a ditch somewhere.

"Crantock." He answers my question. Sadly it

hasn't clarified the matter at all.

"Pardon me?"

"Crantock beach. You'll love it."

"How do you know?"

"I'm taking a guess." He answers matter of fact. Joshua concentrates on his driving and takes us down a maze of narrow lanes. I really hope I don't have to find my way back by myself.

Taking my attention off the sight of his long fingers loosely holding the steering wheel, I try and look anywhere apart from at him. Truth be known it's kinda hard. I've been momentarily sidetracked by the sight of worn woven leather bracelets tightly bound against his tanned skin. I feel my own bangles in response, all fifty three of them.

Fifty three sins.

My eyes travel up from the bracelets on his wrist, to his elbow leaning on the open window. If I look closely enough I can see the defined movement of muscle ripple under his skin with every turn of the steering wheel. Joshua flicks his eyes in my direction and catches me staring. I quickly look out of the window and watch the fields roll pass the window.

I hold in another smile as I take in the scenery around me. It is beautiful, so beautiful, and something about it makes my eyes sting. The fields are full of flowering mustard seeds which are glowing yellow in the sun. Warm air is rushing through the window and for the first time in a couple of weeks I can feel the knot of anxiety I hold in my stomach start to unravel. All the negativity and worry starts to ebb away.

Then I shift in my seat and make a farting sound. *Fuck.*

Joshu-u-a starts to laugh uncontrollably, his fingers grip the wheel of the camper van as he turns to me, his green eyes gleaming, and a smile spread from ear to ear.

"100% PVC."

"You're an arse."

"Takes one to know one."

I can think of nothing witty to say back at all, so I just pull a face instead. A few minutes later I'm distracted from glaring out of the window by Daisy pulling into a car park. This is different from the beach near the cottage, for a start it is jam packed with cars. Alarm starts to flood through my system. I'm not great with crowded places. I would imagine I am even worse with crowded places full of happy holiday makers enjoying a scorching August day.

"Uh, is this a busy beach?" I start to stress sweat. I can feel it prickling along my skin.

Joshua turns towards me his eyes skimming over my face. "Well uh, yeah."

"I want to go home."

"You can't. I promised you a lesson. Now we are going to have one."

Did he promise? I can't really remember the word promise being used, and if it was I'm not opposed to a promise being broken.

I grip the chair with my sweaty hands making my desire to stay in the van clear. "I'm going to be rubbish." This is not a guess on my behalf. I'm rubbish at most things.

Joshua leans in towards me which makes me grip the seat tighter in response. He is right in my space when he offers me a slow smile. "Everyone's rubbish their first time."

I hold my breath while I think of something to say, but I come up frustratingly blank. What is he talking about? It sounded teasing, something implied.

I offer myself a sarcastic laugh and a mental clap on the back. Well done, Bex. Two days in a new town and some twat already thinks you are going to put out to him. *Excellent*. Oh and even better you have gone to a place that you don't know your way home from with him. *Excellent again.*

Josh watches me for a moment. I would imagine my chagrin at myself is clearly painted across my face.

He scrunches his own face in confusion. "No one can stand on their board the first time," he adds, reaching a hand towards me which kind of hovers in the air between us before falling back into his lap. "Or their tenth."

"Hm."

"Are you chicken, holiday maker? Do I need to take you home to mummy and daddy?"

Prick.

"No."

"Good."

I let the air slowly exhale out of my mouth. Joshua chuckles and moves back onto his side of the rusty vehicle.

Swinging out of the car he heads around to my

side. I'm not expecting him to open the door for me, otherwise I would have made sure to get out of the car independently first. As it is he cranks open the door and leans over my body to release my seatbelt.

"I'm not a holiday maker." I say. I seem to be holding my breath as he moves his body close to mine.

He turns, his face inches from mine, and the greens reach deep inside me. "I know, otherwise I wouldn't be here."

I swear on my life I can't help myself, and I only do it because I have always thought of dreadlocks as being really dirty, but I move forward ever so slightly and smell his neck.

He doesn't smell dirty. He smells like the sea, sun and mint all rolled into one.

"Did you just sniff my neck?"

"What a ridiculous thing to say."

He grabs my hand and slides his fingers through mine as he waits for me to jump down from the camper.

I have no idea what the hand holding is about, but the truth is, it's been a damn long time since I had anyone try and hold my hand. I clasp my own fingers around his, tight, like a natural survival instinct.

Walking over the sandy tarmac to the back of the van our hands swing between us. It's just too strange not to comment on. I am turning to ask him why he's holding my hand when I notice that he is looking at my shoulders and the string of my black bikini which is poking out from under my vest top.

"Have you got a cream on?"

"Pardon me? We're only holding hands."

Joshua's lips twitch a little and he nods his head towards our hands. "I know. I meant do you have sun cream on. I think you might need it."

"Oh. Uh. Yeah. Thanks."

"Don't want to ruin that skin." He tugs on my fingers pulling me around closer until we are face to face, and his mouth lowers to my exposed shoulder. Before I can even react his lips gently graze over my skin.

I jump away instantly. "What are you doing?"

"Smelling you."

"What?"

"You did it to me."

"I did bloody not."

"Yeah you did. What do I smell like?"

"I have no idea. What do I smell like?"

"I'm not telling."

Joshua releases my hand and starts to unstrap the boards from the top of the van. I watch as the knot of anxiety that started to unravel earlier during the journey starts to come back with a vengeance. This time it feels different, more intense, a low slow burn.

I don't know what's causing it, but as he easily hoists both boards under one arm and then reaches casually for my hand with his other I lock it away as I always do.

It's just a surf lesson. There can't be anything wrong with that can there?

Joshua

Surfing Lesson No 1

I'm only too aware of how surreal this situation is as I walk along the warm sand with one of my hands holding hers. I keep casting my eyes in her direction. I can't really stop myself. I'm checking she is actually there and I haven't finally lost my last remaining shred of sanity. She is creeping from a nine to a nine and a half. She doesn't seem to notice my glance, so I take the opportunity to absorb the sight of the sun on her skin as much as I can. It glows like shafts of harvest corn dipped in warm honey.

For the first time in a long time I want to do more than just graze my lips against another shoulder.

I can't though.

While she is technically not a holiday maker and therefore hasn't fallen in my 'Not to be Approached' criteria, I know she is not staying. And if she is not staying I know we will never do more than walk down a beach holding hands. I don't do goodbyes of any description.

Last night as we sat on the moonlight flooded beach we told each other everything, but at the same time nothing. She is eighteen, to my twenty. Her family have moved here so her sister can have a life not in the middle of London.

The girl who looks like she is made of the sun is leaving in two weeks to go to university. But that's not all I found out. Without knowing it, she hinted at all the stuff she doesn't want anyone to know. As we sat on the dark sand I found all the answers to the things she wasn't telling me. They were hiding in every moment of silence that hung between us in the night air. She is lonely, frustrated, confused, all of these things and something else. There is something else there. It's in the way she holds her body, and it's in the way her fingers absentmindedly graze over the bangles adorning her wrists.

Something, or someone.

Something that she thinks defines her. She does not want anyone to know it. She does not want me to know it. And to be honest I'm not sure if I want to know either. Well at least I thought I didn't until we reached her gate last night, and instead of giving her a good bye wave I stepped right into her space, holding myself back from kissing her and asked instead if she would like a surf lesson.

Why?

It nearly killed me standing outside the gate to Bridge Cottage last night, especially, as I found myself stepping right into this stranger's space just like I would have done in times gone past. But everything about it was different. Instead of the yielding warmth and comfort I used to know, I was met with this fiery resistance. Resistance I am not used to. Something about it made me feel challenged so I didn't walk away. I asked if she would like a surf lesson. Not quite what I was aiming for.

This morning when I woke up I wanted to cancel. I so wanted to cancel. I wanted to go back to surfing, staring, lying – my normal day. But I also knew I wanted to feel that resistance again. I wanted to feel something, anything other than nothing. So instead of cancelling I drove to Bridge Cottage and knocked on the door and walked through it like I had never crossed the threshold before. Like I didn't know every inch of the place or the history that it has.

She is not a holiday maker. She is a cryptic challenge.

I wonder if she was a holiday maker whether I still would have broken my rule for her. As I watch her settle on the beach, peeling off her cut-offs and stepping those long legs out of a scrap of denim, I can't help but question whether I would have offered a surf lesson regardless of her holiday status.

What are you doing Josh?

Clothing removed she spins to face me. "Do I get a wetsuit," she asks hands on hips.

"Nope."

"You're kidding right? That water is going to be freezing."

"No kidding."

"Fuck."

"I don't think fucking has got anything to do with it. But whatever you want."

She eyes me suspiciously trying to work out if I'm joking or not. I can't help myself. I take a step closer. One step over the sand and one step closer to her.

Bex has already managed to cover herself in sand just taking off her shorts. Tentatively, because I haven't really touched anyone for months, I raise a hand and brush the grains off her shoulder. My fingers enjoy their cautious stroke across her sun warmed skin more than I thought they would. My thumb wants to slide along the groove of her collarbone and try to find the pulse I saw beat there yesterday, but I hold my hand still. My mind can't be stopped and it teeters on the edge of a gutter as I remember the first time I saw her when she was sliding a hand under the strap of her bikini removing stray sand. The memory causes an instant reaction, a spike of adrenaline courses through me which I haven't felt for a long time. Taking a step back, I make a show of sorting the boards out, running my hands over them checking for any dinks that might need attention. Sadly neither of them do, so I have to turn my eyes back to her. She has her back to the sun which glows behind her like a halo, making her features hide in darkness. For one crazy instant I wonder if maybe this girl has been sent to rescue me, but then I remember that she is leaving and I can't be rescued.

"So anyway, you stand on the board like this." I jump on my board to demonstrate.

"You're joking, you don't expect me to stand?"

I laugh at her horrified expression. "No I don't

expect you to stand. Come on let's just wade out and sit on them. That's a good start."

She looks like that might not be a good start at all.

"Scared?" I ask.

She bristles and bends down to grab her board which she struggles to pick up swinging it this way and that. I jump out of the way as it comes towards my knees. I know from experience that a surf board to the knees hurts real bad.

"Nope. You?" She challenges me straight back. Her face is still in darkness but I am sure she is glaring at me.

Yes. But not of surfing.

"Not at all." I try to send her an encouraging smile as we head down the beach towards the sea, but it's hard to be encouraging when I have no idea what I am doing. I just bob my head a bit at her instead.

The sea itself proves to be a problem. Bex spends ten minutes just getting one toe in the water. In the end I get bored of laughing and waiting and swim my board out into the waves.

Eventually, after we have missed at least five good waves, she joins me.

"This is quite hard," she puffs catching up. She is flat on her board using her arms like paddles, she looks like a five year old learning to swim at the local pool.

I bite down the laugh that bubbles inside me. She's doing it all wrong, but I reckon she has a right old temper and I'm not going to be the one to piss her off so I keep my corrections to myself. I can teach her properly tomorrow.

Tomorrow? ? ?

"Turn the board around so your back is to the tide," I explain.

She stops paddling with her arms, allowing her forehead to smack on the board. Her body rests flat on the board and I can't help but notice the dip in the curve of her lower back, just above the edge of her wet bikini bottoms. I grip my own board tighter in response.

Bex raises her head and catches me perving. Thankfully she is too busy grumbling call me on it. "You're kidding right? It has taken me ten minutes to get it in this direction."

"Come here." I grab one of her hands pulling her towards me and then edge the board around with her on it.

My need to laugh intensifies about tenfold. So does a crazy, unreasonable need to kiss her.

Out of the corner of my eye I can see a reasonable swell behind us. Determined not to freak her out so she falls off and I have to dive to the bottom of the ocean to rescue her, I keep my voice level. "Start paddling towards shore, Bex, now."

"Rebecca."

"Bex, just start bloody paddling."

"Rebec. . ." It's too late. She hasn't made distance to ensure she rides the wave and isn't knocked off balance by the swell shifting the board from underneath. I am much stronger than her and it barely makes my board move, but she tips in slow motion straight into the water. We aren't that far out. I'm sure she can put her feet down and stand up but she doesn't. I can't see her for a whole five seconds, and in those moments I am off my own board and reaching down into the water to catch hold of her.

She comes up coughing, spluttering and completely covered in sand, and I'm not talking about a little bit of sand. She is caked in the stuff.

"My nose," she cries.

That's it, I can't hold in the laugh any longer. I grab her up next to me, my fingers tight on her elbows so I can hold her firmly beside me, as she clutches her stinging nose.

"It's good for the sinuses."

"I don't have anything wrong with my sinuses."

"Well now you won't."

Bex glares at me from under sand encrusted hair. "I want to go home."

"Rubbish. Let's get you cleaned up and head back to the beach." I start to cup my hands and fill them with water to splash over her.

"Are you flipping kidding?" She has her hands on her hips again and just looks crazy sexy. Officially she is a ten. There is no doubt in my mind.

"How else do you plan to get it off?"

She hesitates for a moment before offering me a shrug. "Okay make it quick. I'm freezing!"

So I do. I start to gently tip the water over her and she helps wash it off with her fingers as well. I try very hard not to let my fingers graze with too much intent along her skin. We all know sand shouldn't be rubbed, but it's kind of tempting now. I slide my fingers along, and despite the chill of the sea she still feels warm to touch. Warmer than I have felt in a long time. I can almost feel the life pumping inside her. I want to use the flat of my palm to smooth along the length of her limbs, but I reckon that comes under groping so I stop myself and instead take another fractional step closer as I inspect her goose-bumped skin.

The freckles, made of more colours than I can count, and the pale alabaster tone underneath, makes her skin unlike any I have ever known. She really is like the sun.

The girl made of the sun. My girl made of the sun. *What?*

"Turn around," I instruct, my throat in serious need of clearing.

She does, tilting her chin down onto her chest so I can wash the sand off the back of her neck. I am so distracted by the long curve of her neck that I don't see the massive wave coming towards us. This time we are both down. Momentarily we are suspended under the water, our eyes meeting in the murky depths of sand and seaweed. Bex's fingers reach for mine and I link mine through them as I find my footing and pull her up alongside me. This time she is much closer. Her skin is mere millimeters from mine and I am about to slide my fingers down along her arm when my nose starts to sting with the fury of hell.

"Shit my nose." I clamp my hand over my face.

"It's good for your sinuses." She is clutching her

own nose mirroring my action and we both start to laugh. Bex's eyes widen as she recognizes the sound of laughter coming from her mouth. I want to take another step closer, but I am already as close as I can get. The next move would be skin on skin.

"Shall we go to the shower?" I ask my voice so tight I practically croak the words out.

"There is a bloody shower, and I have let you paw your grubby mitts over me for the last five minutes?"

Moving so fast she doesn't see it coming, I hook my foot out around her ankle and she lands back in the water. "There's a shower, race you." I laugh as she comes up coughing, spluttering and glaring.

It isn't a race really. By the time she makes it back out of the sea with her board I am standing there holding her towel grinning at her. Fun on the beach! Who knew Joshua Adams was going to have fun on the beach again? Not me, that's for sure.

"I am beginning to think you are very unchivalrous," she says shivering as the air rushes against her damp skin causing the fair hair on her arms stand on end.

"Here let me wrap you in a towel, my fair lady." I mock a low sweeping bow which makes her crack a smile, and wrap the towel and for a moment my arms around her.

"Warmer?" My voice is low again. What is this? Yesterday it was painting and drinking. Today it's laughing and cuddling.

She raises her eyes towards mine and I see them for the first time in the sun. I would never be able to paint them, they are a deep honey brown with flecks of amber in them. They remind me of one of the amber necklaces that Aunt May always wears.

"Yeah I am." She bites her lip a little and we both stand and stare.

This situation is so far out of my comfort zone. I don't do this — romantic dalliances on the beach. I don't stand with my arms wrapped tight around a girl who I know is going to be leaving shortly.

Picking up the boards, managing both of them under one arm, I link my fingers back through hers, as we turn towards our stuff. I don't have a clear plan in place, but it involves standing under the shower and then lying on the sand next to this strange girl who is making me behave in ways I never thought I would again. In the back of my mind I'm thinking, that if in the space of one morning she has managed to make me laugh, touch her, graze my lips against her, fall to the bottom of the ocean and cuddle her, what on earth could she get me to do by tonight. Part of me wants to find out. The other half wants to run home and slam the door on the strange developments taking place around me.

The plan I don't have is instantly scuppered when I see Dan sitting on my towel making a little sandcastle on it. Andrew is with him both of them watching me with keen eyes.

I feel like I've been caught cheating. Am I cheating? Can you cheat on a girl no longer here?

"Thought you didn't *do* holiday makers," Dan calls as we get close.

Arsehole.
True though.
Bex stiffens next to me and then steps away from my side letting go of my fingers. "I'm not a holiday maker," she bristles as she gets close enough to talk without shouting so the whole beach can hear. Unlike Dan.

He gives her a look that can only be described as a challenge, slowly allowing his eyes to drag up and down her bikini clad body. Something inside my chest tightens in response and I step in front of her to protect her from his devouring look. *Territorial Joshua is new.*

I shift a little uncomfortably.

"Are you the new girl who's moved into Bridge Cottage?" Dan asks her.

She puzzles over Dan's question before replying, "Yeah and?"

Dan turns his attention towards me holding one hand up to shield his eyes from the glare of the sun. I am not sure if he is shielding his eyes from the sun or from the hostile stare that Bex is sending him. Her body is rigid, ready for something. It feels like she is ready for battle, building up her defences. I take another step in front of her, completely blocking the view Dan has. He watches my movement, registering and evaluating me.

"Don't make that mistake, Joshua, she isn't the same. She is definitely not the same."

"Shut up, Dan." I bite out.

"Just saying, mate, I mean we all want you to get it

on, you know do whatever you have to do to forget, use whoever you want, but don't be wasting your time at the beach trying to get around to doing it."

"Shut up," I say again, my voice lower and not with the desire ridden tone I had in the sea moments ago. Now I feel like the clouds are gathering over my head again.

"Joshua, I'm going to go and find the shower," she says, she keeps her eyes averted from mine and I watch her walk away with that strange tightening in my chest again.

"I'll come with you," I call.

"Stay with your friends." She turns and shrugs her hands at me. There is something in her demeanor, in the way she is holding her body, like a fact has been confirmed by her and she is disappointed by it. The sharpness in her gaze makes me feel it too.

I glance at Dan and Andrew who are scrutinising every move I make. I could do without talking about this with them. *Whatever this is.*

"It's cool. I promised you a shower, and then I believe we have a BBQ to get to."

Laughing Andrew gets up off the sand and claps a hand against my shoulder, "Looks like your busy, Josh. Catch up with you later mate."

Dan does not move for a moment, "Don't we all get an invite to the BBQ?" he shouts out to Bex instead of me.

She turns to him, hands on hips which I am sure is driving him crazy. He will be only too aware of her upgrade from a 7.5 to a 10. And says. "No you don't," before continuing her walk up the sand.

I don't stop to speak to Dan, to try and explain what I am doing, what would I say? I just chase after her across the sand and then fall into step by her side.

Once Dan and Andrew are further away from us, the tightening sensation in my chest starts to lessen. I don't know what that's about.

Standing under the cold shower we don't speak a word, and a heavy silence hangs between us until there is only one thing I want to say. I have this whole new feeling coursing through me, something primeval, territorial and completely basic.

I can't fight to keep the words in. I simply have to say them. Something about her makes me want to say them. "Bex?" I reach my hand to her arm under her shower.

"Mm?" She has her eyes closed to the sky allowing the water to trickle over her face.

"Don't let Dan close to you. He doesn't treat girls that aren't staying very well."

Her eyes snap open and the ambers glow at me. "Do you?"

I offer a snort as a response but when she continues to glare at me I realise this may not be answer enough. "I don't even talk to girls that aren't staying."

"Why you talking to me then?"

Why am I talking to her? "I don't know."

"Lovely."

We stand in silence again for another few minutes and out of the corner of my eye I can see her raising her arms above her head as she attempts to wash the sand out of her hair. The motion sets me thinking about Dan looking at her that way again.

"Bex."

"Rebecca."

"Okay, Rebecca, don't let Dan get to close to you. Okay."

"What if I want him to?" She pops one eye open to gauge my reaction.

"That would be your choice I guess."

Bex, Rebecca, whoever, starts to smile slowly. "What's it worth?"

Anything.

"What do you want?"

"I want to know what he meant about my cottage and that I am not the same?"

I don't know what to say. I can't open my mind up to the complicated matters that lie under that simple question. *I used to be in love with the girl that lived there, but she's gone. Maybe I could hang around with you instead for a while?*

I don't think so.

"I used to know the family that lived there." I shrug eventually. "It's kind of complicated." How do you tell a strange girl under a beach shower that once you thought your life was going to be intricately linked with that cottage and the residents of that cottage? That you expected that one day you would live in that cottage and have a family of your own in it and now you're not. Nothing even close to that.

"You're keeping secrets."

I give a sarcastic laugh and think of the unspoken words in the silence that hung between us last night on the beach.

"Aren't you, Bex?"

"Rebecca."

"Aren't you though?"

The ambers flicker with something. "How about you keep your secrets and I keep mine? It's only twelve days."

It is only twelve days. Twelve days until she is gone. Can I do that? Can I spend twelve days with her and keep my secrets and let her keep hers? Can I spend twelve days with anyone again, or should I go back to my life of nothing. No laughing, no touching, no lip grazing, no falling to the bottom of the ocean and no cuddling.

I don't know if I can, but then I also don't know if I can't. "Deal."

ELEVEN DAYS TO GO

Bridge Cottage
St Agnes
Cornwall

16th August 2013

Dear E,

I can confirm that surfer dudes smell of the sea, salt and mint. I can also confirm that they randomly hold hands, smooth their lips over your skin and endure an endlessly painful BBQ with your parents.
Well Josh. Josh-u-a, does anyway.
His name sounds funny doesn't it? Josh-u-a.
Why am I sharing this with you? I can't help but think you should be doing this. This should be your life and I should be where you are. You should be lying on a beach with a boy who looks like he is made out of the moon and sea. No I'm not losing it. He does. In the dark his skin shines like he is lit by something deep inside him.
I like him.
I know I shouldn't.
I don't deserve it.
I almost wanted to tell him about you. We were careering

down this tiny winding road in his decrepit old VW and the warm wind was blowing through the window the sun was shining, and for a moment I started to relax. I nearly told him how I lost you. I didn't. I can't. It's my secret to carry.

I think he is keeping secrets too. I wonder if they are as sad and as dark as mine.

I wish you were here, smelling the salt, feeling the sand and giggling on beaches with me. If you were then I would truly be able to enjoy it.

Miss you as always.

B. xx

Rebecca

Breakfast

I am not even going to bother going downstairs, what's the point? I have nothing to get up for today. Last night was an unmitigated disaster. Joshua looked most bemused and was grinning as I walked him out to Daisy.

Once we were in the lane outside the cottage I leant against the garden wall, completely loitering. I didn't want to say goodbye to him. For some completely irrational reason I wanted him to lean in and kiss me. I was waiting for it, holding my body tight with expectation. He didn't. He lifted his hand smoothing a piece of my crazy orange straw hair behind my ear, and then grazed his thumb ever so lightly across my mouth.

I've never wanted to be kissed more in my life. Actually I don't ever remember wanting to be kissed before. Not consciously. Kissing is just a natural progression an evening can take when you have run out of conversation with a complete stranger.

Last night I felt myself leaning in towards him, proper movie style. He just stared at me in the darkness then offered me a wide smile.

"See you soon, Bex."

"Rebecca."

"Bex," he whispered into the night before walking around Daisy and roaring the old engine to life.

I went straight up to bed and let sleep claim me until the nightmares came again. Last night the words were muddled all wrong.

"Rebecca, will you just learn to behave, and get in the damn car?"

The word *"Bex,"* echoed around my dreams turning the nightmare into a deep dream where I didn't know where I was, or what I had done.

Josh didn't ask to see me today as he left, which is really annoying because I want to see him. I want to know what that prick at the beach meant yesterday about me being different to the person who lived here before. I want to know who lived here before. I want to know why Joshua has secrets about it. But more than that I want to know what his secrets are. I want to know what that wanker at the beach meant by Josh needing to forget. I just assumed at the time he was insinuating that Josh should just sleep with me and get it over and done with. And yes while that's rude, I'm not unused to those sentiments. But as the evening went on, I watched Joshua's body language in this house, and around me and my parents and I realised that's not what that knob was hinting at. He was telling Joshua it was time to move on from something.

This sensation is new to me and I am not sure how

to handle it. I've never had this really irritating desire to see someone again before. All I am doing is pacing my room trying to work out how to initiate a meeting, and then hating myself for even thinking it.

I don't want to like anything about this town. I don't want to like anyone in it. I especially don't want to like tall well-built men with huge smiles, dreadlocks, inappropriate facial piercings and all sorts of factors that could jeopardise my nine grand. And I especially don't want to feel like anything, other than my sister will make me want to come back to this town after I leave.

11 days to go.

***

I've wasted time showering, using up all the hot water in the taps, and am now twitching about in front of Emily who is drawing in the garden.

It's kind of weird this hanging around thing, but I don't have anywhere to go. It feels like every second is ticking by in slow motion. Every second of the next eleven says stretched out in front of me. Before, back in London, before my self-imposed imprisonment in my bedroom, I would have called up a dodgy connection, slipped out the house and been up to no good for the afternoon. I have only hazy recollections of what the no good afternoons involved but I know they centred around smoke filled rooms and the clinking of glasses.

That's one of the promises I have made my parents for the next two weeks. No Alcohol. The last time I touched the stuff I lost an entire night of my life. The images I do have of the night are the ones I am trying to fight from behind my closed eyelids.

Part of me could do with a drink now though. It's easier to drink myself into oblivion then it is to face every second of time painfully ticking past.

I didn't feel like this yesterday. Yesterday was not a bad day, why is that? *Joshua.*

I shake any thought of him and his distracting abilities away. Mum and Dad scared him off last night. That's the last I am going to see of him.

Or is it?

"Want to come to town?" I ask Emily instead of scouring the cupboards looking for any drop of alcohol.

"No I'm busy." She does not bother raising her eyes from her pad. Emily is oblivious to the constrained, suffocating feelings I'm battling. She just continues sketching away as I nearly combust in front of her.

Ah sketching!

"Need anything from the art shop?"

This makes her put down her pencil, her blue eyes glance over my twitching form and a frown dimples between her eyes. "Do *you* need anything from the art shop, Bex?"

I flush instantly, which is really bloody annoying. "What are you implying?"

She picks up her pen again. "Nothing."

Clearly she does not need anything from the art shop. Bollocks. "I'm going to go buy a sausage roll."

Emily keeps her gaze focused on her sketch. "Have

fun, Bex." She starts to giggle that annoying flower fairy laugh she owns.

"It's not what you think." *Sort of.*

I attempt to walk calmly to the garden gate, but when I am ten steps away I break into a run.

"Sure sure," she shouts back. Who knew her voice could get that loud.

I make a point of going to the bakers first and purchasing a sausage roll – seventy pence! How cheap is that! And then I start to loiter on the small high street.

The fact hits me that I know nothing about Joshua at all. Apart from the fact he works at the Art Shop that his aunt owns and he looks like he is made with the light of the moon and the depths of the sea. I don't know what he would be doing if not at the art shop.

Maybe he even has a girlfriend, but I'd like to think the random hand-holding and lip grazing that took place yesterday counts against this theory. But I know nothing about dating so perhaps that's how it's done. And to be fair to him I haven't asked him if he has one. Why would I? We are just hanging out, well we were until my parents frightened him off with their crazy Gestapo BBQ.

Maybe he is just super friendly to all newcomers to town. Maybe he gives everyone a surf lesson and then slides his hands firmly over their skin when they come up from a trip to the bottom of the ocean.

I remember what his dickhead friend said yesterday at the beach about him trying to forget something and

I realise that Josh may not have a girlfriend right now, but he may possibly be trying to forget one. Does he want to forget though?

I am aware that my street cred rating I once used to own in London goes down the pan as I sneak my way across the road and try to peer into the shop window. Damn it, the sun is reflecting on the glass and obscuring my view. I know I may have been spotted so I straighten my shoulders which allows my string vest top to fall down on one side and expose an expanse of skin, and jingle the bell on my way into the shop. There is no music on, so I instantly recognise that he is probably not going to be here, a fact which I find crushingly disappointing. *What the fuck is wrong with me?*

Glancing about the shop, my eyes once again absorb the pictures hanging from every available space of wall. Dark hair and eyes, mixed with smooth limbs. Limbs that the artist knew well, very, very well.

Joshua painted them.

The realisation smacks me over my head and I am frozen to the spot staring at them. Changing my focus I try to read something in them. Anything other than pure love and devotion, which is how I read them the first time I saw them, when they made my eyes sting with unwanted tears. They make tears sting again now, but only because they still read like perfect poetry to me and the thought burns inside my brain.

I shake it away. Who gives a crap? *I am leaving in a handful of days, does it matter? Why am I over thinking this anyway?*

"Can I help," a voice sing songs. I watch as a young woman walks through the back door with a cup of something steaming in her hand.

I glance between her and the paintings and the similarity is impossible to ignore. The woman in front of me has a sheet of glossy jet black hair and dark almond shaped eyes that are replicated about thirty times around the shop.

Blank brain syndrome.

After appraising me up and down, she casts her gaze towards a canvas behind the till which is covered in an orange themed rainbow.

She flicks her eyes over me again. "Are you looking for someone?"

"Um, nope. I don't think so."

"Well yes or no?"

"That would be a no."

Spinning, I dash out of the jangly door before I can open my mouth and ask if she is the girl in the pictures. And if she is, why did Joshua lean up against me along our garden wall and sweep his thumb across my lips in a completely erotic stomach churning manner.

I am marching back along the limited High Street when I hear someone calling "Bex." It's a man and I know my dad would never make the mistake of calling me that, not that he would probably bother to call after me in the first place. It can only be one person, the pinch in my lower stomach as I move my feet faster in the opposite direction confirms my guess.

Power walking in flip-flops is near on impossible and I don't get more than a few paces before the boy made of the moon and sea catches hold of my elbow and spins me round to face him.

Joshua leans down and gazes at me, the greens deep and calm. His lips have a slight curve and I find myself focused on them. I lick my own lips in response.

"Where are you trying to run to?" He grazes his hand down my arm stopping at my wrist, which his fingers loosely slip around. The entire trip his hand makes down my arm makes my skin burn like it's caught on fire. I drag my hand away from his and the heat that generates from the touch.

"I wasn't running?"

"Attempting to?"

"If I was running you wouldn't have caught me."

Joshua throws his head back and laughs. I don't want to laugh, I want to ask who that girl is and why the hell she is working in his shop surrounded by paintings of herself.

There is no way to ask that question without sounding like a crazy so I lock it inside me instead.

Joshua runs his hand along my wrist again, his thumb against my pulse as he waits for me to come up with something to say, which I can't. I can't pull away either. I am just frozen there, with my hand in his, words stuck inside me and my feet unable to move.

"You're not jangling."

"Pardon?"

"You're not jangling." He lifts my hand and motions his head a fraction towards the wrist he is holding.

I stare at my wrists which are not adorned with their usual fifty three bangled statement. I feel my lungs empty and then wait for them to inhale but they don't. I just stand there empty.

'Rebecca, will you just learn to behave and get in the damn car.'

"Bex?" His voice pulls me back to the present and I gaze up into his green calm eyes.

I have no words, all I can think is 'I forgot them.' I forgot my fifty three sins. And I know I forgot them because from the moment I woke up the only thing I could think of was Joshua. I start to feel a burning rage build up inside me.

"Bex?" Joshua moves his body closer to mine but my lungs still won't take air, not even to breathe in his sea, sun and mint scent.

"I've gotta go." I don't stop to discuss further. I yank my hand from his and start to pace away as fast as my stupid flip-flops will allow. I am going to burn them as soon as I get home, well just as soon as I have my bangles on.

I know he is still behind me as I push through the gate and head around the back of the cottage.

"Hey." Emily starts to smile when she sees me but the smile falters on her lips as she watches me rush past her in the house.

"Hey, Em," Joshua greets her.

"What's with her?"

"Bangles."

"Oh," is all I hear her reply. I am in the cottage away from them and taking the stairs two at a time. I crash into my room and dash for the dresser, grabbing the bangles off the side.

My lungs start to burn and a sob builds in my throat as I start to count them on. I have to do it individually. Fifty three reasons to know I am bad.

My eyes are closed but I hear the door give a small squeak as I assume Joshua walks in to my room. What must he think? And I was worried about him thinking I was crazy earlier?

What does it matter? I am quite clearly crazy.

Finally I get to fifty three and lean on the dresser as I catch my breath and try to bring my emotions under control. I don't like to show weakness and it's fair to say Joshua has just seen me at my most vulnerable.

I open my eyes and look for him in the mirror. He is lying on my bed, his hands linked up under his head, a steady cool green gaze resting on me. I turn to face him but he does not say anything. He just continues to watch me. I let out a deep, slow breath as the quality of the air in my room becomes heavier, denser almost, charged with an emotion that I don't recognise.

Sitting up Joshua moves onto his knees before shifting across the bed towards me. My lungs start to feel tight again but in a completely different way.

He runs a hand along the bangles. "What are the bangles for, Rebecca?"

He just called me Rebecca? *That sounds surprisingly*

wrong.

"They are so I never forget something."

The green gaze warms my cheeks and my breathing starts to hitch unnaturally fast, heart attack fast, as I watch him edge himself even closer.

"Can you tell me what?"

I so wish I could. I wish I could I speak the words to share the burden in my heart.

"No."

Joshua thinks about this for a moment, weighing up my secrets in his mind, then he offers a small shrug.

Holding my breath I watch him step up from the bed and move himself into my space. My focus is on his mouth which is surrounded by an unshaven scruff. My lungs have that inhaling, exhaling problem again and I stand there suspended in the moment waiting for him to say something; waiting for him to speak and ask me about the dark secrets I have hidden inside, ask me again about the bangles that lock my mistakes into my soul.

"I'm going to kiss you now, try not to hit me."

He's going to what?

I don't have time to think anything else, because before I can react or move, or even speak, he slides one of his hands up into my hair weaving his fingers into my loose bun as he moves his lips towards mine.

The kiss is so sweet and slow, his lips tantalisingly warm and firm. All at once I can smell the moon, sea and mint scent that I discovered yesterday. It fills my head until I feel like I am swimming in it, until I feel like I am tingling all over with the sensation of his warm lips teasing mine and the mint smell swirling around me.

I should move away, but I don't. I move closer, pressing against him and breathing him in as I allow his tongue to slip into my mouth and entwine with mine.

This isn't how kissing normally is. I don't normally have a problem with dead legs when I kiss. But then it's been a while since I tried it sober.

I run my hand up his back and along his shoulders feeling strength and solidity beneath my fingertips. Impulsively I move my body until there is no space between us. He trails a hand down my face and throat feeling his way with warm dry fingers to my shoulder. I don't want the hand to stop. I want it to carry on exploring. It does stop though and his lips pull fractionally away from mine.

"It's just as I thought." His voice is a low murmur next to my ear.

"What is?" I don't even recognise my own tone. It's not one I have ever heard come from my mouth before. It sounds deep and wanton and all things dangerously good.

"You. You taste like the sun."

The boy who looks like he's made of the moon and sea thinks I taste like the sun. What does that even mean?

I am about to say something in response. I am about to ask that if he thinks that I am one thing, and I think he is the opposite whether that is a good thing or a bad thing, when my bedroom door flies open and I look instead at my dad standing on the other side.

Dad stands with his mouth hanging open and whilst we aren't locking lips, Joshua still has his body pressed up tight against my own, one hand still firmly entwined in my hair.

"Uh," I say.

Joshua, tries to take a step back but his legs are against the bed, so instead of creating space between us all he manages to do is lose his balance and pull me on top of him as he lands on the mattress.

I wait for my dad to explode, I am expecting it. But instead he opens and closes his mouth a few times before pulling himself together. "There is lunch on the table, if you can manage to bear the company, Bex." He walks away from us, but then pauses at the door. "Josh, you're more than welcome to join us if you wish." He offers a smile, but I can't help thinking it is directed at Joshua not me. A little pinch of disappointment settles in my stomach that the first friendly emotion my dad has shown around me in months is directed at the stranger by my side rather than me.

I can't stop myself. "It's Rebecca," I shout after him as he walks out the door.

As soon as I turn my focus back onto Joshua I realise that I am still lying on top of him. That's not good. Well, it's not all bad either, but I shouldn't be rolling around on my mattress with anyone right now, especially not a dreadlocked, super fit boy with green eyes that read my face like his are right now.

"Do you need me to go?"

I pretend to think for a moment, not quite able to move myself off him. His hands slide down my back and along the curve of my spine.

"I am pretty sure I am going to get a bollocking."

"Why?"

I wave my hand between the two of us.

"Aren't you eighteen?"

"Yes but there are terms I have agreed to, and I am not sure being found in flagrante with you is one of them." *Ooh, that's actually quite a big word.*

"Why did you need to agree to terms?"

"Because I need to leave."

"But you just got here."

"Exactly." I groan a little and allow my head to land gently on his chest. I take the opportunity to breathe in that mint scent of his again. It's intoxicating.

His hands don't move from my lower spine, and I'm finding it strange that it's not that odd. I'm not used to people touching me. Who would want to?

Joshua slides his nose along the edge of my ear and I start to get that low burn again in response. "I'm starting to want to know just what it is you have done, Bex, to get brought here," he murmurs into my ear, warm breath licking along my hairline.

I give a shiver and try to screw my eyes shut against the images that barrage inside my mind at his words. The things I did to get bought here.

"I can't tell you." I whisper back, my words barely audible.

"Why?"

"Because then you would not want to do this again."

I feel his lips curve into a smile against my throat.

"Well I might."

"But you might not."

"So do you want to do this again?" he asks.

No. But then maybe a whole lot of yes as well.

"Maybe."

He leans back and I see the first true smile I've seen from him, it's wide, open and breathtakingly beautiful. It's so beautiful I almost blurt out some of my awful truth.

He slides his thumb along my jaw, tilting my gaze to meet his. His green eyes bore into me, trying to find something there. He won't find the truth, no matter how distracting he is, those are tales I'll never tell anyone.

"Should I leave so you can have your bollocking?" He lowers his lips to mine but stops just before they touch.

I lie there like an idiot waiting to be kissed, like a teenager on her first date. Not that I ever had a first date.

After ten seconds of waiting for a kiss that is not going to arrive I open my eyes.

"What you doing?"

"Watching you."

"Why?"

He laughs a short burst of sarcastic laughter, "I'm not sure."

"Charming."

"I try."

So it's going to be like that is it? Fine.

"Well if you have finished staring then perhaps I can proceed to go downstairs to participate in my telling off."

"Well, I would hate to get in the way of your parental discipline." His voice is low, dark and wicked. "I'll come back later when it's over."

He's joking right?

"Yeah, don't bother. I will be on a lock down for at least five days."

"No can do. I only have ten days left with you and I am planning to have them. I'll be back later."

Joshua rolls me off him and springs from the bed heading for the door. "Try not to get grounded, Bex, It will be hard to give you your next surf lesson if you're locked in the attic."

I watch him leave, but I don't bother replying. I know I'm not going to see him tonight or tomorrow, I need that nine grand too much. Dreadlocked boys are not part of the plan.

"Bye, Joshua," Emily calls as we get to the front door.

"Bye, Em," he shouts back.

"Bye, Joshua," shouts my mum and dad followed by what sounds like sniggering. *That's odd.*

"See you later," he whispers low into my ear.

"No, Josh." I start but he is out of the door and down the path before I get all my words out.

I close the door and lean my forehead on it for a

moment. I need to prepare my sulky teenager look. This is a huge problem because I have a wide, cheek splitting grin plastered all over my face like a bloody dosey. Now I am going to be told off for smirking as well.

Joshua

Drain Pipes and Window Sills

The kissing is going to be a problem.

Why did I do that? Now it's going to be the only thing I'll be able to taste until I get back to see her tonight. And I will see her tonight. I know there is little chance of me doing anything else.

It was the bangles. I am blaming the bangles for the impromptu kissing / groping. Something about watching her standing there with her eyes screwed shut, hardly breathing, completely unraveled any damn reserve I had.

Kissing Bex.

Not that I'm complaining, it was different, so different to anything before. She's like burning fire, no coyness, no shyness, just come right at you hot.

Too hot.

I restrain myself from walking back to the front door and knocking to ask if I can hang around permanently for the next few days. I just need to give her some space with her parents and then as soon as darkness falls I will be back with the girl made of sun.

I don't know what the deal is with her parents, but

I am beginning to understand that she must have done something pretty damn bad. Not just for the fact that they have bought her here, but the way she is around them. Her body is tense like she is ready to fight or take flight. I reckon she always fights.

When her dad walked in to her room she did not look him in the eye, her body just tensed next to mine. Nor did she move away like I would have expected. She just stiffened her shoulders, like she was ready for battle. That was embarrassing, pulling her down on me like that. Embarrassing but at the same time all levels of hot. For a moment there she was pressed against every single inch of my body, and didn't my damn body know it. Six months with no physical contact at all and then I go into overdrive and manage a lingering kiss and a full out body press all in one morning. It's a miracle I didn't explode there and then.

The need to know more about her is burning under my skin. What is that with her parents? What is the thing with the bangles? I have never in my life watched someone count on fifty three bangles before. I know there were fifty three because I counted along with her. Watching her stand there with her eyes screwed shut I realised she was clearly remembering or recanting for something. Fifty three what?

Not knowing is going to torment me.

The one thing I am beginning to realise is that whatever she thinks her parents feel, I am not sure that they actually do. Whilst she avoided all eye contact with her dad, I on the other hand made sure to look him in the eye when he walked in. I don't want him to think I am some shifty character after his daughter's virtue, because that could not be further from the truth. When he glanced over us, it wasn't anger that lined his features, but more relief. Relief and amusement. That is strange in itself.

My feet stop their long dragging walk from Bridge Cottage and Bex, and I look up in surprise at my destination. I didn't even know I was heading here, but now I find myself standing outside a door I haven't walked through in six months. Although I have walked passed it probably a thousand times, I've never even glanced at the door that so much of my past is shut behind. Now I am standing here sliding my keys out of my pocket and into the lock. I hear the click of the Yale as the key slides home, it's a noise that used to mean 'home' to me but now sounds strange to my ears.

Taking the stairs two at a time I walk into the sunlit room. Someone has been here since I last was. Everything is covered in sheets to protect it from the motes of dust spinning around in the shafts of light coming through the glass ceiling.

This is my studio, which was once my home. The place where I used to spend all day and all night. Now it is a just a room, a room on top of a shop covered in dust.

I pad through, breathing in the musty scent, trying not to touch any of the past that lies around me, and head towards my stack of new canvases that I keep rolled in a drawer. I pull one free from the bundle and clip it on an easel before pulling the entire thing into the centre of the room, directly in one of the beams of sunlight. I spend a few minutes watching the sun shining a pale yellow on the canvas and think about just what it is I am here to do.

Am I really going to paint again, when only a few months back I swore that I was never going to put myself on a canvas again?

I can't hold it back. The need to paint moves my hand and I slide my fingers over the blank canvas. As I do I recall what it felt like only half an hour ago when I was doing the same thing to Bex's skin. I know that in just a few hours time I plan to do the same thing again. And I will. I know there is little chance I will be able to stay away tonight, the need to see her is burning inside me and I know that I will spend every day with her until she leaves. When she is finally gone I will get back to my old self, the self that no longer paints but until then I am going to find out just who Josh is who lives to see the sun again.

I head to the kitchenette grabbing my paints from cupboards and then I start to mix and blend until I have created all the colours of a late summer harvest. Until I have created Bex on my pallet.

I close my eyes for the moment when I feel the touch of the brush against the canvas, I wait for the emotion to hit me, but it doesn't. I start to paint instead, just like I never stopped.

***

Dusk is drifting through the skylight when I hear a sharp knock on the door down the stairs. I bet its Aunt May wanting to know where I have been since breakfast time. Whilst 'Joshua Panic Watch' has lessened, if I don't check in every few hours she does tend to flip out and start scanning the beach looking for my washed up body.

I pace down the stairs and swing open the door. Dan is leaning against the frame, a smirk on his face.

"There you are, mate. I told them I would be able to find you."

He leans in slightly and I get a whiff of rancid stale beer from his breath. I'm guessing it's been one of *those* afternoons.

I hold in the sigh trying to escape and instead move away from the door, starting to walk back up the stairs. I want to cover my painting but I can't use a cloth because the paint is still wet. If I turn it around it will look like I am trying to hide something. This would make Dan even more interested. Best to ignore it and hope he is too pissed to see.

"So you been here all the day?" he asks casting his eyes around the studio. Back in the day we all used to hide in here and smoke roll-ups and listen to terrible music. That was a long time ago now. The memory feels like it is veiled in my mind and I can no longer get a clear visual image of it.

"Yeah most of it," I shrug. I am unwilling to admit the beginning of the day involved kissing the girl made of sun.

I don't need to. Dan's eyes fall on the canvas standing in the middle of the room. Let's be honest there was no real way he was going to miss it.

He turns a calculating gaze on me and I can't get a read on his expression. He looks puzzled, cross, and something else. What is that? Disappointment?

"So you all fixed now, Josh?"

"What on earth do you mean?"

"Well, what I mean is." He takes a step towards me. "For months we haven't seen you. We've all been dealing with the shit from that night, it's nearly destroyed us all, and then suddenly some redhead turns up with biker boots and you are painting again and running around on the beach holding hands like nothing ever happened. What about Faye? Don't you think she deserves more?"

The air rushes out of my lungs.

"What? That's not it at all. Fuck, Dan, I can't believe you just said that!! I straighten my shoulders as anger rushes through my veins. "It's not like I woke up two days ago and forgot everything. And leave Faye out of this. She is her thing and I am mine."

My fists are clenched, anger isn't natural to me, but something in his accusatory tone is pushing my buttons. His words swirl around my head. What does he mean, redhead with biker boots, Bex was wearing flip-flops at the beach yesterday. Then I remember the first time I saw her, after Dan rated her a 7.5 and I realise he was watching her far more closely than I thought. Far closer than I would want.

"How do you know she wears biker boots?" I ask. I know there are far more important questions to ask but I am stuck on this one.

Dan gives a laugh that comes out almost like a sneer. "Shit, Josh, the whole town is talking about her, the see-through tops, the make-up, the fact you are running around up and down the high street after her, like a school boy."

"So what, is everyone watching me to find out what crack-pot thing I do next?"

"No, everyone is waiting for you to break again, because she will break you. You know she's going. We all know she is going. That girl is never going to stay in a town like this. And let's be honest mate, why would she? You will never do anything more than hold hands with her."

His words make my chest get that unfamiliar tightness again. I push it away. I know she is going, I went into this with my eyes open, I won't be the one to ask her to stay, even though I may want to.

"I know." I sigh. "I just find her interesting."

Dan is staring off into the distance, his mind on something else before he snaps his attention back onto me. "Maybe I should spend some time with her, see if she can fix me too, hell maybe she can fix us all before she leaves."

Bile rises in my throat.

"Stay away from her, Dan."

"What? She's a holiday maker, that makes her my territory not yours. I'm sure I can show her a good time. Something to remember St Agnes by."

I know he is drunk, but I've never wanted to hit my oldest friend so hard in my life. I'm going to kill him for even thinking of touching the girl made of sun.

"Stay away from her." I repeat again.

Dan focuses on me, "You do like a challenge don't you, hey, mate?"

"What do you mean?"

"Well you know, you spent years chasing Ai—"

"Don't you dare say her name." My body literally throws itself into his space as anger pulses through me.

"Just saying, maybe you should aim for something a bit easier this time. I could hook you up with someone in your league and you could leave the redhead to me."

I shove my hands against his chest forcing him towards the door.

"Get out, Dan, before I do something I'll regret." My teeth are clenched and my limbs are burning with a need to thrash out.

Dan laughs and turns for the door. He is halfway down the stairs when he calls back up, "You'd do well to remember your friends who've been looking after you for the last half year. Enjoy your fling mate."

I don't have anything to come back with. I am just standing there burning with anger as I look over the painting in the middle of the room.

Bex.

I need to see her right now. I need to make sure that no one else has touched her. I need to make sure she is safe at home where I left her.

Grabbing my keys I dash down the stairs, a faint thought lingering in my mind that I hope Dan has got away because otherwise I may punch him as I run past.

It only takes a few minutes to reach Bridge Cottage, once there I screech to a halt unsure how to proceed.

I have no idea how I am going to be received after the fall on the bed situation from this morning. Truth be known, I don't really want to be ostracised from Bex's life for the next few days, so instead of knocking on the door like a sensible person, I decide to break and enter instead.

I look for the drain pipe that leads to her room; I know it is there, I have climbed it before. I place my foot into the familiar foothold and hoist myself up. It's been a while since I negotiated the walls to this cottage but I still clearly remember where every dent in every brick is. It only takes me a couple of minutes and before I know it I am perched on her window sill wondering just what the hell to do next.

What am I going to do now I am up here? I did not think this through at all.

I peer through the window like a peeping-tom upscaling his criminal activities. She is not here. That's good, it gives the sensible part of my brain time to kick in and make me go back to the solid ground below.

Or not.

The crazy part of my brain wins, and instead of shimmying my way back down the drain pipe I open the sash window. Swinging both feet into the room I sit there for a moment contemplating what to do next. Am I going to sit here waiting for her until she has finished whatever it is she is up to downstairs? Part of me wants to creep down the passageway and find out what she is doing, but thankfully I don't have to worry because Bex walks into the room just as I am making my master plan.

"Ah!" she screams.

I bounce off the window sill and come towards her, my hands reaching for her skin, eager to feel the sensation of it against my fingertips.

"Shh." Instinctively I pull her in towards me until our bodies are aligned, her breathing is rapid and I can feel her chest rising and falling against my own.

"What the fuck, Joshua, what are you doing here? I nearly had a heart attack." She looks like she is going to continue, like she might be working up into a rant so I stop her words with my lips, coaxing her closer and closer as I do.

There is the briefest moment of hesitation and then she kisses me back hungrily, like having a surprise visitor through the window is the best surprise she has ever had and I should be rewarded for my efforts.

"I'm doing that," I say once I have pulled my lips away.

"But, how?"

I stop her words again. This time as I move my mouth against hers I run one of my hands up her spine and along her bare shoulder. I can't resist it. I slide the strap to her vest top off the curve of her shoulder and lower my lips to the smooth skin. She smells delicious, and feels warm like the sun, as I knew she always would. My concentration is focused on my lips against her skin, but in the back of my mind I register a gasp escaping from her mouth and it makes me pull her even closer. Lifting her in my arms I step for the bed and lower us onto it, leaning my body into hers. I can feel every bit of her against me and it makes me feel this dark urge to be with her. I slide my hand along her belly and up and over her ribs. I want the crazy short shorts off. I want to slide her top over her head and feel her skin meshed with mine, burning into mine. More than that I want to feel what it would be like to be inside her. I know I could lose myself inside of her, and I want that. I want to feel nothing, apart from the sensation of being lost inside her.

Bex pushes me back slightly and her amber eyes seek mine. Slowly she traces a finger along my eyebrow, brushing it over the ring on my brow before sliding the finger along the side of my face all the way to my jaw. Her eyes never break their hold over mine. It is the single most intimate thing anyone has ever done to me. The gentlest of touches which somehow brings me back from the dark edge of need and want I was teetering on. Pushing myself away a little I glance over her face. The amber's are still trained on me, waiting for me to make a move.

"Sorry." I let out a slow breath with my words. The blood pounding through my system eases with the release.

Bex smiles but gives me a firm nod, her hand

grazing down my waist.

I shift myself away before her touch reaches the waistband of my board shorts. I may have gained some resistance but it's not that strong.

"Bex, no." I say as she reaches for me.

Sitting up a little she pushes a hand against my chest. "I don't know what you think. I'm not that kind of girl."

Something about her anger makes me want to laugh. "What kind of girl?"

Her entire countenance changes instantly. The angry girl defending her virtue seconds ago is gone. Her eyes flicker with a direct challenge and she slides another hand down my torso, her reach determined and firm. There is something in her expression I can't read. What is that? Determination? Repulsion? Acceptance? I catch her hands easily in both of mine and lift them above her head. I lean my mouth back down to hers and flick my tongue along the edge of her lips tasting the sun and fire that linger there. I lower my mouth and kiss along the arch of her throat and then all the way back up to her lips.

"Why are you stopping??" She pouts with her words.

"Okay." I take a deep steadying breath. This is uncomfortable. The guilt crushing me is breathtaking. I never thought I would be back in this house, wanting something from someone, not from a person that I don't even know. Believe me I want it. I want her hand to reach their goal, I want to feel myself in her firm grasp and find some form of guilt ridden release in it. But that flicker in her eyes just moments ago is pulling me back.

It hits me in a blinding moment of clarity. She thinks this is what she *should* do.

I feel sick. And then a little bit more. I move my body away from hers creating some space from the heat between our bodies. "Bex. I don't want anything from you." I try to smile with my words, I'm not sure I succeed.

"What do you want then?"

What does she mean, what do I want?

"Uh." Another long breath. "I just want to spend time with you, I'm not expecting anything. You know?"

She looks at me blankly. The ambers gazing at me widely.

"I just," I lean in back towards her. I can't stop myself. "I just want you to want to be with me, to spend time with me, and see where that goes."

In that moment I say words to someone that I never expected to say again. "I want you to be with me."

That's it. I didn't know it, but now I do. I am not going to rush one moment with her. I have ten days to make the girl made of the sun *want* to be with me. Not just do it because it is something that is expected. I have ten days to be with the girl made of sun, and not just want to lose myself inside of her because I want to erase old memories. I have ten days to find myself inside her.

"First base only?"

I grin in response. "Maybe second."

"Am I allowed to take some clothes off?"

I chuckle as I glance down, she is barely wearing anything, just bare feet and tiny shorts with a stretched out vest top that leaves little to the imagination. I know this because my imagination has already had them removed and on the floor.

"What do you plan to take off exactly?"

"All of it."

"Well then that would be a no." But the voice in my head is screaming *yes yes yes*.

She gives a dramatic sigh and gets up from the bed. "I'm going to clean my teeth, and then I am coming back for my make-out session. Be prepared."

"Can I stay over?" I ask as she walks away.

Please don't make me leave.

She turns and looks me over, her eyes dark and intent.

"I wouldn't let you leave."

And as unexpected as it is to me, I know that I wouldn't want her to let me leave.

TEN DAYS TO GO

Bridge Cottage
St Agnes
Cornwall

17th August 2013

Dear E,

He knows about my bangles. I feel kind of bad because they are our thing, me and you. He doesn't know what they stand for but he knows how much they mean to me. I don't know how I feel about that.

After he watched me count them he kissed me. And the truth is I don't know how I feel about that either. At the time I felt guilty. Guilty about you, guilty that he had distracted me from my bangled punishment. But then he distracted me and made it feel like my guilt and worry just washed away. Later when I went to talk to mum and dad about it they weren't even bothered. I thought Dad would be, especially after what happened the other week but he just look amused. I don't get it. It made me confused so I made a huge mistake and called Joshu-a my boyfriend. I know he's not.

He came back later and did it all over again. I don't know

Gone

how he got in my room but I think he may have climbed the wall outside. He strode across the room and grabbed me, kissing me, making me feel something deep in my centre, a feeling I'd never had before. It burnt so hot in my stomach it felt like I was going to catch alight.

It made me want something. Him. Then I remembered all those things people were saying about me in London and I tried to stop myself. I can't be that girl. I know I never have been but I don't want people thinking that I am like that. I don't want him thinking it.

I wish I could talk to you.

Miss you as always

B.xx

Rebecca

Breakfast

I didn't mean to call him my boyfriend in front of my parents. That was a huge error and I regretted it instantly. I saw Mum pull that 'Happy Mum Face' where for a split second she thought I could be like other daughters and manage to make it through a few days or weeks without getting in some form of trouble. But we all know I can't. My dad looked like he was not going to be fooled into believing I could be changed. But then I guess out of the family he has seen me at my absolute lowest; a vision that my mum can't even contemplate. Emily sees me as some form of warrior protector. I don't even think she truly realizes I am the reason behind most of her troubles. My mum sees me as a girl that she used to know who got lost somewhere. It's only my dad who has seen enough to know the truth.

Even last night I could feel London Bex start to rear her ugly needy head.

The switch flipped when he asked me "What sort of girl" I was.

I feel repulsed at myself this morning.

Gone

Joshua stayed all night and the whole night I battled the switch. Part of me hating him being there and wanting him to touch me. The other half of me trying to edge him into taking it further.

He didn't. No matter how hard I pushed in my darker moments.

Finally he pulled away from me, a wide smile stretched across his face, a beautiful smile.

"Rebecca Walters. Stop trying to steal my virtue, a no is a no."

I could feel against me that he didn't really want to say no. The fact that he did instilled in me some calm that I haven't felt in a long time. I don't have to be anything that I don't want to be. I don't have to give anything or do anything I don't want to.

Finally I was able to relax and not live by one of my labels, even for one short night. In doing that I started to experience thing's I'd never felt before. My skin was just burning with my need to have him next to me, skin on skin. The moon shone on his shoulders like silver as he leant down to kiss me, his lips firm and sure as he explored me with his hands. It felt like I wanted to die from needing more.

He was gone this morning when I woke. Next to me on the pillow was a sketch of me on a folded piece of paper. It shows me lying on the bed with my eyes closed, my hair spread over the pillow and half of my face.

I looked at the piece of paper in my hand and the peaceful expression on my face. And then with a shock I realised that with all the strange things that happened last night; a boy in my bed, and mammoth kissing sessions. There was one thing that didn't happen. I didn't have any nightmares.

Ten Days to go.

Cream Tea

After I've showered, I take a long and hard look at myself in the mirror. If I could be that girl from last night maybe I could lose one of those labels after all? Maybe the people here would never know to call me that? Unable to find any profound answer to my question in my mirror image I trek down the stairs. The cottage is deserted so I am guessing the Munch Bunch are out for the day. That's a bit annoying, I would have asked Joshua to stay for breakfast if I knew they were going out early.

I scour the kitchen looking for something to eat. I find a bloomer of bread and hack off a doorstep which I butter and jam. The first mouthful does not go down well. It tastes like, well like bread and jam, but it is not what I want. I am feeling a little restless, more so than normal, and I know the reason why and it is very annoying. I just want to see Joshua again. I want to find the boy made of moon and have breakfast with him. I've never shared a meal with a guy in my life, especially breakfast but today I want to. I find my door key on the sideboard and slip on my flip flops and head out. I am sure I can track him down somewhere.

I go by the shop but it is closed, a sign on the door

saying that it will be open again in twenty minutes. I turn my attention up and down the limited row of shops. The tea room beckons me with steamy windows so I head towards it, not entirely sure what I am looking for. Am I still looking for Joshua? Or am I now in search of a sticky bun and a cup of tea?

A sticky bun wouldn't be bad.

Checking my pocket I make sure I have my left over change from my bonus fiver – I have officially only spent seventy pence since being here. It's a miracle.

I don't find a sticky bun, but I do find Joshua.

He is sat at a far corner, one elbow on the table his head propped in his hand, looking across at the girl from the pictures.

I feel a little wave of sick wash over me and my body does this annoying rigid thing where I get stuck on the spot unable to move.

So did he, or did he not spend most of the night with his hands over a vast percentage of my body, working me into a crazy frenzy?

This completely explains the lack of removal of my clothing. He has a goddam girlfriend. I hate myself first, for being so weak and pathetic, and then I hate him nearly as much.

I can see a glimmer of silver blonde hair over in the far corner and I know instantly it is Emily, which means the Munch Bunch are here. There is no way I am going to go and sit with them and do the whole pretend happy family thing while Joshua is over in the other corner staring lovingly over a cup of tea at the girl from the paintings.

I'm going to turn and leave but the girl with the dark eyes notices me glaring by the door and says something to him. He spins and the green eyes pin me to the spot. I want to move but my feet aren't listening.

"Bex, come over." He gestures to me. Is he mad? He waves again, and my cursed feet just walk towards him.

Has my bloody brain gone on holiday?

I think it must have done, otherwise I would never have got into that situation last night. I don't do evenings of romantic intimate dalliances. It's just not my scene.

"Rebecca," I state.

"Bex, this is Faye." He waves between the two of us and I hesitate for a moment. Is he really introducing me to his girlfriend?

"Hi, Rebecca." The girl with the shiny dark hair smiles at me. "I'm Josh's oldest friend. It's good to meet you finally."

"Yeah why's that?" Pleasantries are not on my to-do list right now.

The Painting girl, or Faye as she is called is undeterred. "Well, we are all pleased that you have broken through Josh's painting brick wall. It's a problem when an award winning painter can think of nothing to paint. Now apparently he can. You." Her words sounds strange but her tone is even and friendly.

"Shut it, Faye." He laughs and shushes her with his

hand.

Hmm.

"Well maybe he should stop," I say.

"Stop what?" she asks.

"Painting me. He won't be able to in a few days when I am gone. Maybe he should go back to painting you." And with that I walk back towards the door not making a second glance in the direction of my family or the sticky buns.

"Bex, wait." He catches up with me out on the pavement, and the door to the tea room clinks shut behind us. One of his hands slides along my arm to grasp hold of me. I hate the tingle that accompanies his touch. Right now I am so mad at myself for allowing myself to be made a fool of. Fourteen days, that's all I had to do before I could leave again. Fourteen days and I could not manage to get through them without getting into some sort of dilemma or trouble.

Did I think that I was going to spend two days with a guy and suddenly all my problems would be gone. No more nightmares, no more screaming? Who am I kidding? I don't deserve that sort of peace.

Fuck, I am so mad at myself I think I am going to explode, or implode. "Is that the girl from the pictures in the shop? The pictures that I couldn't afford to buy apparently?" I keep my voice low, my anger at myself trapped inside.

"No, you have it so wrong. Faye, is a family friend. And I didn't mean it that you couldn't afford it, I just meant they weren't for sale." His face flickers as he clearly remembers his words in the shop that day. "If you would just come back in and sit down and have a cup of tea like a normal person you would realise that Faye is a friend."

Fuck. Did he just say I am not normal?

"What did you say?"

He hesitates, clearly scanning his memory for the error that has made my cheeks flame red.

"Is this about the paintings, because I can't remember what I said, but I didn't even know you then?"

"It's not about the fucking paintings, Josh, it's about me and the fact that I shouldn't have trusted you." I try and take a step back. "I shouldn't trust anyone."

"Bex." He links his fingers through mine but I pull away.

"It's fucking, Rebecca!" I scream.

He moves a step closer into my space. "Rebecca," voice low. "You are the one who said you did not want to share secrets."

Secrets. My whole life is secrets.

"Is she the reason you did not have sex with me last night?"

Joshua leans back from me slightly, his dark green gaze flicking over my face. "No. Not at all."

"Because truth is I wanted to fuck you, but you did not seem that keen."

His eyes widen a little but then become steely with a resolution that I don't understand. He steps right up against me pushing me against the window of the tea shop, one leg pinning me in place.

"What did you say?" his voice is nothing more than a whisper.

Mine, is not. "I said I want to fuck you."

He moves another step closer and the low burn I am beginning to associate with him flames into an outright ache. "Lower your voice, Rebecca, your parents and sister are right through the window. Just how far do you want this to go?"

This makes me hesitate. For a split moment I wonder how this must look to them, how it must look to Emily sat on the other side of the glass pane. Me standing there glaring at a boy with dreadlocks who is right in my space, his taut body just mere millimetres from my own. Then the Rebecca switch is flipped and I lose all sense of propriety.

I want to shout, I want to push him, at him, move him out of my space.

"I wanted to go all the way, you know, shag, fuck, have S.E.X."

He is so close I can feel his breath on my skin. "Don't be cheap now."

Ha. Cheap if only he knew.

I take a deep drag of air, and then another and the red rage starts to ebb away. I push my hands against his chest. "I don't want to see you again. Okay."

And I don't. Trusting people is always my biggest mistake. I'm not going to make that mistake with him again.

The greens sweep over my mouth, then to my eyes one last time.

"Fine. Enjoy your holiday, Rebecca." With that he moves his body away and walks back into the tea room and I am left with an ache that is centred in the pit of my stomach and goes right down to the tip of my toes.

"Fine." I shout after him.

I start to march away, away from him, away from my family and away from my fake home.

Joshua

Girls Lost at Sea

I can't believe she said that in the middle of St Agnes.

"I want to fuck you."

Who taught the girl made of sun to speak like that anyway? It makes my stomach twist to think that she may have said it to someone else before me.

"I want to fuck you."

It keeps reverberating around my brain and every time I hear it I also get this deep stab of longing somewhere inside me. Not just physical but something other; a flicker of recognition at her words and the look on her face as she said them, that sheer defiance and hatred that she had stored up. It made me feel something deep. I just don't know what it was. It is not an emotion that I recognise.

After I swung back into the tea shop I went straight up to her parents' table. Her mum looked like she was on the brink of tears as she worried the rings on her fingers.

"I'm sorry about that." I said.

Bex's Dad looked up at me a look of resignation on

his face, "That's okay, Joshua. You don't really need to apologise to us, we should to you. She will calm down in a bit. If I was you I'd steer clear for a while."

I offered him a smile and walked away. Every step I took I could only think one thing. What on earth has she done for her parents to treat her like that? Like she is a bomb just waiting to go off. I walked back over to Faye. I did not say a word. I just shoved my hand into my pocket, grabbed some change and gave it to her.

"See ya, Josh," she called after me as I walked back out the door.

I know the news will have spread like wildfire. 'Joshua Adams, the poor soul has found someone nearly as fucked up as he is.'

Thing is I don't feel like a poor thing. I feel alive for the first time in ages. I feel challenged. I feel like I want to track her down and do exactly as she asked until I lose myself inside of her. I feel like I want to kiss her every two steps down the high street. I feel like I want to walk up and down it holding her hand, not caring who sees. I feel everything but in the same moment I don't know what she feels, or if she even feels anything at all.

"I want to fuck you."

Now I am staring at the painting in the middle of my studio I feel a distinct urge to darken it. Not because of the words she said, because, let's be honest, I so did want to do that to her last night. Even when she was really pushing me to give in and take her, it was ultimately what I wanted to do, and that is why I didn't.

But there is something else there, a darkness inside of her. I don't think its evil. I can't believe for one moment that she has anything that bitter and twisted inside her, but I think she believes it is there whether it is or not.

I mix some dark paints, adding some grey for a stormy sky, just like her mood this morning and I brush it over the burnished gold. An hour later I have changed the entire mood of the painting. Even Bex herself is now swathed in dark, the edge of it glimmers from under her skin. She is no longer like a sun kissed harvest, now she is something else entirely, something that I can't put into words. A goddess, half the side of light, half, the darkness she can't control. Two elements at war with each other.

The studio is in darkness when my phone starts to ring. The noise wakes me from my reverie and it hits me that I have been in here all day without anything to eat or drink. It's been a long time since that happened.

Faye is on the other end, shouting something at me as soon as I answer. For a moment I can't make sense of her words. They are just a jumble of sounds battering my ears.

"Rebecca," she shouts.

My brain snaps into action on that one key word. "Rebecca."

A sinking sensation fills my stomach and for a moment I can't place myself, am I now? Or am I back then? Is this the phone call that's going to end everything in my life, just like it did six months ago? But Rebecca is not the right name. Rebecca is the name of the girl made of the sun.

"I'm coming now." I shout as I search desperately for where I threw my keys hours before.

I don't even stop to double lock the door, I run straight down the stairs and head for the beach where Faye has told me Bex is.

As soon as I get to the top of the beach I see Faye waving at me. I ditch the flip flops and sprint over to my rock. I can see a shape on the floor but I don't recognise what it is until I get closer and see that Bex is passed out on the damp sand. The sea is about stone's throw away, a child's stone throw.

Jesus Christ.

"How did you find her?" I try and get Bex's head up on my lap, but she is entirely out cold not even registering that she is being moved.

"Andrew and I were going for a walk," she says. I glance up and even in the shadowy light I can see her cheeks flush slightly.

"Thank god. Did you see anything?" I cast my eyes about and notice an empty bottle of vodka.

A little piece of the mysterious jigsaw that is Bex clicks into place. She acts out, but not because she is trying to get attention. If she wanted attention there would have been an empty packet of pills and she would have been further away from the sea.

A single bottle of vodka just tells me that Bex, for whatever reason is trying to forget something. She just can't handle her vodka.

"Bex, wake up." She does not respond to my voice at all.

I direct my attention to Faye. "I'm going to go and get Daisy. Can you sit with her until I get back?"

Faye bends to her knees on the cold sand. "Sure, Josh."

"I don't want to ruin your date."

"Shut your face."

I don't stop. I sprint back over the sand and dash up the lane to Aunt May's to get Daisy who cranks to life with a thundering roar.

What was Bex thinking?

It's all I can think as I negotiate the dark lanes back to the beach.

What was she thinking?

I get back to the beach and find Faye with Bex's head resting in her lap. "She threw up."

"Throwing up is good, we won't have to get her stomach pumped. I don't think her family should hear about this."

"Get her to drink some sea water, remember when. . ." Faye stops talking. She doesn't have to say anything else. I all too clearly recall the memory she is thinking of. It's just one of our many shared memories.

"I remember." I tell her, my eyes meeting hers in the moonlight. Then I lock the memory away, back in my box of things to never be discussed.

I turn my attention back towards Bex and away from the past. "Bex baby." *Baby? Really?* "It's time to wake up, Bex. We've got to get you home."

She groans something and then throws up again, all down my shirt. Clear liquid soaks through to my skin, but I ignore the accompanying chill and slide my hands and arms under her neck and knees, lifting her easily. For a girl so tall she is alarmingly light.

I sink my way back over the sand to Daisy and open the back door somehow managing to wrestle Bex onto the back seat over a mass of rubbish lining the floor. I switch on the middle light which flickers to life with resentment. Bex has some more colour now. Breathing a huge sigh of relief I just grab her into my arms. Shit. The girl who is going, was nearly gone without me getting the chance to say good bye.

I wrap my arms around her tight, and so wish I could take back those shitty words I said to her today "Enjoy your holiday, Rebecca." Who the fuck was I kidding apart from myself. I should have followed her, chased after her. Anything.

I also wish I could take back the stupid arsehole comment I said to her the first time in shop. She must have thought I was a complete wanker. I don't even know why she has been spending time with me. Her words outside the tea shop come back at me "I shouldn't have trusted you," and I realise her spending time with me is as unique to her as it is to me. *Dickhead.*

As I breathe in the scent of sea water lingering on her skin a simple, enlightening fact hits me. I don't want the girl made of sun to go. Not now. Not now she nearly washed away in the sea. I want her to stay on land right by my side.

"I'm gonna go, if you have this?" Faye's voice is tight enough for me to glance up at her, wrenching my attention away from Bex. Faye's eyes are shining in the dim light.

"You okay?"

"Yeah I am, and it looks like you finally are too." She offers me a small smile and then steps away before I get a chance to ask her what she means. It doesn't play on my mind long because I instantly turn my attention back to Bex who is making a strange gurgling sound.

"Bex, you need to open your eyes."

She does not answer but waves her hand at me, which in itself is answer enough in the circumstances. Then she is sick again. She gets poor Daisy's floor this time not me. I rub her back as she retches and coughs.

Leaning forward I place my lips against her hair. "What the fuck were you thinking?" I feel her move a little so I shift back to give her some space. She glares at me through her matted red hair.

"You said," she slurs but then stops, glaring at me instead.

"I said." I can't help but smile. She looks so bloody adorable sitting there all soaked with wet sand, matted and covered in sick.

"I said." She starts again but does not finish.

I squeeze myself onto the seat next to her and slide my arms around her tight tucking her into my side. "Ignore me. Sometimes I am a prick."

She starts to laugh, well at least I think she is

laughing but when my shoulder starts to feel damp I realise she is crying with her arms clung around my neck.

"I'm sorry," she murmurs so low I can barely hear her.

This is so not the Bex I thought I knew. I laugh when my thought registers with me. I've known her three days. Three bloody days and she has spun my entire world on its head. It's still spinning to such an extent that I think I would rather ask her to stay than to be by myself like I was before. My arms tighten another notch.

"Why are you crying?"

She snivels into my neck before responding. "My parents are going to kill me."

I chuckle and push her back to I can see her wide amber eyes staring at me.

"Nah, come on, let's get you sorted. I can't have you grounded. I've got plans for the next few days."

Bex continues to stare at me. "I'm sorry," she says when she has been watching my face for a few moments. She reaches one hand out and slides one of my dreads behind my shoulder.

"I'm sorry too." I link my fingers through hers. "Ready to face the music?"

"No."

"Come on, we are making a stop off first."

Bex does not argue any further she gets up from the back seat clutching her head as she does and clambers over to the front seat resting her head against the window. I climb over as well and then lean against her as I buckle her in. I go to tell her that I am going to take us to my studio, but she has gone straight back to sleep again.

Two minutes later I pull Daisy straight onto the pavement outside the shop and jump down to let Bex out. She still has her eyes closed so I shift my arms about her again to lift her out of the car.

"I can walk."

"I can carry you."

"I should walk."

Reluctantly I release my grip on her and she places her feet on the floor. I expect her to move away from me but she surprises me by sliding her hand into mine. I clasp hers tightly in response tying us together with our entwined fingers.

"Thank you, Joshua," she says. Her voice is low and the way she says my name makes it sound like she is singing a song.

"We haven't got you home yet, one thing at a time."

Opening the front door I lead her up the flight of stairs to the studio. Something happens to the atmosphere on the climb and by the time we are at the top the air feels much heavier, like we have climbed a mountain instead of twenty steps.

"Through here." I motion my way through the door and flip on the light. Swathes of brightness land on us, and I instantly regret the bright bulbs I put in for my late night painting sessions.

Bex has her eyes fixed on the easel in the middle of the room off the small hallway. I hear a small gasp escape her lips as she walks towards it.

Watching I wait for her to say something. She stares at my first work in half a year, and I feel a nervousness I've never encountered with my work before. Normally I just paint and expect people to like it, to gush over it, to want it. I don't think she is going to do any of those things. She says nothing. And then a little bit more nothing.

Finally after what feels like an age she turns to me and the damp track marks of tears are painfully obvious on her face.

"Is that how you see me?" she says."

I look between the real her, and the picture I have drawn of her on the beach in her bikini the first time I ever saw her. The goddess I created today when I made her half-light, half dark, and a continuous contrast.

"Yeah it is."

"I wish I could see that too." Her voice breaks on the final word and the note makes my stomach tighten. I push it away and reach my hand for hers.

"Come, let's get you showered."

I lead her to the small shower room Aunt May put in when she got fed up with me stinking out the place. A five day straight paintathon will do that to a guy.

I turn the dial of the shower and reach my hand under the water making sure the hot still works and then step back.

"Don't leave me," she says.

"I'll wait on the other side of the door," I offer.

Best try to make a stab at gentlemanly behaviour.

"Just stay here, okay."

Something about the way she says it roots me to the spot and I don't move a muscle as she peels off her damp shorts, top and underwear.

Shit.

My throat is ridiculously tight as I watch her get into the shower and stand under the water with her eyes closed. She is so beautiful. I am not even going to offend her by describing her as hot, because that just would not be adequate. Beautiful. It's the only word to use.

"Wanna get in?" She still has her eyes closed.

"No. You're still sandy."

"You could help me wash it off."

I reach one hand into the shower and slide it up her arm, brushing at some of the sand. For a girl who was passed out an hour ago she moves surprisingly fast. Her hand snakes out grabbing mine and before I can form any level of physical resistance she pulls me into the shower with my clothes on, fitting her naked body against mine.

She does not make any moves at all. She just pulls me in tight and wraps her arms around my waist as the water slides over the both of us.

"Thank you for finding me."

I say the words before I can stop myself, "I will always find you" But what I mean is that I will always want to find her. Even after she is gone.

NINE DAYS TO GO

Bridge Cottage
St Agnes
Cornwall

18th August 2013

Dear E,
She was back. London Bex. The one you got so cross with that night. I've been winning my fight against her, mostly, but yesterday I did something so crazy stupid.

You will hate me when you know, but I can't not tell you. It was so silly but I saw Josh-u-a sitting with another girl in a café and I just flipped. I know I had no right but at the same time I couldn't stop it. I couldn't control it. I don't think I will ever win my fight against her. London Bex.

I drank a bottle of vodka and passed out next to the sea. I can hear you shouting at me. I can only think what it would have done to mum and dad if I'd been swept away in the sea. What would have happened to Emily? Would they have been relieved that the problem that is Bex had finally been taken care of?

Josh-u-a found me, took me home, cleaned me up, made me

safe.

I don't know why. I don't deserve to be rescued by anyone.

He stood with me for the longest time wearing all his clothes under a steaming hot shower and his arms were so tight around me it felt like he may always be able to rescue me no matter what happens.

Crazy right?
Miss you as always
   B.

xx

Rebecca

Breakfast

The sun is streaming through the windows and it burns into my one open eyeball like a red hot poker. *Bloody hell.*

Then I remember the bottle of vodka, the throwing up, the shower and falling asleep in Joshua's arms.

"You're awake." I feel the pressure of lips against the top of my head and I tighten my arms around his bare chest.

"I wish I wasn't." There is a second of hesitation while he tries to work out what I mean. That came out so wrong. "I mean my head hurts, quite badly." He chuckles beneath me and kisses my hair again. In response I do something I have never done before. I snuggle. That's right I snuggle against him, allowing my lips to gently brush against his skin with my movement.

I want to avoid eye contact for as long as possible. What must he think? To all intents and purposes it must have looked like I was trying to top myself. Who drinks a litre of vodka that close to the tide?

I do.

Of all the times I wished I was dead, this morning is not one of them. Tears sting the back of my eyelids when I think of what could have been. What I would have done to Emily if that sea had crept up the sand another metre or so.

Joshua lifts my face with his fingertips so I have to look at him.

"Morning." He smiles, his green's dazzling in the sunlight.

"Morning."

"What do you fancy for breakfast?"

The thought of eating anything makes my stomach roll. Joshua wiggles himself so we are level, his nose touching mine. He stares at me before allowing one corner of his mouth curve up in a smile. "No more vodka."

Vodka.

I must turn a funny colour because he chuckles as he skims his nose along my cheek. I breathe him in, how can he still smell of the sea and mint? My hands move from around his waist and I slide them down his chest. It might be my imagination but I am sure I see the greens darken fractionally.

"Be. . ." he starts but does not get to finish because there is a loud knock at the door.

"Rebecca?" Shit. It's my dad.

We look at each other in shock, and then in a move worthy of the GB gymnastics team Joshua rolls off the bed and underneath it before dad has turned the handle and slowly pushed the door open.

"Who you talking too?" he asks hovering in the

doorway, clearly unsure whether to come in.

I pull my duvet up and offer him a smile. He looks confused at my smile, but I guess my family aren't that used to having a beaming Rebecca around.

"No one, Dad. I was having a debate about what to do today."

"What are you going to do today?"

Snog boys with dreadlocks.

"I don't know yet."

Dad walks over and lowers himself uncomfortably to the bed. Before he has a chance to investigate closer and find two head shaped dents on pillows I throw myself back onto them.

"Bex, can I talk to you about something."

"It's Rebecca and yes you can." My voice sounds uncomfortably tight. There is something in his tone which is making me very aware of the fact Joshua is under the bed able to hear everything my dad is about to say.

"I wanted to talk to you about what happened on the high street yesterday, and what you said to that young man."

Crap.

"Dad, I already apologised to you guys yesterday, and I also apologised to Josh." For some reason I can't explain I can't call him Joshua in front of my dad. There is something strangely intimate about it.

"Yeah, I know and that's what I wanted to talk to you about. It's just you seem a different girl to the one that we dragged kicking and screaming into the car just a few days ago in London. I just wanted to let you know that I kind of like her."

Blank. My brain is completely blank.

There is a split second of uncomfortable silence as I scramble for something to say. "Dad, you of all people know that I am not going to change my mind about leaving, money or no money, I can't stay."

"Why?"

"Uh, because of Emily. She's gonna start that new school in a few weeks and it won't be long before I am the reason she gets teased again. When it does, I won't be able to help myself, again, and the family will be back to square one, again. Everywhere I go everyone will look at me as the girl that causes trouble, and every time they look at you they will think, there is the dad of that girl that causes trouble, or the sister, or the mother. I don't want that anymore. I'm always going to be ruining everything for you all."

"Rebecca, none of us blame you for what happened that night, we have only ever supported you and believed everything you told us."

I glare at my dad. We are never ever allowed to talk about it. That and the fact I know Joshua is under the bed listening.

"Dad the only reason you say that is because I am your daughter and you are obliged to. If I wasn't you would believe the same as everyone else."

My heart squeezes as I remember the night I earned another label. Well, not the night itself, because I still can't remember that, no matter how hard I try. But I recall only too clearly the next day.

The day I lost everything including myself. The night that resulted in the bangle prison sentence that hangs over my heart.

"Rebecca, will you just learn to behave and get in the damn car." I lock the voice away.

Dad stares at me intently watching my face. "One of these days Rebecca you will realise how much your mum and I love you. I just hope it's before we lose you for good."

"Love me?" I shout. "How can you love me? What about the other week? What about what I made you see??" This is the clincher. It was the events of the night two and a bit weeks ago that sealed our move to the country and upgraded the move from something that my parents would like to do, into something that they had to do as soon as they could.

Dad shifts uncomfortably and turns to face me. Squaring his shoulders he reaches for my hand. "Rebecca, you just need to promise me that you will never get yourself into that situation again, because the truth is, if I believe that, then I may be able to let you go."

I stare long and hard at him, my eyes reading the new lines around his mouth and across his forehead and I know I am the one who put them there.

"I'm sorry, Dad." My throat tightens.

"So am I. I'm sorry that your mum and I never taught you to value yourself."

"What do you mean?"

"You're beautiful, Rebecca, we should have told you every damn day until you saw it yourself, so that you could see the light instead of the dark. Then you would never have trusted people who would use you and abuse you."

Although I hate crying more than anything in the world, hot fast tears slide down my face. It's the second time I have cried in as many days and with every drop of saltwater I feel like I am coming undone.

"I'm sorry you lost your job." The words wrench their way out of my throat.

Dad reaches for me and smooths down my straw hair. "Are you kidding me? It's the best thing I've ever done. Well that and the act that necessitated my freelancing."

I grimace and compulsively shudder.

Gently he tucks my hair back behind my ear, something he hasn't done for years. "You know, Rebecca, you need to stop living by what other people tell you about yourself."

"Maybe." I concede.

"Spend time with your sister before you leave, she's going to miss you."

Oh god. I start to cry harder.

"I'm going to miss her too, Dad, that's why I have got to go."

Dad pats my head again and then gets up from the bed. "Family dinner tonight?"

"Since when do we have family dinner?"

"Since tonight. You can bring Josh if you like."

"Dad!"

"Okay, I'm going." He raises his palms in a

surrender motion. As he gets to the door he turns and faces me. "We want you to stay, Rebecca, but we also understand why you've got to go." And with that he lets the door swing shut behind him. I watch it for a moment and wait for Joshua to come out from under the bed.

Joshua kneels on the bed next to me and touches his fingers under my chin lifting my face to his. My face feels damp and sticky from my outburst of tears and I clamp my teeth down on my lower lip to stop myself from crying anymore.

"What happened, Bex?" He leans down and kisses along my cheek, gently fluttering kisses all the way around my eyes, absorbing my tears with his lips. Slowly his fingers link through my hair and he lowers his mouth to mine. It's a different kind of kiss, this is slow and tender like he is trying to unravel all my secrets with the taste of his mouth.

"I can't tell you." I pull my mouth away my heart thudding uncomfortably.

"Why?"

"If I told you, then you would judge me and I probably wouldn't see you again." The thought of not seeing him again makes me get this unfamiliar ache in my chest.

Joshua pushes away from me slightly. "It's okay, we said we would keep our secrets. I'm not going to push."

He slowly lifts one side of his lips into a crooked smile and the green's read deep into me.

I speak without thinking. "Two weeks ago my dad

was worried about me because I didn't come home from a party."

Joshua leans back further still, the green gaze steady and intent. His hands hold my shoulders, smoothing circles with his thumbs. "Yes?"

"The party was at the flat of the son of Dad's boss. Dad didn't like me spending time with him because everyone knew he was a druggie and something really bad happened a while back. I promised Dad that I wouldn't see him anymore. But." My voice falters.

"Yes?" Josh keeps his gaze steady.

"I was just bored. I hadn't been out in months. I'd just been sat around doing nothing. I didn't know where else to go. So I called him up, grabbed my stuff and legged it. Thankfully I left a note in my room." I hesitate again.

"Why are you thankful about that Bex?" I stare into the pool of green as I cast my mind back to the night a couple of weeks ago, the nightmare evening that changed the course of everything. The night that consequently lead me to be sitting on a bed with Joshua, laying bare some of the horrible things I've done. "The party was manic, as they always are. I should have known better. The last time I left one of those parties everything was destroyed, this time was no different. I drank a bottle of vodka. I hadn't drunk in months, hadn't touched anything in months. Then someone offered me a spliff and I thought, fuck it why not? I mean shit happens to me anyway, why should I try and stop it?" It's hard to explain, it's like there's a switch in my brain and when it's flipped I can't hold myself back.

It ends in destruction."

I don't tell him that yesterday on the high street was the switch being flipped. That I can't stop it, that I need to push until people leave me or don't want to be around me anymore. Joshua's fingers are still rubbing their soothing circles. "And?"

"And well that's kind of it. Dad came to find me in the end. Found me doing some stuff that I shouldn't have been. That I wish I hadn't been. He decked his bosses' son and dragged me out."

"Fuck, Bex."

"That wasn't all. Dad got the sack and well I got rebranded. I mean I've been living with labels so long it almost wouldn't have mattered but I couldn't let Emily go through it all again."

"Go through what?"

"Being blamed for who I am. Teased for who I am."

"Can you tell me why?"

"No."

His voice is so low I can barely hear his next words. "What did they call you Bex? Before you came here?"

"A whore." The words hammer into the air between us and I feel the slice of every syllable cut me deep.

I start to extract myself from his embrace, thinking it better if I am the one to do it. But instead of letting me move away he grasps his hands around my arms and holds me still.

"Don't run." His voice is so low I can barely hear

it. He holds me firmly as I battle my emotions on the inside.

"Don't run," he says again, his voice firmer and a fraction louder.

It's hard because every cell in my body is telling me to move away from him, to run as fast as I can and don't look back. I don't do sharing secrets, and I don't do heartfelt conversations about the mistakes I have made.

I don't even tell people the mistakes I have made. I just hide, so no one will ever know them. Know me.

His fingers don't let go and I squirm against him. I want to hide my face and duck away from the shame that I feel. It's been over two weeks. Two weeks of continual hell, a hell that I only really started to forget about when I met the boy made of the moon and sea. The limited memories I have assault my brain, my Dad's face when he told us about losing his job. The guilt and the blame that is stamped on my heart because I have repeatedly caused grief for my family and the fact that I know that the only way I can protect them is by leaving them.

Tears start to course down my face again, and my breathing takes on a strangled feeling as it attempts to fight its way out along with my gush of emotions.

Joshua slowly, so slowly, pulls me in towards him and I bury my head in his chest as sobs rack through me. This is why I don't like to think about the things that I have done. It's never pretty. I can feel his lips against my hair and he makes a shushing noise.

We kneel like that for what feels like an age on the bed,

until I start to feel his body go rigid under my touch. This is going to be it. He must have realised what I was doing at the party. What my dad found me doing.

Now he's going to go.

"Who was it?"

"What?" I look up through my sore eyes and try to read his face.

"Who was the guy whose party you were at?"

I give a humourless laugh, "I don't think it matters."

"It matters to me, because I want to kill him." Joshua is staring at me earnestly, no bravado behind his words. Just a flat resolution.

"It doesn't matter," I say again. Joshua continues to evaluate me, his gaze level with mine. His face is so close to mine our noses are touching, which in any circumstance other than me baring my soul would be quite amusing.

I see it click inside his mind before he speaks. His eyes give him away. "This isn't the secret that you think defines you is it? There is something else?"

'Rebecca will you just learn to behave, and get in the damn car?'

I laugh, a crazed sound I am unable to control. "Joshua, with me there is always something else. That's why I have to go."

He thinks over my words for a moment, weighing his response, our faces still millimetres away from each other. "Will you stay with me until you go?"

"What do you mean?"

"You and me, give me the next nine days to show you, you're not a girl to be labelled."

"Bu—" He cuts off the rest of my words with his

lips. His kiss is something else, not the playful game from the other night, nor any other shared moment we have had. It's hungry, and demanding and all consuming. His tongue teases inside my mouth and entwines with my own and he presses his body against me tight. With one hand he gently reaches up and touches my face. I pull away and stare into the pool of green. "Yes."

Joshua catches my face in both his hands and flashes me his wide smile. "Rebecca Walters, I am so very pleased you said yes."

I smile back at him, my own cheeks feeling like they are going to split.

"I'm going to be back in half an hour, you and Emily be ready."

"Emily?"

"Yes. You need to spend time with your sister before you go, and as I am unwilling to relinquish any of my time, it will be a day trip for three."

He doesn't explain further, he heads over towards the window and slides it up.

"You're crazy."

He winks at me as he dips over the side of the window ledge and I stand there for a good five minutes smiling to myself in the middle of my room.

Nine days to go.

Joshua

Castles in the Sand

I was smiling as I went over the window ledge, my smile frozen on my face, but as soon as I was out of sight the bitterness that was eating into me took over. I can't believe what she told me. It's making me feel something I have never felt before. Rage. The thought of anyone labelling Bex and making her believe something like that about herself makes me want to kill, or maim.

I held it together in front of her, but the moment she said the words and revealed her secret I wanted to kill the fucker who thought they could mess with her. She didn't tell me exactly what it was that her dad caught her doing, but she didn't really need to. It was painted in disgust all over her face and in the label she divulged. This is what she meant the other night when she gave me the death stare and told me she wasn't that sort of girl. I don't think for one moment she is. She just can't control herself, this much was evident last night in her unconscious form on the beach. Some fucker took advantage of that.

I'm going to kill someone. It's burning through my veins. Jesus a few days ago it felt like I'd been part of the living dead for months. Today I am burning with such a fury and with so much adrenaline pumping through me I feel like I could run all the way from here to London just to punch some twat in the face.

I want to know who it was. I wonder if I can find out on Facebook? Shit she doesn't have a Facebook, and now I know why. I doubt she has any internet presence at all if that's what people have been saying about her.

I could ask her Dad, find out where he used to work. I could track the bastard down that way.

Who am I kidding? What can I do anyway?

I never planned on asking her to spend her remaining time here in St Agnes with me. I felt like an idiot asking, but I couldn't not. I need to show her how I see her. I want her to value herself for what she is, not what people say about her, and I want to show her that sometimes you can be loved the right way. I am no expert, but I feel it deep inside me that together we could be something else. I have nine days to show her what possibilities she has open to her.

The sick bit is that after she told me I wanted her even more. I wanted to take every inch of her and show her what she is worth to me. Everything. I wanted to possess her and in that moment for her to find and possess me too.

I've got nine days left to make the girl of sun value herself. Nine days to show her what it means to have someone worship you. Nine days left for her to fill my life with sunlight.

I don't have a plan, so I head back to Aunt May's. I

haven't been back home in days and I know I need to check in and get some clean clothes.

Aunt May is standing in the kitchen when I get back. I watch her shoulders lower as I walk through the door.

"Hey," I call.

She turns to face me and I can see the worry etched on her face. "Hey, Josh, did you run out of clean pants?"

"Very funny." I walk up to her and wrap my arms tight around her. "Am I in the dog house?"

"Bah, get away with you, bloody big softie." She waves me away. "Eggs?"

Oh god. Aunt May is obsessed with eggs for breakfast. According to her you can't face the day without eggs. This morning it looks like she is creating Eggs Benedict. To be fair to my only living relative she is creative with eggs, and she is an amazing cook, so it is not often I have to worry about what may be served up. Normally I would love this and be scraping seconds out of the bowl. Today my stomach feels off, like I am standing on a boat and the roll of the waves is setting my digestive system on edge. I can't stop thinking about what Bex told me, nor my murderous need to kill the people who made her believe that about herself.

"Are you going to the beach?" Aunt May asks. She pushes a cup of tea in front of me. She does not believe in coffee and is of the staunch faith that a cup of tea can fix most things and that is a stance she will never change.

This means I normally have to get my cup of Joe from the overpriced coffee shop on the way back from the beach. It's not such a problem though. I don't normally have a huge amount of pressing engagements to worry about.

I used to. I always used to be under a deadline – must get this project completed, or, must make sure that I am in this place or that for a specific time. Not so much of late.

Aunt May is still letting me coast but I know my time is running out. She has been my guardian since I was five and I know her well enough to know that my stay of grace from her sharp tongue will not last a huge amount longer.

"Yeah I may go." I shrug a little, keeping my answer vague. For some reason I am unwilling to admit that I am going to see Bex.

"You going to see that new girl again today?" she asks reading my thoughts.

"Doubt it," I lie.

"She looks like trouble."

I swallow down the surge of anger that rises. "Why? Because she wears black and has a love of bangles?"

"No, because girls who say what I hear she said always are."

"What? How do you even know that?"

"The whole town knows, Josh." I ignore her pointed look and butter some toast. I don't want to fight with my only relative who has seen me through so much. "What are those bangles about?" she adds almost to herself.

The bangles. The bangles are important, I just don't know why. I give another half-hearted shrug. "I am not sure, but they mean something to her, she counts them as she puts them on."

Aunt May instantly raises an eyebrow. Damn it. I don't want to start that rumour mill off. "Not what you think, I saw her put them on the other day, she counts each one on whilst screwing her eyes shut like she is trying to block something out, or maybe keep something in."

"She is odd, be careful."

"Yeah, yeah." I am not sure Aunt May really gets to have the final say on who is odd or not.

I dash up the stairs to the shower and stand under the hot water. I can't get the vision of Bex in the shower at the studio out of my head. It is doing nothing to settle the waves of alien emotions that are washing about inside me. That moment when she pulled me into the shower and wrapped her arms around me, that was something else. It wasn't even sexual, although it could have been. Instead it felt like she was clinging onto me, and holding on for dear life. There is a very small part of me that hopes that she was.

By the time I am out of shower and dressed I have a clear plan for the day. Emily will love it. All young girls like castles don't they? She can draw the scenery and I can draw Bex so that when she has gone I still ultimately have her.

***

"What are you doing?" Bex is lying on her tummy her gaze transfixed over the edge of the cliff at the sea rolling below.

We have wandered along the castle walls, our fingers entwined as we watched Emily skip along like a lost flower fairy, her hair glistening in the sunlight. The weather is warm and dry, perfect conditions for lounging about enjoying the Cornish coast and the remarkable castle I have brought them to, which is built into the rock. Bex was squealing with delight when she saw it, until she realised the noise she could hear was coming from herself, then she clamped one hand over her mouth, her freckles scrunched around her eyes as she attempted to stop smiling.

"Wow!" Is as all she said as she twirled on the spot looking around her. It's funny because I thought Emily would be the most excited out of the two, but Bex won that competition hands down. She gave so much of herself away in those few minutes, more than she did with her big secret reveal this morning.

"Do you not have beautiful places like this in London?" I asked.

Bex thought about this before giving a small shake of her head. "Not that I ever saw."

I smiled. "Well that's a pity. We should take a photo for you to take back."

Now she is chewing some long stems of grass, her amber eyes trained on the sea as I attempt to draw her. Emily has already insisted that I draw the both of them together, which I did happily. It can be a gift for

Bex when she leaves. Something to remember our day trip by. Now I am cursing that I only brought my charcoals with me, I am gutted because the sun is lifting off her skin like an iridescent glow and I know if I try and capture it when I get home I won't be able to. Not properly anyway.

"You're not drawing me are you?"

"No, ma'am."

"Joshua?" God the way she says my name kills me. It makes me want to take her apart. I cast my eyes about and look for Emily who is off in the distance distracted by a formation of rock. Bex is looking up at me shielding her eyes from the sun. Placing my sketch pad on the ground I move myself towards her. "Josh." Her voice holds a warning and I know she is glancing towards Emily. I don't care. I wrap my fingers around her wrist, my thumb placed against the faint pulse that beats there. Although she opens her lips, with a slight curve lifting one corner and closes her eyes, I don't kiss her. That is what she is expecting. Instead I trail my index finger around the outline of her mouth, memorising their shape. She bites down a smile, her nose wiggling as she does. Perfect. Gently I lean in and kiss the tip of her nose. Bex tilts her mouth up towards mine and although I wasn't going to kiss her I end up doing it anyway. She is warm and fiery and I need to feel her against me. Edging myself as close as possible, I release her wrist and slide my hand up her spine. My body responds to hers and as she shifts herself against me I know she feels it too. It's like every fibre in my body which is touching hers is super aware of how close she is to me. Smoothing my hand along the curve of her waist, my thumb runs along the edge of her ribs and I am gutted that I am on the edge of a cliff overlooking the sea. If I wasn't then I would probably lower my hand further to the waist band of her shorts which I would slide my fingers inside, not too far, just enough to make her push her body into mine even closer. Just like she did the other night when we did this for hours.

"Do you guys mind?" *Uh. Emily.* I'd completely forgotten about her standing a few feet away.

"I don't mind," I call out, my lips still against Bex' mouth. "Do you? I say lower, so just Bex can hear.

"Not minding at all." She smiles the words back against me. I start to pull away but she grabs me round the neck and plants a smacker full on my mouth. "I don't mind in the slightest," she murmurs.

Emily peals a ring of laughter. "Bex and Joshua, sitting in a tree," she chimes.

"Shut it, Midge." Bex scowls at her sister, it's not the scariest scowl I have ever seen. It's ever so slightly undermined by the enormous smile beaming from her face.

I don't want the day of revelations, castles and kissing to end. "Any chance you will be allowed out with me tonight?"

Bex leans back and looks at me. The ambers absorb the sun and throw it straight back out at me. I am blinded by her. I can't see further than her and I wait holding my breath for her answer. I so want her to go out with me. As in properly, not just random kissing and hand holding.

"What, like on a date?" she asks.

"Maybe."

"A real date?"

"What does a real date involve?"

"I don't know I've never had one."

I concentrate on the ambers for a moment to see if she is being serious. I think she is. *Jesus.*

"A real date it is." I state firmly.

A little silver head pops between us. "Someone's going to have to ask Mum and Dad."

"Do not." Bex frowns. This time the frown is far more realistic.

"Josh, you'd better do it. They like you." Emily laughs again with her words.

In a move I would never envision her making Bex starts to chase after her sister, both of them screeching as they run over the grass. Laughing, I watch them chase each other until I see them get very close to the edge of the wall. Shit. I can't have them falling into the sea. I'd never be allowed to take her on a date then.

Rebecca

To Date or Not to Date

"What you going to wear?" Emily is sat on my bed, her legs swinging as she watches me pull a comb through the orange straw that I sadly have to call hair.

"This?" I wave at my clothed body.

Emily looks me up and down. "But that's what you wore to the castle?"

"Yep."

I had my shower and dried myself off before putting back on my dirty clothes. I put clean pants on. Just in case.

Excitedly Em throws herself back onto the mattress and with great enthusiasm starts to kick her legs on the bed. "Bex, you are so ridiculously clueless, it's scary. I am thirteen and I know more than you!"

"Yeah, how many dates have you had?"

"Two."

Oh. That's a bit of a bitch.

Concentrating on parting my hair in the middle before working out just what to do with it, I glance at her in the mirror. "What am I doing wrong then?"

Crossing her legs Em sits back up on the bed and stares at my reflection. "Okay, do I need to go over basics with you?"

"What are the basics?"

"What sort of date is it?"

I give a sigh and twist my hair up out of the way to start my make-up. "Is there more than one kind of date, because no one has told me that?"

"Is it casual? Dinner? Drink? Oh no you're not allowed alcohol."

"Very funny." Splodging a squirt of foundation on my make-up sponge I grimace at her little blonde perfect self.

"Firstly stop what you are doing. You don't need the make-up."

"Excuse me? I think you'll find I do."

"No you don't. Secondly, just in case you haven't noticed, Joshua is crazy hot, scorching hot, volcano erupting hot."

I blush instantly. Nope, I had failed to register that fact at all. *Not*. "That's enough from you. You're too young for thoughts like that."

Em sticks her tongue out at me before continuing my date lecture. "You can't go out in the same shitty clothes he saw you in today. He needs to know you want to go on a date, and that you have tried to make an effort despite the fact you two have been rolling in the grass all afternoon."

"Why?"

"Because guys like to feel they are not the only one's doing the chasing."

"Well I'm not chasing."

With a dramatic eye-roll Em gets up from the bed.

"I'll organise your outfit, you get your hair to behave and do something."

"Yes, Miss." I make a strange sound and Em turns and looks at me in surprise.

"Did you just giggle?"

"No." I don't giggle. Ever. Although that was a weird noise I just made.

With a superior rise of her eyebrow she turns back to my cupboard and I continue to stare in the mirror. No make-up, really? She must be mad! Maybe just a little bit of eyeliner then, that's a fair compromise between all and nothing.

Ignoring my hair I set about darkening my eyes while I watch Em pull together an outfit.

"There," she announces proudly.

I look at the green scarf and skinny jeans.

"I can't wear that!"

"Why?"

"Because I can't wear a bra with it!"

Marching over to the window she slides the pane of glass up and peers outside. "No. I can't see them."

"Get back in from the window before you fall on your head. What can't you see?"

"There should be pigs flying past because Rebecca Walters has just said she is worried about going out without a bra."

"Okay, that's enough, get out!"

Giggling Em heads for the door, she is halfway down the stairs when she shouts up, "Better hurry up, Bex, I can hear his van outside."

"Shit!"

I scramble to fit into my jeans and quickly tie the scarf into a halter neck top. I am running down the stairs to get to the door first when I remember my hair. Crap. Up it is.

Rebecca Walter is going on her first date ever, with mad hair and no make-up, and I thought I was supposed to be making an effort!?

Joshua

The Date

I'm grinning like a lunatic as Daisy comes to a shuddering halt by the front gate of Bridge Cottage. I've been unable to stop grinning all afternoon. What a geek. It's the date. The date was approved by Bex' mum and dad who looked slightly confused when I dropped the girls off earlier, after our castle jaunt, and asked if they would mind me taking Bex out for the evening.

There is a minor problem in the date scenario. I've never really been on one either, not something I was willing to admit to Bex this afternoon.

To make this feel like something other than hanging out with each other at the beach I am wearing jeans. Obviously I still have my flip flops on with them, my hair tied back in a loose band and a slightly smarter T-shirt, but I like to think I have made a half decent effort at dressing up for our date.

When the front door to the cottage opens I realise I have not made enough of an effort, because Bex is standing there looking mind-blowing. Hair twisted up with loose strands falling around her neck combined with skinny jeans and a dark emerald green silk halter neck top that when she turns I can see exposes all of her back.

Shit.

There is no way I'm going to be able to keep my hands off the smooth expanse of skin exposed between the two ties keeping the top in place. Suddenly the date seems like much more of a challenge.

"You okay?" she asks. I am standing on the doorstep with my mouth hanging open.

"Um, yeah. Uh you look nice. Uh, I mean beautiful." *Just call me Mr. Smooth.*

Bex hesitates like she is not sure what to do next. "I'm not quite ready. I need to finish my make-up." She holds the door open making room for me to walk in which I do, taking a step closer to her.

"Stay as you are." Okay, even I can hear my voice is noticeably a pitch lower.

"You're kidding right?"

I move my hand towards hers clasping our fingers together. "Nope."

"Told you," shouts a voice from a different room.

"Shut it," Bex shouts back.

"You kids ready then?" Bex's dad walks into the hallway and I try to drop her hand. She doesn't let go of mine, she holds onto my fingers tighter. I stand a little straighter in response.

"Yes, sir." I say. *Yes sir? Yes sir?*

"Be back by midnight please, Bex." He gives Bex a smile and watches as she registers his words.

"Midnight? But the coach will turn back into a pumpkin."

Her dad laughs a loud burst of laughter. "Go before I change my mind."

"But what about my ball dress?"

"Eleven thirty."

"Glass slippers?"

"Eleven."

At this Bex gives a screech and pulls me by the hand to the door. "See you at midnight, Dad."

I am just going through the door when her dad touches me on the arm. "Take care of her."

I turn and look him straight in the eyes, "I plan to." And with that I am through the door and about to go on my first real date, in what could possibly be classified as forever.

"So where we going?" Bex is practically bouncing with excitement as she buckles up her seatbelt.

"First you have got to apologise to Daisy for calling her a pumpkin."

"I'm not apologising to a car."

I turn the key halfway in the ignition and let the engine falter on the start. "Nope, she is going to need a stroke, or an encouraging word."

"Okay, are we talking about the car or you? Because if you want me to stroke you, you really just have to say."

I turn and raise my eyebrow at her until she scrunches her face at me. "Sorry."

"Say it louder so Daisy hears."

"For fucks sake, I am sorry. Can we get going

before I change my mind?"

I start the engine. "Now that wasn't too hard was it?"

Bex pulls a face and looks out of the window.

"I can see you in the wing mirror."

She pulls the face more.

"Very attractive."

"So where are we going anyway?" She turns back to face me.

I leave her question hanging there for two minutes until I apply the brakes and pull the handbrake up. "We are here."

Bex looks out of the window and peers into the darkening evening. "It's the beach."

"Yep."

"Really? I put my best top on, and squeezed into my jeans for the beach?"

"Stop moaning and come and see." I jump out of my side of Daisy and make the point to get to her door in time to open it before she does. She slides out and offers me a smile that is borderline shy.

"Bex?"

"Yes?"

Stepping her back against Daisy's door I press my body tight against hers. "Thank you for coming on a date with me." I lower my lips and kiss under her ear where I can catch the faintest hint of a floral perfume.

"Well you know, I don't wear this top for just anyone." She smiles at me again, this time the smile has a taunting edge to it.

The blood pulses in my veins. *She had so better not.*

"Well that is a good thing." My voice has that low unique depth to it I only heard for the first time today. "Because I think I would be very jealous if you did."

This is quite an ironic statement because I think it's the most clothes I have ever seen her wear. It's kind of sexy, but I have a distinct urge to take them off.

Bex reaches up and places her lips against mine, grazing her teeth against my bottom lip which makes my stomach tighten. "You've nothing to be jealous of, Joshua." she sing songs my name and my stomach tightens even more. "So are we doing this date?"

"Come on then, Miss Walters." I grab her hand and lead her over to the sand. I slip off my flip flops and she does the same so I pick up both pairs and walk us down towards the rock where we sat talking the first day I met her, and where I found her just last night before the sea tried to steal her away from me. Christ was that only last night? It seems like forever ago.

Bex gives a little gasp as we pull closer and I give myself a mental high five like a complete loser. Before I went to pick her up I set up about fifty tea-light candles, hoping to god they would not go out. Blankets are laid amongst the candles and I have a stash of driftwood ready to burn.

"Ever seen blue flames before?"

"Yeah on a gas hob."

I burst out laughing. "Funny and good looking, is there anything you can't do?"

"Surf."

"Well that's true. We're working on that."

I snag a lighter out of my back pocket and set light to the tinder in the middle of the fire. Grabbing her hand I pull her onto her knees on the blanket. "Watch." I point to the fire as the crackling and spitting starts.

"Watch for what?" She moves herself right into my side and I wrap a firm arm tight around her as we settle on the blanket.

"Wait."

"I'm not good at waiting."

"Well I can help with that." I tilt her mouth towards mine and kiss her with the slowest most lingering kiss I can manage, while also trying to keep one eye on the fire.

"Look now," I say.

She turns her head towards the fire and gives a loud gasp. "Shit its blue."

"Yep and no gas around."

"I would ask for you to explain, but really I just want to snog."

"Well, that, I am more than happy to help you with." I push her back against the blanket and climb over her lap as she grins up at me. "Now you see, the salt from the sea crystallises and when the fire—"

"Josh, very pretty, now just kiss me Goddamn it."

So I do.

An hour of dedicated snogging later I can hear her stomach rumbling above the waves rolling on the sand.

"Hungry?" I ask against her mouth.

Bex hesitates twirling one of my dreads in her

fingers. "Yes." The way she says it makes it clear she is not hungry for food.

"Excellent, I have dinner." I drag myself away from her touch and reach into the cool bag I left on the sand hours before.

Digging deep I find cans of coke, and packages wrapped in foil. "Here." I chuck one over at her.

"Very romantic."

"I aim to please."

I watch as she opens up the foil packet. "A cheese and pickle sandwich?"

"Only the best for our first date."

"No cider?"

"I figured you wouldn't fancy one after the vodka last night." I watch as her skin turns a notch paler and then a red fiery burn lights up her cheeks.

"Well that's true I guess."

She lifts the sandwich to her nose and gives a little sniff. I grin into the can of coke I have popped open. "I'm not going to poison you."

"Well you can never be too sure."

"So what was with the vodka last night?" I curse myself silently. I promised myself that I wasn't going to ask, but the question slips out into the night air.

Bex leaves me hanging for a moment as she makes a long job of chewing her bite of sandwich. "Sometimes I get really angry at myself." Her face flickers with an internal thought. I wish I knew what it was.

"And vodka helps because?"

Bex looks intently at the sand surrounding her toes

as if she is trying to find the answers to the universe there. I don't want to ruin this date by talking about sensitive subjects so I change the subject before she can answer. "Fancy a swim."

"You're kidding right? If it's cold during the day, it will be bloody freezing now?"

"It's warmer now." I know this for a fact.

"I don't believe you."

"Try it."

"I don't have my bikini."

"And? You have underwear on?"

"Joshua, you are more than aware of the fact I don't have any underwear on my top half."

"Really? I hadn't noticed?" The schoolboy giggle I make ruins my outrageous lie. I am so aware of her lack of underwear it is almost painful.

I need to see my challenge through though so I stand on the blanket and start to undo my jeans. "Well I am not scared, and I have more to lose by the water being cold than you do."

This makes her laugh out loud. "I think you may be covering your own back. Are you making an excuse for a teeny tiny?"

"Maybe." I wink at her and quickly push down my jeans and stand on the sand in my boxers and T-shirt.

"Joshua, anyone could walk along!"

"Better run then." I turn away from her, strip off my remaining clothes and the dash for the water's edge.

Fuck that's cold.

Okay, this may have been a mistake. It really is very

cold. I hear her call from the water's edge. "You forgot your towel!"

Well this could be very embarrassing.

I wade out further and then turn to face her. She is standing on the damp sand dressed only in her knickers.

Good grief.

Cute knickers though.

"Turn around," she instructs. I don't hesitate but follow her direction. I try and listen for the sound of splashing or gasping, cursing even, but there is nothing. I am about to turn to see if she has run off with all the towels and my clothes when I feel her wrap her arms around my waist from where she is standing behind me. Her lips kiss along my shoulder blades and I feel goose-bumps not caused by the frigid water spread over my skin.

"You know I have seen you naked before."

"I know." I feel her lips smile against my skin.

"So can I turn around now?"

Instead of answering she edges me around with her hands until we are face to face. The sea is as still as a pond, the water covering us just to our waists. I slide my hands around her back and pull her in towards me until we are pressed tight together. The cold water has no effect on me as I feel her breasts pushed up against my chest.

Bex is watching me intently and the silence between us is so deafeningly loud I can't even hear the tide on the shore any more. "You look like you are made out of the moon," she says. The girl made of the sun thinks I am made of the moon.

I use my fingers to tilt her mouth up to mine. Her lips open hungrily and I move myself closer still. She lowers a hand and slides it along my hip, for a brief moment I think she is going to aim lower but then I realise she is touching my tattoo.

"What is your tattoo, Joshua?"

I catch her fingers from my skin and raise them to my lips. "I'll show you one day."

"I want to see now."

"Patience, Rebecca." Finally I crush us together until I can no longer feel anything except her skin burning into mine and I know that I will always feel her skin burning into mine even after she is gone.

EIGHT DAYS TO GO

Bridge Cottage
St Agnes
Cornwall

19th August 2013

Dear E,

Did you ever think I would be the sort of girl to skip around a castle? Me neither.
What about a date?
Skinny dipping?
How can I be doing all of this without you?
You'd like him. You'd probably like him a bit too much and we would end up in one of our twenty minute strops Do you remember those?! Remember the time we sulked the whole way through Hollyoaks until my dad came in and told us he had ice cream and then we both went running through to the kitchen screaming our heads off. Then we fought over who got which flavour.
If I had the chance again I would give you the chocolate. I would give you the chocolate every time.
I wish you could meet Josh-u-a. I wish that more than you

will ever know. I wish I didn't have to keep him from you but if he knew about you, I don't think I would get to do the things like I have today again. And I can't give them up quite yet. Not quite yet. Just a few more days of this and then I will go back to how things were before.

Before him.
Miss you as always
B.
xx
Ps: Did you know driftwood fires are blue? I know! Me neither!

Rebecca

Breakfast

"Pancakes."

I am asleep but I am pretty sure I just heard someone mention pancakes.

Oh yeah I so did.

"Pancakes are the best way to start the day."

I roll a little and face Joshua who has a sleepy smirk on his face. Last night after I got in from the date I said a quick hello to Mum and Dad before running up the stairs to my room where Josh was waiting for me. He lay on the bed as still as a statue while I counted off my bangles. Then I pounced on him.

"Pancakes are a fattening way to start the day. Muesli is far better for you."

"Well you could do with some fattening up." He slides one hand up along my bare midriff, running his fingers along my rib cage.

I hold my breath in expectation of where his hands may go next. I am not disappointed. He smoothes his warm touch over my right breast and I feel my entire body respond exactly the same way it has all night. Like I am smouldering with anticipation.

We haven't slept a huge amount, just lying in the dark talking, kissing and touching. Not much else than that. Joshua is determined that whatever this is we are doing for the next few days we are going to do it properly. No regrets, he told me. Nothing to look back on and wish that we had done things differently.

It's frustrating but also making me smile like crazy.

Too much smiling. I am going to have to hide from Mum and Dad today, otherwise they will turn on their parenting super detective skills and work out that I have been skinny dipping, and spent the night practically naked alongside a boy with dreadlocks. I am pretty sure that will surely be the end of my tuition fees.

I must remember the tuition fees. It keeps slipping my mind but I must focus on it.

I should probably clarify that it is me who has been 'clothes off' all night. For some reason that I can't quite explain, I still have not managed to get close enough to Joshua's tattoo to find out what it is. Last night in the sea it was too dark and all night, every time my hand strayed to investigate he pulled me away. It's a little annoying. Why won't he let me see?

"Okay, so I have got to go before your dad catches me sliding down the drain pipe." Joshua kisses under my ear with his words. In response I slide my legs around one of his thighs and edge myself closer.

"Then what?"

"Then what? Let me think. I will pick you up, take you for a surf lesson and introduce you properly to my friends, if that is okay with you? And possibly my

Aunt May."

I scrunch my face a little at this. During the night as we whispered and touched, Joshua told me all about his parents being killed when he was young. It made me feel sick to my stomach. He went on to tell me all about his Aunt and about meeting his friend Faye the first day. I still think she is the girl in the paintings but I didn't bother saying anything. We did agree to hold our own secrets and at the end of the day, what does it matter? I haven't told him everything about me either. I am not sure his Aunt is going to like me though. Something about the way he held his arms tighter around me as he described her to me makes me realise that she might not be my biggest fan. Not that anyone ever has been.

"Okay. I can do that," I say. Although I am not sure that I can. I am not the kind of girl that gets introduced to friends and family.

"How quick can you get ready?"

"Why?"

"I fancy a race."

"No."

"Half an hour, lets go." He jumps from the bed and catches his jeans up from the floor. I use the opportunity to conduct a full out ogle of his washboard stomach. I have a distinct urge to trace my tongue along it.

I give my head a shake when I realise he has been talking to me. "Sorry what?"

"Do I even want to know what you were thinking then?"

"Probably not, no."

"Okay. See you in thirty minutes."

He levers himself out of the window and I wrap myself in my duvet and follow him over to the window sill. "Okay, crazy hyper person." I whisper/shout after him.

At the bottom he grins up at me and offers me a salute which makes me snigger as I watch him jog down the lane back towards town.

After he is out of view I turn back into my room and catch a glimpse of myself in the dressing table mirror. I don't recognise the girl covered in orange freckles, her hair is standing on end and she has a wide cheek splitting smile all over her face.

I avert my gaze from the stranger in the mirror and focus on the wallpaper behind it.

Bloody hell. I've never noticed how truly terrible it is. All giant pink roses. I stand up and slide my finger nail under the edge of a panel. It takes a few moments but eventually I get a good grip and rip the whole lot off. I work another section and pull that off too. Leaves of rose painted paper land on the floor by my bare feet.

I've cleared half the wall when I realise what I am doing. I am decorating a room I never expected to stay in.

***

"Emmm!" I am standing at the top of the stairs to the attic screeching as loud as I possibly can. Joshua left twenty five minutes ago and all I have done since then is managed to strip half the wallpaper in my room.

"What?" Emily comes to the bottom of the stairs and looks up at me expectantly. I am still wrapped in a duvet which I am sure looks odd in itself, but she chooses not to comment.

"I need your help," I state.

This makes her hesitate. They are possibly words I have never said before. "Doing what?"

"Come and see."

"What on earth is going on?" Mum walks along to join Emily at the bottom of the stairs, stopping in surprise when she sees my duvet outfit and stares up at me inquisitively.

"Oh, you can come too." I wave at them both and then quickly head back into my room to fling some clothes on and fluff my pillows removing all trace of my overnight – not sleeping a wink – guest.

Mum walks in the door first and comes to a halt just inside. Emily is hot on her heels and looks about admiringly at the mess I have made.

"Aren't you supposed to be seeing Josh?" asks Emily.

"Yeah, how do you know?"

"He is in the front garden talking to Dad."

Shit.

"Good maybe he can help too," I say.

Mum looks about the room, her quick light brown eyes taking everything in. The unpacked suitcase, my biker boots in the corner that I haven't worn in days and my bangles which are still on the dresser.

Double shit.

I walk over and sweep a handful up and shove them on my wrist. I don't have time to count them now.

"So I was thinking, we could paint it white and then let Emily loose with her paints and artistic flair.

Emily has a frown furrowing her forehead and mum looks completely perplexed.

"Why don't you ask Josh to paint it?" asks Em.

"Paint what?" Joshua slips back into the room and it feels like he has never been gone. He walks right up alongside me until the skin of his arm is touching mine causing the hairs on my arm too stand to attention and mesh with his. "Wow." He turns and stares at the walls which have giant strips of paper hanging off them. "You have been busy!"

The thought hits me immediately, and I can't believe I didn't think about it before. Joshua knows his way into this room, via a drain pipe which means he used to know the person who owned it. For whatever reason the owner of the giant pink wallpaper is no longer here but I have ripped it off the walls with no regard. Sometimes I truly wonder if I have a brain at all.

Joshua is staring at the walls, his green eyes burning. I can see his Adams apple bob in his throat as he swallows repeatedly.

I untangle his clenched fist and slide my fingers into his. "I'm sorry. I did not think."

Surprisingly he turns to me with the widest grin I

have seen yet stretched right across his face, his white teeth glint and his face look so open, honest and happy, I want to kiss him. And I do. I can hear Mum give a little gasp as I tiptoe up and plant a kiss on Joshua's lips. For a split second he smiles against my mouth and squeezes my hand.

"This is perfect," he says. He turns to the closest wall and finishes yanking off a strip of paper I have left hanging. "Roses are so not your thing."

"Rebecca, I don't understand. You are going in a few days, why do you want to decorate. I was going to make this into an office for your father." Mum is looking at me, her expression still muddled. First there was the wallpaper, then there was the smiling and hand holding, then the kissing. It's a miracle she is not on the floor dealing with a 'my daughter is normal' heart attack.

For some reason her words make my eyes sting, and I notice Joshua's back stiffen. I think about my dad using my room as an office and am not sure I like the idea at all. *My room?*

"Well surely, I'll come home during the holiday's wont I?"

Mum's frown deepens a bit. "I don't know, will you?"

"Well maybe, if my room is not covered in roses."

Emily steps in between us. "We had better get these roses down then." Em, goes to stand near Joshua and whispers something which he nods his head at. *That's not annoying at all.*

"I'm going to go and make some coffee, anyone

want some?" Mum walks towards the door, clearly this situation is beyond her.

"Two sugars," Joshua turns and blinds her with one of his super wide smiles. "Oh and, Bex, we are going to need to go and get some white paint."

"That's okay, we have some in the shed." Mum adds.

"Excellent, let's get going."

An hour later the five of us, yes Dad has also joined in, have removed every single spec of rose wallpaper. Joshua is doing this weird thing with my parents where he is actually making conversation with them. He has realised that Dad is a graphic designer and they have been talking software programs, design ideas and god knows what ever since.

I tune back into their conversation when Dad laughs out loud at something Joshua has said. To my complete shock Dad walks over to me and then puts his arm around me giving me a squeeze, explaining to Joshua that I don't know anything about art and that I shouldn't be let loose on the blank walls.

"I know, Mr. Walters, that's why Em and I are going to do it."

Dad waves his hand at him. He has already told him to call him Andy twice.

"You're going to paint my walls?"

Ooh that sounds a bit dirty.

Joshua's lips twitch like he may be having the same thought. "Yep. Come on, we've got to let this dry. Lets go for our surf lesson and then come back later and do more."

I wait for Dad to step in and tell me I have to clean up my mess or something, anything, but he just laughs and says. "Have fun. Do you guys want dinner later?"

To which Josh says, "I have plans to take Bex out tonight if that's okay."

Plans?

Dad says, "Sure, why not."

Excuse me?

Josh says, "Actually we need to leave really early tomorrow to drive along the coast to the place I want to take her, about six in the morning."

Six? Is he mad?

Dad says, "Well, Josh, why don't you stay in the spare room tonight so you don't have to get up too early to come and get her."

At this point I realise I drowned in the sea last night and this is not real.

"Thank you, that would be a huge help." Joshua turns to me sending me a wink and reaches for my hand. "Shall we go and get some stuff from the studio Bex?"

"Rebecca."

Joshua grins and raises his pierced eyebrow at me.

Sadly I have nothing else to say. Nothing. My come-backs seem to have been seriously crippled. I follow him down the stairs, aware that there is dead silence in the room we have just exited which means they are all standing there wondering where their daughter and sister is, and do you know what, I am wondering where she is too.

Joshua

Surf Lesson No #2

I hold her hand the whole way down to the beach. Something feels different. When I walked in and saw her pulling the wallpaper off the wall I thought that maybe she had flipped. Maybe the crack that has been present in her countenance since I first met her had finally broken. I'd only been gone for half an hour, but half an hour away from Bex is beginning to feel like an age. Anything could have happened. Her Dad could have mentioned about that prick's party that left her tainted and scorned. Whatever it is about those bangles could have tipped her over the edge. But no. She just doesn't like wallpaper with roses on it, and to be truthful neither do I. That paper has always given me a headache.

We don't really need to go to the studio, or to the beach but my need to touch her and kiss her was getting too intense to ignore. While her parents seem to be accepting of me, I don't think they would appreciate me kissing her, using my tongue to explore her mouth and my hands to explore her skin while they are in the same room. The beach will be a welcome respite from my need to touch the girl made of the sun.

Walking across the sand in silence I skim the beach looking for people that I know. I have made enough small talk today, I just want some alone time, well, alone with her.

The beach is busy but it is just holiday makers enjoying the warm August sunshine. No one is on my rock so I guide us through the towels and laughing children until we get to the spot that is close to becoming 'ours.'

"Don't we need boards, if this is a surf lesson?" she asks, breaking the silence. Laughing I pull her down onto the sand in front of the rock. We don't have towels or a blanket but the sand is warm to touch and we are hidden from the view of the rest of the beach by the position of the rock. As soon as she is on the ground I lean her back into the sand and slide one hand along her body from her thigh to her shoulder. I move myself so I am pressed all alongside her.

"We don't need boards."

Bex giggles a little, her eyes opening in shock at the sound. "So what sort of lesson is this then?"

I move myself closer still until my body is practically on top of hers. "No lesson." I slide one hand under her neck weaving my fingers into her hair, and tilt her face up to mine so I can gain full access to her mouth. I start with a slow kiss, teasing the very edges of her lips with my own, she wiggles herself against me in response running one firm hand down my torso and stomach which makes my stomach quiver in anticipation of her touch. I know I want her to go lower.

This is not what I had planned with her. I was never going to give in to my intense need to be with the girl made of sun. But now it feels like something has changed. Hunger and need are burning in my veins and I can feel the same radiating off her.

What is the change?

Her warm breath mingles with mine as our mouths hungrily explore each other. It feels like I am going to drown in desire. Our bodies are so tight together, there is no way she won't be able to feel the effect she is having on me. I pull away a fraction trying to get any thought into my head other than 'Must shag now.' "Bex." I try to say her name normally but it comes out like a low croak.

"Don't you dare," she kisses back.

"Dare what?"

"Stop this." With that she moves herself one final centimetre so she is pressed right up against me and I can feel myself straining to move against her body, preferably with her, and inside her.

I hold myself still as she creates some steady friction with a subtle movement from her hips.

Shit.

"No, way. Not on the beach." I catch hold of both of her hands and pull them up above her head moving my body away from hers slightly. It doesn't help hugely. I can still feel the blood pulsing.

"I think you may need a dip in the cold sea, Joshua." She bites her lower lip and the action nearly kills my limited self-control.

"I think maybe we both do." Ignoring the glaringly obvious bulge in my boardshorts I jump away from her body and pull her up after me. In one easy move I lift her from the sand and sling her over my shoulder, making sure to keep my back turned from the rest of the beach so I don't scare any children with my monster erection. I charge for the sea, my feet sinking in the sand as I splash into the water.

"No!" she screams.

It's too late, not that I would have listened anyway. I dump her in the water and wait for it to ease the fire I have burning.

"Joshua," she sputters as she comes up from under the water and reaches a hand for me.

"Sorry, but you know that sort of behaviour is illegal on a beach?"

Pulling as hard as she can on my hand Bex tries to drag me into the water with her but she can't move me, laughing I lift her clean out of the water, and she slides both legs around my waist as I walk us back into the deeper depths out of view.

"That was mean." she says the words against my mouth.

"So were you." I am teasing. Obviously.

"Were you not enjoying it?" I know she is not talking about splashy time in the water.

"Believe me I was."

"What are you scared of, Joshua?"

Losing you.

"I'm not scared of anything. I just want it to be

right. I think you're amazing and you deserve to have someone show you how it can be."

"Are you the guy for the job, Joshua?"

I watch her for a moment, the sun glistening off the water droplets on her skin as I think of my response.

"I am the only guy for the job."

Two hours later I have covered Bex in small trails of sand that I have trickled from my hand onto her skin. Bex is ticklish in various places, something I didn't know, but I am storing the information away for use at a later time. The beach has emptied and there is only us and a family with two young children left.

"Do we need to go home yet?" Bex has her eyes closed against the late afternoon sun, a sleepy smile playing on her lips. Moving myself a little closer I use the palm of my hand to slide over the skin of her thigh and brush off the sand I placed there.

"It's your room we are decorating?" I leave the words dangling there. Truth be known I am unwilling to move from the beach. I want to lie here until the sun has faded and stopped glowing on her body. Then I want to move myself right up into her space until she makes me feel like she did earlier. "We could go to the pub, if you fancy it?" I suggest instead of initiating some skin on skin contact.

Bex opens one eye. "You want to go to the pub with me?"

"Sure why not?"

"I thought you just liked to hide behind rocks with

me."

"Well that's true. I like to do that too."

"I'll think about it." She shuts her eye again but her lips curve at a smile.

"I'll buy you a cheese and pickle sandwich?"

This makes her open both eyes and lean onto her elbows. "If you are offering a cheese sandwich does this mean it's our second date?"

I start to grin. "Maybe. Do you want it to be?"

Bex frowns slightly as she weighs something in her mind. "I need to know what base we are reaching before agreeing."

"Third, max."

"Then I'm gonna need chips with my sandwich."

Jumping from the sand I offer her my hand. "Agreed, come on, the pub does the best cider in Cornwall."

"Ugh, cider."

"I'm going to spank you for saying "Ugh" to cider."

"Now, Joshua, spanking is not technically third base. Do we need to clarify this?" She starts to giggle and run across the sand.

Seriously, she thinks she can make it across the sand quicker than me? Six paces later I rugby tackle her to the ground, pinning her to the cooling sand with my hands firm around her arms. I slide one of my legs in-between her thighs and she watches me with burning hot ambers, not blinking or breaking eye contact.

"Then I think we need to redefine exactly what the

bases are." My voice has taken on that unique low tone I only get with her.

"So what base is this?" The ambers are still intense and I am more than aware of the location of my knee.

"One and a half."

This makes her laugh and wiggle her arms free from my grasp. "Come on, a girl could die of thirst around here."

Unwillingly I peel my body away from hers and catch hold of her hand in mine. I think I had better make my drink slightly stronger than a cider and combine it with a cold shower. A very cold shower.

Bex can't drink cider. She's had two pints and her face is glowing bright red. We caused a stir when we walked in with our fingers linked tightly together but now we are old news and everyone is leaving us in peace at the corner table.

Unfortunately I can hear Dan before I see him. Bex who is sat facing the pub stiffens automatically.

"Josh, there you are, buddy." Dan grabs a spare chair and moves it to our table. "We are going to Newquay in a bit, why don't you two love birds come along. Faye's coming, Josh, she's probably missing you, she hasn't seen you in days!" Bex stiffens again, and I notice that Dan is watching her reactions closely. He turns his attention to her. "Ah, so Josh hasn't told you about Faye, and their weird friendship they have maintained over the years."

I glare at Dan over the table. I have nothing to hide, well not really but I am beginning to understand how Bex reacts to challenging situations and I could do without being puked on again anytime soon.

"He's told me enough," she says.

"Are you getting a drink and joining us, or passing by?" I can't keep my annoyance out of my voice. We have been sitting here having an amazing time flirting over our pints, and now Dodgy Dan is going to ruin it.

"Well if you are offering, mate, I won't say no."

I wait for him to make a move but he doesn't so reluctantly I get up from the table and head to the bar.

I try and make small talk with the guy next to me at the bar as I order Dan a pint but it's a bit tricky because I have one ear trying to listen in to Bex and Dan at the table. I can't hear a damn word they are saying because the crazy old guy with the dog won't stop twittering on at me.

Pint purchased I walk back over and can see instantly that Bex looks on the edge of either angry or upset.

"Josh, I was just saying you guys should come out tomorrow night so Bex here can meet everyone." Dan says.

"Rebecca."

"Rebecca." He nods his head in assent at her and I really dislike the way her name sounds coming out of his mouth.

"We can't tomorrow we are going on a road trip."

"Where are you going, maybe we will all come."

"We are leaving at six," I let my words sink in.

"Still want to come?"

"Fuck that." He downs half of his drink.

"I thought so."

"Night after then?" He suggests draining the end of his glass. Dan can sink a pint in a clear four minutes. It's what makes me sure he is part animal.

"Sure," I agree. Although I have no plans to see it through. I have a week left with the girl made of the sun, I am not going to waste it watching my friends get trashed while trying to shag strangers.

"Good chap." Clapping me in the shoulder he starts to get up from his chair but not before turning and placing his hand on Bex's arm. "Remember what I said." Leaving his words hanging there he chuckles to himself and heads for the door shouting goodbye to the pub as he goes. One of these days I am just gonna have to tell him to fuck off. I don't care how long we've been friends.

The moment he has gone a deathly silence settles over our table. Bex is watching me but she does not seem the same as earlier. She is radiating the Bex I met on the first day, not the girl I was at the beach with just a couple of hours ago.

"What did he say?"

And yes I will kill him for it, whatever it is.

"Nothing, Joshua, don't worry."

"What did he say, Bex? Otherwise I am going after him myself."

She sighs a little and leans back in her chair with an air of resignation. "He said," she takes another breath. "He said that I shouldn't feel offended that you haven't had sex with me yet, because you don't shag holiday makers unless desperate, and that you are still in love with someone else."

Well that was worse than I thought.

But she is not done. "He also said, that next time I'm in town I should hook up with him, because he is guaranteed to give me a good time." Bex displays no expression at all and just takes another deep sip of her drink.

I, on the other hand, can feel a bubble of rage build up inside me. I try and lock it down before it erupts.

I don't know what to say apart from 'Sorry my oldest friend is a complete pig and doesn't know how to treat women right,' and I don't think that really covers it.

Choosing silence instead I watch as she takes another sip of her cider before saying, "It's okay, Josh, I'm kind of used to it."

"What do you mean?"

"Well, for some reason, that is how guys see me, it always happens."

"What do you mean for some reason?"

Bex lets out a sarcastic laugh. "The truth is, that I have never technically had sex with anyone." She says this very loud and the pub automatically stop talking to listen. "So if you discount the odd sexual favour I've given I'm technically quite innocent." Deathly silence permeates around the room, which she fills again with the sound of her own voice. "Don't get me wrong, I might be known for blowjobs in back alleys that kind of thing, but not technically sex. Actually,

Josh, if you are interested I can meet you out back and sort you out right now."

Fuck.

The girl made of the sun glares at me, her entire body rigid as she battles whatever it is she has on the inside. Her colour has heightened another notch of red and this time I don't think it is the cider making her flush. Before I can say anything in response she scrapes her chair away from the table across the bare floor boards and stalks out of the pub. Without hesitating I chase straight after her into the cool night air. She hasn't gone far and is stood on the corner of the lane. She must be working out where to go. Reaching for one of her hands I turn her to face me.

"Can I show you something?" I ask.

"No."

"Bex, two minutes, and then you can decide whether to strop off again and waste whatever limited time we have together." My words make her hesitate. She swings around glaring at me with her frown back on her face.

"Two minutes."

Keeping her fingers in mine I lead her down the lane towards the high street heading for my studio. Walking through the door a heavy silence settles between us and slowly I take the stairs with her one step behind. At the top I don't bother turning on the light. I walk her instead to the large room that just holds the one canvas. I haven't touched it since the other day when I darkened all the gold. The moon is shining through the sky light and it makes the gold of her skin in the painting turn to bronze.

"This is all I see when I look at you. You are neither one thing nor the other. Not dark or light. You are just you." I try and stop myself from saying anything else but the words, "Only you," fall out of my mouth before I reign them in.

Bex stands and stares at the painting her shoulders still set and determined. Leaning towards her I place my lips against the back of her neck, inhaling the sweet scent of vanilla mixed with a lingering hint of the sea.

"You know," she says, her voice small. "I used to be quite a good girl." She stops speaking and I edge around to face her. Tears are sliding down her face. Reaching a finger I catch one on my fingertip.

"What happened?"

Bex reaches for me, sliding her arms around my waist and pulling me in towards her. "I'm going to tell you but I want to do something first."

Carefully she kisses me on the lips, her mouth firm and sure as she grips her arms tighter around me so I can't move away. Then slowly, ever so slowly she lowers herself down until she's kneeling on the floor right in front of me. *She's got to be kidding me.*

"Don't move," she whispers as she starts to untie the knot on my shorts. It's kind of hard not to move in the circumstances. The moment her fingers start to tug on the tie I feel desire claim me, along with a heavy dose of repulsion at myself.

The tie undone she lowers my shorts until she has revealed the tattoo under the waist band. Fingers graze over the inked skin and I hold my breath at her touch, and then a little more as she leans forward and places her lips against the mark. Gently she flicks her tongue over the compass inked on my skin before leaning back and looking up at me, her eyes shining in the moonlight.

"What does it mean, Josh?"

Slowly I lower myself to the floor so I am kneeling in front of her. Taking her hand I place it firmly on the skin.

"It means that I don't know where my home is yet."

The ambers watch me, reading me, assessing me. Eventually she leans in and kisses me, her hand still under the waistband of my shorts. "I wish I could help you find it, Joshua."

And in that very moment, it is all I wish for too.

SEVEN DAYS TO GO

Bridge Cottage
St Agnes
Cornwall

20th August 2013

Dear E,
I was so close E, so close to being normal just for a few days. Yesterday was the best day ever until some twat had to ruin it by goading me into telling a pub full of locals I was good for a blow job out back should anyone fancy it.

What's wrong with me?

I know what's wrong with me? It's because I know that's what people see when they look at me and it's what I believe is there because of that.

Josh managed to reign me back in, bring Cornish Bex to the forefront and quieten London Bex back into her place.

He showed me his tattoo. Do you know what it is? It's a compass, I asked him what it meant and he said he didn't know where his home is. That heart-breaking thought helped me fight back to the surface. How sad is it that? A man as beautiful as Josh-u-a doesn't know where his home is. It echoed inside me that I don't know where mine is either. It's not here in this sun filled place with giggling, kissing and tattoos.

Gone

It's somewhere dark with you.

Later when we had crept back into the cottage he told me he was glad that he was going to be my first. As I went to sleep with my arms tight around him I had one thought. That I wish he could be my last.

Miss you as always
B.
xx

Rebecca

Breakfast

"I said the spare room." Dad marches in, standing with his arms folded over his chest. I am still wrapped tight in Joshua's arms where I have been the whole night without moving. The good thing is that we have our clothes on. The bad bit is that I still have my hand over Joshua's tattoo, which effectively means my hand is down his pants.

Joshua struggles to sit up, pushing his dreads back out of his eyes. "Mr. Walters, I am so very sorry. I ... fell asleep."

Dad wets himself laughing. "It's half six you were supposed to go half an hour ago." And with that he leaves the room.

"He didn't say I was grounded." I lean my face closer to his and skim my nose along his jaw.

"He didn't say I was banned." Butterfly kisses land on my cheek.

"He—" He cuts my words off with his mouth and I laugh against his lips. And then. Well then I nearly tell him I love him.

I don't. I perform a ninja roll off the bed and stand

on the floor, my feet firmly planted on the honey coloured floor boards.

"Are we going?" says Joshua.

"Shower?"

"Together?"

"In your dreams."

Joshua catches hold of me, firm strong arms around my waist. "I don't have to dream, I am with you."

"Who knew dreadlocked surfers were such romantics."

Chuckling against my skin, his teeth nibble my neck as his nose skims along my jawline. "Oh, Bex?"

"Yep?" I am ever so slightly breathless.

"Don't forget you have some stuff to tell me today."

Well I am going to try and forget.

"Yeah, yeah. Let's rock and roll. I am sure we can wash in the sea later!"

"Clothes on or off?"

"What would you prefer?"

Joshua sends me one of his cheek splitting grins along with a wink that makes me momentarily forget whatever it was I was doing.

Oh yes getting dressed.

"I'll pack my soap." I swing for the door before he has a chance to come back with another quick fire reply.

Downstairs I head into the kitchen. I am not overly excited to face my dad, but the sensible part of my brain knows that I am legally an adult, and I am sure if I managed to act like one every once in a while things in the home roost may not be that bad – all of the time.

"Hey, Dad?" He is sat at the worn pine kitchen table with the paper in front of his face.

"Hello, Rebecca." Dad does not lower the paper. *Well this is a little awkward.*

"It's not what you think." I'm kind of twitching around in front of him, not entirely sure what to do with myself. "We were talking, and then I guess we just fell asleep. You can be grumpy with me later, please don't make Josh feel bad."

I've had to use that P-word again. Given the circumstances and what with the fact that three weeks ago my dad found me in a far worse situation, using the word *please* in the hope he does not overreact is not a bad choice to make.

The paper shakes a little and I can hear a weird snorting horsey noise.

Oh dear here comes the anger explosion.

Slowly Dad lowers the paper, he is bright purple, but not with rage. Tears are streaming down his face as his body convulses with laughter. "You should have seen your face."

"Are you taking the piss?"

"No."

"So you're not annoyed with me?"

"No, not particularly." And by this, I know he means not yet.

"Am I still allowed out?"

"What a crazy thing to ask, of course you are still

allowed. Go enjoy Cornwall, it's a beautiful place, you may notice when you are not so distracted by handsome painters." He makes a strange chortling sound and gives his paper a brisk shake before lifting it back up again and obscuring his face from my view.

I hesitate in the middle of the kitchen, not sure if this entire weird situation developing around me is real or not.

"I made you a flask of coffee." Dad waves his hand towards the kettle and the flask standing next to it.

"Uh thanks."

"You ready, Bex?" Joshua bounds into the kitchen, his hair is pulled back into its familiar low ponytail and he is wearing a vivid green T-shirt that makes his eyes stand out. My mouth pops open and I snap it shut. I'm too slow, way too slow and Joshua starts to break out in a sexy wide grin.

Turning ever so slightly I try to catch a glance of my dad's reaction to Joshua after finding us in bed together this morning. He is peeping over the top of his paper but he must sense my movement towards him because he quickly lowers his head again. "Don't forget your coffee?"

"Thanks, Dad," I say. Grabbing the flask I walk over to Joshua who quickly links his fingers through mine tugging me in beside him so our bodies are touching.

"Have a great day, try not to get washed away in the sea or sunburnt," Dad calls after us as we walk through the door.

Out on the pavement by Daisy I hesitate. "Did my

Dad seem a bit odd to you?"

"Not really." Josh starts to unlock the door handle with his keys.

"Really? You didn't think that it was a bit strange he didn't shout?"

"I don't know, Bex, do you expect you parents to shout about everything?"

"Well yes, you know why."

Josh starts his slow wide smile again. "No, I don't, not really but you are going to tell me today." He watches me scrunch my face up into a frown. "You promised. You don't break promises as well do you?"

"Sometimes."

"Well then you are a naughtier girl than I first thought."

"Do you like your girls naughty, Joshua," my voice tinkles over his name which makes my comment completely pointless. I'm not sounding overly naughty right now. I sound like an over excitable six year old.

Joshua grins at me the green piercing. "Guess you'll have to find out." He swings the door open wide and sweeps his hand aside, "You may enter my rusty vehicle."

I clamber up into the van biting down as hard as I can on my bottom lip trying to stop myself grinning back at him. If I carry on the way I am people are going to start thinking I am normal. Dates, sleep overs, early morning surprise trips. That's normal right isn't it?

We are heading out of the peaceful, quiet village

when I finally think to ask just how long this trip is going to take. "About an hour, traffic allowing." He tells me with a smile from the driver's side.

"An hour! A whole hour in this van? Are you joking? I thought we were at the end of the world anyway?"

Joshua turns to me the greens pinning me in place. "We are not at the end of the world yet, but I am going to take you there."

Something about his words makes my stomach tighten with a low unexplainable burn. I shift a little on the pvc seat hoping that it will disperse a little. Thankfully I don't make a farting noise so I assume the seats haven't warmed up enough yet. It's chilly and the weather looks a little misty. Giving my arms a rub to reduce the goose bumps I give my weather forecast. "It's going to rain."

"No it's not."

I peer further out of the window. "Yes it is."

"No, it's not. It's going to be a scorcher. I hope you brought your bikini with you." He turns a little to face me and rakes his eyes along my crossed legs and crochet vest top. He can clearly see the tie of the halter neck so I don't bother replying. It's going to rain anyway so I doubt I will need it. I continue to stare out of the window at the passing scenery. It really is rather beautiful, once you are on the main road you would never really know you were by the sea. It's just green fields everywhere. At the same time there is something quite unique about knowing that they sea could appear at any moment. I turn to the boy made of the moon and sea sitting by my side.

"Where are we going anyway?"

"Everywhere?"

"Including the end of the earth?"

"Including that."

"Why?"

"Because I want you to see all of this place before you leave."

"Why?"

His knuckles grip the steering wheel a little tighter and he keeps his attention focused out the windscreen. "It's the nearest thing I have found to home." He says finally.

I don't really know what to say because I know that this place, with its rugged landscape and never ending winding lanes was never meant to be my home.

Twenty minutes of heavy silence have passed when we start to head towards what looks it could almost, just about, resemble a town. I swivel a little in my seat and perform the obligatory fart sound. It must be warming up. I glance up at the sky through the window and sure enough beneath the layer of hazy cloud a vivid blue is starting to seep through.

"I think you may be right about the weather."

"I'm always right."

I roll my eyes in response and turn my attention towards the town we are driving towards. A tall spire dominates the view. I lean forward to get a closer look, cranking my neck into an unnatural angle to see through the window. "What's that?" I ask.

"Truro Cathedral, I'm going to show you right

now."

I have been so busy watching the Cathedral getting closer that I haven't noticed Joshua negotiate Daisy into a pay and display car park.

"Everything is going to be closed," I say. I glance at my watch which confirms that it is only seven thirty, technically a time that no sensible person should be up and out of the house.

"I know, it will just be us." He grins a little as he jumps down from his seat and slams the door shut.

"Okay," I shrug.

"Come on, Bex, where is your sense of adventure?"

"Reb—" I don't get to finish because he pulls me around by the hand and presses his lips against mine. I edge myself a step closer until I feel my body fit into the grooves of his that I am starting to recognize. I feel the burn I experienced earlier in the car reignite in my stomach.

He slowly kisses around my lips with the lightest of touches. "Driving seriously hinders my capacity to do that," he murmurs. His lips kiss along to the lobe of my ear which he lightly tugs on with his teeth.

That's it. The burn in my stomach explodes and rushes over my entire body.

Reluctantly I inch myself away from him, although I can still feel the hand he has resting on my hip through the material of my clothing. *God damn clothing.* "Did you park the car to finally have your wicked way with me?"

"You wish. I parked the car to show you the sights and get to the bakers before the tourists get there."

I have no idea what he is talking about. "I don't understand."

Joshua links his fingers through mine and tows me towards the car park exit. This is a minor problem because my legs feel a little like jelly after the kiss and earlobe nibble move he just made. "You will later. Come on, stop dawdling, we've got a lot to do."

"That's rude. You were the one who stopped the proceedings to kiss." *And make my legs go dead.*

He stops again and rounds back into my space. "Well in that case." His lips come back to mine, his tongue teasing.

I place both my hands on his shoulders and break away a little. "What's with you?"

"What do you mean?" He leans back a little so his cool green gaze can appraise me.

"You seem different." He does seem different. Wild, carefree, and definitely different.

"What because I keep doing this?" He reels me back in, this time his right hand slides under my vest top and along my tummy. "And this." He lips are against my mouth but I can hear the tone in his voice. His hand slides up and over my right breast which is quick to respond as his thumb grazes against my bikini covered nipple.

"Uh. Yes. This."

Joshua laughs and moves away, leaving me standing there with flames scorching over my skin. "I don't know. It just feels good to be away from St Agnes, it feels like I can get air into my lungs again."

Seriously he can breathe? Because right now breathing is not high on my to-do list.

"Come on, Bex, let's go and explore, or do you want to make out in a deserted car park a little more?"

I flush what feels like a vibrant shade of red to match my burning limbs.

We move away from each other turning back for the path we were on, and find an elderly couple standing watching us.

The red cranks up another notch.

"Hey, good morning." Joshua grins at them as we walk past and I concentrate on my flip flops.

As we move further away I can hear the old lady say, "Remember when we were like that, Ed?" To which the old man replies, "My memory is not that good."

We are too far away to hear her comeback but her words make me hesitate. Do people looking at Joshua and I see some perfect ideal of Love's Young Dream? Because that's not what this is, is it?

Yet as we giggle and walk towards what must be the high street it's all I can think. What if this is it? Loves Young Dream.

Joshua

Half Truths and Sand Castles

To be honest I'm feeling pretty bad about touching Bex's boob in front of an old couple in a car park. That's not really my thing. Although I reckon it could become a new thing if I wanted it too.

I tug her hand and lead her towards the high street. This was supposed to be a quick pit stop to buy some pasties and show her the sights. Not a grope in a public place. Bex is laughing, the early morning sunlight bouncing off her skin and hair. I wonder if she has noticed that she has completely forgotten to put any make-up on? Not a single scrap. I know she was distracted by her dad this morning, but part of me wants to claim that it is me who is making her forget to cover up her beautiful skin with that terrible foundation. Her amber hair is piled on top of her head in a loose bun, strands escaping and trailing down the back of her neck. The exposed flesh of her long slim neck makes me want to slowly kiss my lips up it, and I so would, but I don't want to shock any other locals straight after their breakfast.

"Come on, we have got time to look at the

cathedral before we have to move on with the day trip."

Bex matches her pace with mine and I tuck her in close to my side winding my arm around her waist.

"This place is beautiful," she says. Her gaze is taking in the wide high street which sweeps into a large circle.

"Not all of Cornwall is like St Agnes."

"I'd say."

"Come on, we have got to get to the bakers, or all the old biddy's will get there before us and steal our lunch." I increase the pace of my footsteps with my words.

"Who on earth will be buying stuff at the bakery now?" she questions.

"Everyone! That old couple had already been. I could smell the pasties from over the other side of the car park."

"Oh, I've had Cornish pasties in London."

"No you haven't."

"Yeah I have."

"Believe me you haven't."

Bex grinds her feet to a halt. "Are we going to have our first disagreement about a pasty?"

"Not at all, I am just stating a fact which you don't agree with."

"That's an argument in my book."

"No one argues about pasties."

"Well, I have had one."

"No one apart from you." I sigh a little to hide the grin I want to break out over the fact we seem to be having an argument about pasties, of all things. "Okay you have had one. Can we go to the bakers now before they sell out of the bloody things?"

"Fine." With her words she starts marching down the high street.

"Bex," I shout after her. "It's this way."

Bex turns on her heel and stomps back along in the direction I am pointing. "It's Rebecca," she retorts.

I can't help myself I just laugh loudly and break into a jog to catch up with her. I am so distracted by her stroppy little hip swinging walk, and the laughter that is bubbling inside my chest that I don't even register the words before they are out my mouth and hanging in the fresh Truro air. "I'll make sure to tell our kids that our first row was about a pasty."

Bex stops her stress walk and comes to a halt her back turned towards me. I am expecting a retort, a classic one line Bex comment but she picks up her feet and starts walking again.

I fall into step at her side and we walk in silence to the bakers. I head in first and she follows me through the door. "Wow, that's a load of cakes," she says.

The bakers is full of freshly made cakes in every size and flavour you can imagine. "That's why I brought you. It wasn't all about the pasties." I smile at her and wait to see her reaction, she hasn't looked at me since I made the 'Children' booboo.

"Can I have a cake as well as a pasty?" Her eyes gaze up and down the counter. I so know which one she wants to get, her eyes light up as she spies an enormous Chelsea bun dripping with icing and crowned by the biggest cherry I've ever seen.

"Yeah, and breakfast," I say maneuvering myself closer and touching my arm against hers.

Turning my attention to the lady behind the counter I start to reel off our order. "Two giant sausage rolls, two Chelsea buns, two Cornish pasties and two cups of coffee."

"For you and whose army, love?" the lady asks.

"Oh just me and her." I reach my hand to Bex and link my fingers through hers.

"Day trip is it?" she asks.

"Yep, to the end of the earth."

The lady glances up at the clock behind the counter. "You'd better get running along then, my dearie."

"Yes you are quite right, we had." I agree handing her a twenty.

She then spends five minutes counting out my change into the palm of my hand. This is the Cornish idea of 'better get running.' Nothing is ever a rush.

Once I have my change safely in my pocket and made it out of the shop I guide Bex to the cathedral. I have no idea why I think she will like it, I just do. I am not wrong. As we walk along the river that runs alongside the landmark she does not say a word. Her gaze is on the tall spires piercing the sky and I am happy to watch her take it all in. She does not even notice when I leave her standing there and sit on a bench.

"It's beautiful." She turns her gaze to find me and realises that I am not standing next to her. I grin as I wave at her and she walks towards me. She looks almost abashed that she has been caught out enjoying something of beauty.

"It's even more breathtaking inside." I say.

"Think I can see?"

"We could try the door?" I don't reckon it will be open but I guess there is no harm in trying.

By some miracle, and no that is not a play on words the door is open. I soon realise why when I see a printed note on a wrought iron stand announcing 'Morning Prayer."

"Want to go in?"

Bex gives a miniscule nod of her head and we walk into the cool shadows of the church. Bex automatically looks up at the arched stone vaulted ceiling. "Wow."

"It's beautiful isn't it?" I ask, but I am not looking at the church I am gazing at her as she stands on the spot and spins slowly taking in the stained glass and the sheer expanse of space above and around her.

I head towards a pew and she follows me in and for the first time I take my eyes off Bex and absorb our surroundings. There are about twenty people scattered throughout the first few pews. I am surprised about the amount of people out early in the morning with their heads bowed in prayer. But then maybe my cynicism has come from the fact that I no longer think there is anyone to talk to out there. I turn my head to Bex to comment on this but notice that her head is bowed down and her lips are moving with words that are not reaching my ears. I don't see at first because I am so surprised by her action, but after I have been concentrating on her still form for a few moments I notice splotches of wet spread on the crotchet stitching of her vest top.

Tears.

The girl made of the sun is crying in a church on what was supposed to be our fun day out together. That's a backfire of note.

I want to touch her, hug her, talk to her but I don't do any of those things. Instead I slide off the bench and walk back towards the door and the sunlight outside leaving Bex to her silent conversation.

It's only a few minutes later when she steps back out into the courtyard walking towards me with a neutral expression. "You're right it's a beautiful town." She smiles and instantly the atmosphere around me brightens.

I open my mouth and words just fall out of it again. "There is a Uni here you know?"

Bex's forehead squeezes into a frown and she gives her head a little shake. "Did you buy breakfast earlier?"

Well that's one way to change the conversation.

"Yeah, come on, let's eat and drive otherwise we will never get to our destination."

"Just where is our destination exactly?"

"You will see soon."

And with that we walk back to the car park. I link my fingers through hers again but this time she does not clasp mine back, at least not as tightly as I would like.

Finally we reach our first stop, well the second stop if you include the teardrop inducing visit to Truro Cathedral. I crank Daisy's handbrake and swivel in my seat to face Bex. She has barely spoken the entire journey.

"I'm sorry," I say.

"What for?"

"For taking you somewhere that upset you."

This is not what I mean. What I mean is that I am sorry for whatever it is that makes her cry, or get drunk enough to want to be washed out to sea. I'm sorry for mentioning the local Uni and hinting at the fact that she could stay. You know if she wanted to.

"Oh that." She waves her hand at me. "I always cry in church, always have done since I was little."

"Really?"

"Really."

"Well in that case I am not sorry at all."

"Prick a dick."

"Do you practice your rhyming?"

"Five minutes every day."

"You should make it ten."

We both stare at each other for a moment before her lips start to twitch at the corner and I lean forward and kiss the tick. "Come on, I promised you the end of the world, now I'm going to take you there."

"Really here? I thought you were making reference to a sexual mind blowing move you were going to make."

I shoot her a wink. "Later," and then take great delight as she flushes beetroot.

Bex opens the door and steps out slamming it with a resounding bang behind her.

Stroppy!

I can't help myself. "Promise not to throw yourself off a cliff?"

"Promise not to talk to me then?"

I pretend to weigh up the option. "Done." I start to walk away and head towards the footpath past the tourist trap pub sitting right in the middle of the view.

Bex does not say anything, but I can hear her flip flops flapping behind me so I know she is following my path. I head down right onto the rocks and then start to jump from one to another. The flip flops stop.

"You coming?" I call over my shoulder.

"I'm sorry. What?"

I turn and face her. She is peering over the edge of the rocks. It's a long way down.

"Are you coming?" I hold out my hand to her but she ignores it and jumps for the rock. Defiance radiates off her. The girl made of the sun is more of a challenge than I ever would have guessed. I honestly don't know where I stand with her. This morning we were giggling and snuggling, now she is this independent beam of light that seems to be trying to repel me. Not that it is working. It makes me want to move closer.

I resist the urge, and sit down on the rock. "Welcome to Lands End." I wave my hand at the sea and rock formation in front of us, the most southerly point in the British Isle's. "Or as I like to call it — The World's End."

Bex does not say anything her face is turned out to the sea and her shoulders are rigid. I know not to push. Whatever it is that is making her act this way it's brewing under the surface and I can sense there is a battle taking place inside of her.

Instead of touching her which is what I really want to do I sit and listen to the waves crash onto the rocks and the deathly silence between us.

It doesn't last long.

"You know I am leaving, Joshua, don't you?" She doesn't look at me with her question, her gaze is focused on the tide.

Yeah I know she is leaving. I also know that I really don't want her to. I also know that she is the only good thing I have found in what seems like an age and what I once thought would be forever. I clamp my lips shut and wait for her to continue.

"The thing is, I can't stay. Even if I wanted to, I can't."

"Why?" *Ugh, I need to touch her.* I place my fingertips on her elbow, just the lightest of caresses. Her back straightens in response.

"Two years ago Emily started High School, the same one as me." Her eyes remain focused on the sea as she starts to speak.

"Yes?" I can't see where this is going. All siblings go to the same school. I used to hate it when I was growing up because I never had a brother to make the trip to school with.

"Nothing happened at first. It was all normal. I was in a good place, doing okay, top sets in most subjects and working towards my exams. I had a boyfriend and friends. It was all normal..." Her voice trails off.

I want to ask more but I hold it back, I just concentrate on the feel of the skin of her elbow against my fingers.

"One day, it was last period and the class was really lively. It was chemistry, which I never really understood. Everyone was messing about with the Bunsen Burners. Suddenly the fire alarms started going off, and you know what it's like, we all trooped out onto the playground to get into line."

I have the most terrible tightening in my stomach with her words. It feels like a cold shiver seeping into my abdomen. I still don't say anything.

"I thought some idiot had set fire to those wooden prodder things you use in science but as we walked towards our line I started to hear rumours that someone was on fire. I didn't really understand at first but I soon noticed everyone was looking at me. I don't really know what made it click but before I knew what I was doing I was looking for Emily. Her class line was right over the other side of the playground so I ran over there. Matt, my boyfriend, came with me, but I couldn't find her."

Bex still is not looking at me. Her shoulders are squared and her head upright as she visualises the scene in her mind. When she starts to speak her voice is quieter. "I couldn't find her, I started to panic and scream her name. Her whole class was staring at me, some of them looked shocked. There were a group of three girls who saw me coming and turned their back towards me. I didn't even register it at the time. I ran into the school and straight for the lower level where Emily's classroom was. She still wasn't in there, then I noticed the school secretary running down the hallway towards the girl's toilet and I followed her and went through the door."

Bex stops again and takes a deep breath, a breath that she holds for the longest moment before allowing it to exhale. I edge myself closer so that the skin of my arm is touching hers.

"Emily was in there, the sports coach and the Head Mistress were in there too and they had Emily's head under the sink tap and water was spraying everywhere. I started to shout at them to stop, wondering what the hell they were doing, then the smell hit me. Burning. It felt unreal but I walked up to the sink and looked at Emily. She was crying silently half of her hair gone and her scalp bright red."

"Shit." It's the first word I have to say but it is not the one I really want to use. I slide my arm around her and lean her into me with her back resting against my chest. Her breathing is ragged and I hate myself for making her drag all this stuff back up. Along with that I feel a deep burn of anger inside me.

"I went with her to the hospital. She didn't speak once the whole way. The doctors said she was in shock. They also said that the Head Teacher and other teacher had saved her scalp with their quick action. She only has the tiniest scar now. She was incredibly lucky."

"What happened then?"

"Nothing."

"What do you mean nothing?"

"She wouldn't tell who did it. She admitted that she had been bullied since the start of school, just petty stuff first, someone asking for money, pushing in the corridor, scribbling on her stuff, all pretty minor, but I think it was probably quite often, but she would never tell us who had set fire to her hair."

"What did you do?" I have no doubt in my mind that she would have done something. Fire burns in her probably brighter than it did in that school toilet that day.

"For some reason I kept thinking about those three girls who turned their back on me in the fire drill line. I knew it was them. The next day I caught up with them in the toilets, and I don't really know what happened but this rage just took over me. I broke one of the girls cheekbones against the sink, the others didn't fare much better. I got expelled and mum and dad pulled Emily. It's not something I am proud of. I never wanted to be the kind of person who would hurt another, especially young girls. Even if they are bitches."

"Shit"

"The rumours followed us. I was known as the girl who broke other girls' faces, and it didn't take long for me to be invited out by the wrong people. Let's be honest, I wasn't in touch with anyone else. No one wants to be friends with a girl who goes crazy like that."

"I'm sorry, Bex."

"Nah, it's over now. But you need to understand that's why I can't stay. The second school we went to I couldn't stop myself. I trailed Emily everywhere making sure she was okay, every person that came near her got scared off by her big sister. But worse than that, she ended up getting teased more and more because of me and because of the things that I'd done. The labels followed me everywhere. Rebecca Walters the dangerous girl. What with the new label I picked up a couple of weeks back. I can't have Emily carrying that around. It's not fair."

I so get it, and with her words I know that she will be gone in a few days, but I also know that I would never ask her to stay. How could I?

"I understand."

She turns to me and the amber's hold my gaze. "Do you get it, Joshua, do you understand that I have to leave it behind and live my own life and let them live theirs?"

I lean myself forward and place my lips against hers, nothing more that the shortest of kisses. "I get it. I hope that you get what you want." I mean this, but I know that in saying it, I will never get the things that I want. Her.

By the time we've driven to our final destination, a secluded beach that can only be reached by a sharp descent on foot, she has told me everything. She has filled me in on the ensuing two years, the crowds she has been mixing in, the trips home with the police for drunken behaviour, the shop lifting, the vodka, and finally up until the day when her dad found her doing something I'm guessing he didn't want to see. "I don't want Emily thinking that's normal and following my example, she's at an impressionable age, imagine if she turned out like me just because I am the only role model she had." She'd said with a look of resolution set in her features. It made me grip the steering wheel tight enough to make my knuckles ache as her determination seeped through me.

"So did you not have any friends who tried to help you?" I ask as we look out at the shimmering sea. There is a heaviness in the air between us. Bex has told me everything and I have told her nothing.

"Yeah I did."

"And?"

"I can't really talk about it, Josh." Bex has turned herself from me. I slide a hand along the skin of her back, feeling along every notch of her spine.

What can't she talk about? Surely she has told me the worst? "Why?"

There is a heavy moment of silence before I see Bex's shoulders slump in defeat.

"Because she left."

"What? How?" The questions shoot out of my mouth with me unable to control them.

"I took it one step too far."

I button in any further questions. Obviously she does not want to talk about it. I can't blame her. I know there are plenty of things that I still can't talk about. Or wont.

"Do I repulse you now, Joshua?" she turns and asks.

I read her face, the crease between her eyebrows, the slight scrunch of skin around the corner of her eyes. Repulsion is not a feeling I have strongly right now. It's something else that is claiming me, emotions that I don't understand very well are surging inside me, the need to protect, the need to fix. Anything apart from repulsion.

I slide a hand along the smooth expanse of skin over her hip, up along her rib cage and move myself closer.

"You would need to do something very bad to repulse me." My voice lowers automatically but I notice that she flinches a little at my words but then quickly clears her face of all expression. I realise that she has not told me everything. There is something still there, lurking in her past, something darker than all the other secrets she has spilled this afternoon. Something that she really doesn't want me to know.

"How bad?" she teases obviously hoping I did not notice her expression change.

"Oh, really really bad."

"Like what?"

I shift over on my knees and grab the bag from the bakers. "Like eat your lunch in only four mouthfuls."

Bex eyes the large Cornish pasty steadily. "Easy."

"You're so going to fail."

"It's all about tactics." She tears the crust of the pasty and breaks it into two shoving one into her mouth. Once she has swallowed it down she pops in the other and then spends another three minutes chewing the overload of pastry.

Next she splits the remaining pastry and mixture of meat and potatoes into two. "You're going to have to turn around for this, you won't want to kiss me again if you see me do this."

"No way, you might cheat."

"One thing I am not is a cheat." Her shoulders stiffen again.

"Calm down, and I assure you I will still want to kiss you." *Like forever.*

"No."

"Do it, do it, do it, do it, do it." I start to drum the sand with my words and she shoots me her frowny look and then just shoves half of the pie in, squidging it in so far she has to cover her face with her hand because she can no longer close her mouth.

I start to laugh, no not laugh, I start to giggle like a ten year old as I watch her munch it down.

"By the way I am finding you very sexy right now. I just want to throw that out there."

"You're weird," she says when she has finally stopped chewing.

"Maybe, but my question is can you do it?"

Bex eyes the remaining chunk and then shrugs and shoves it in. I sit and beam a ridiculous grin at her as she finishes the pasty in the allocated four mouthfuls. When she is done she leaps from the sand and starts prancing about. "I am the champion, I am the champion."

Standing I grab hold of her hand and ease her bikini clad body into mine. "You certainly are."

"Have you ever done that?"

"Nope I fail every time."

"Really?" She starts to dance over the sand chanting "Loser," at me. Like I am going to let her get away with that.

In five easy strides I have my arms locked around her squirming body and have walked us towards the sea. The day is scorching hot as I predicted and I know the sea will be ice cold in contrast. Oh well. I dump her straight into the water, not deep enough to go under but far enough to get her wet all over.

"Josh!"

"Who's the loser now?" I pull her up from the water, hoisting her high and she wraps her legs around my waist, leaning in to kiss me with lips that taste a combination of sea salt and Cornish pasty. Something about her kiss seems different, playful almost, she slides her tongue along the curve of my top lip, smiling against my mouth.

"That really wasn't very kind."

"Well you know, I never said I was perfect."

Bex smiles at me, a true smile, and I understand the difference is in her kiss. She has told me her worst bits and shown me she is not perfect but I am still here, still holding her, still kissing her. How many friends must she have lost after what happened. How lonely has the girl made of sun been?

I walk us back out of the sea and head back to our hiding place behind the rock. Slowly lowering us onto the towels, I gently let her lie flat against the sand before leaning into her and catching hold of her lips with my own. For the first time I go into the kiss with my eyes shut, waiting for sensation and need to lead me to make the right moves. Bex shifts herself slightly beneath me and slides her hands up along my back before linking her fingers around my neck. I can feel her body rub against mine, slightly. I move myself back in towards her, pushing her further into the soft sand underneath us. Ever so slowly and with my eyes still closed I lower my lips down her throat and plant soft kisses along her skin until I reach her collarbone which I kiss along to her shoulder. All my senses in the absence of my sight are heightened and I can smell the sunflowers on her skin and taste the salt drying in the sun. More than that I can feel, I can feel the warmth of her against my lips and it makes me want more. I want more so badly, it is like a steady throb inside me. I lift myself back up to her lips and kiss her one more time before opening my eyes to the startling daylight. The ambers are watching me.

"Don't stop." She says.

"What do you mean?"

Bex does not answer she shifts herself against me again using her hips to move her pelvis against mine and the movement alerts me to what she wants me to do. My body reacts instantly, not that I wasn't excited already but now I feel the blood flow swiftly to my dick and I know what I want to do with it.

"Bex, we are on a beach." It's not an outright no.

I couldn't say no now if I tried, but then I also

know I don't want our first time having sex together to be on the beach.

"Use your imagination then?" She grins at me, her eyes taunting me and believe me I want to use my imagination, but at the same time I think about all the stuff she told me earlier and I know that the girl made of sun needs more than a quick roll in the sand.

"Well if you say so." I murmur as I roll us over and then over again wrapping the blanket around us tightly, binding us so closely together there is not a single spec of space between us.

"I feel a bit like Cleopatra," Bex giggles. She goes to say something else but I stop her lips with my mouth prising her own open as I quickly dart my tongue against hers. She comes right back at me, kissing me with an intensity that makes me feel heat burn up the back of my neck. I strain with a need to move against her but I hold my body dead still. I want it to come from her. This has to be her choice. I open one eye, just a fraction, so I can get a read on her emotions and find that she has her eyes tightly screwed shut. I instantly smile against her lips, the look of concentration on her face is the cutest thing and it makes me realise that she is probably trying to hold her body as still as I am. With one small peck on the lips I roll us over one last time so she is lying on top with her body pressed against mine. I anchor my hips into the sand, determined not to make the first move. I don't have to worry, with the spin of our bodies her eyes fly open and stare at me hard. Then Bex gives me a slow one sided smile as she realises what I have done, handed her the power to allow the moment to play out as she wants. She shifts herself against me as much as the tight blanket will allow, rubbing herself against the length of my erection which feels like it is pulsating against the material of my shorts and against her. Bex's smile grows ever so slightly as she closes her eyes again, and I move my hands as much as the constricting blanket will allow gripping either side of her hips as she sets up a steady motion, up and down, using me to stimulate her. I'm thinking the blanket was a terrible idea because I want to be able to run my hands along her skin and into her hair. I roll us a little again so I can release the tightness.

"Don't stop," she says.

"I'm not stopping," I kiss against her mouth. I demonstrate clearly how I am not stopping by running my free hands down her back, using both my thumbs to glide along her spine, feeling every vertebrae as I lower to the edge of her bikini pants, pulling both my hands down firmly on her hips again and pushing her pelvis in towards me so that the pressure she creates is almost to the point of being painful, the sort of pain I can cope with. My touch against her skin sparks her to move faster and firmer against me and for a moment I forget to watch her face as I close my eyes and concentrate on the feel of her sliding along my shaft. The movement and sensation is so intense I can feel myself edging higher and higher. That won't do, this is supposed to be about her, not me.

I catch hold of her shoulders and roll us over one last time so now I am on top and can drive the motion.

I lift my head and check the beach is still clear before lowering my lips to her throat which I kiss down until I reach the trim of her bikini top. Ever so slowly, using tentative fingers, I edge the material back until I have freed a nipple which I gently catch hold of in my mouth, rolling it with my tongue. Bex gasps out loud and lifts her legs wrapping them around my back. Raising one hand I use my palm to stroke firmly along her midriff, up and over her rib cage and along her throat until I can slide my fingers around the back of her head and lift her mouth gently up to mine. Bex strains herself against me, her hips lifting higher and higher with every movement she makes. Her hands splay into the sand so she can lever herself higher still and I start to put more intensity into my own actions and move my own hips faster in response.

Deep inside me I know I want to reach down and move her bikini bottoms out of the way so I can feel her properly, but I know I need to stick to my original intention. I watch her face and know that she is focused on whatever she can feel on the inside, lips slightly apart her breathing more ragged with every thrust I make. Shit I want her bad. I literally can't stop myself from crushing her with my body as I put every bit of myself into riding this out.

"Josh," she gasps into my ear and I feel her lift up against me, her back rigid and her arms tight around my back as she spasms against me, and that it, that's me done. A huge surge takes over me and for a moment there is darkness all about me, as all I can feel is Bex tight in my arms.

Seconds of silence tick by as we lay in complete stillness. I breathe through my mouth a little to clear my head and kiss my lips along her throat to her mouth. It's a tame kiss, considering. I feel oddly shy, unsure how she is going to react, but her lips kiss mine hungrily which gives me the confidence to open my eyes and look into the ambers which are shining at me. I bite my lip a little and try to think of something to say other than "Sorry I took advantage of you on a beach."

"Are you shy?" she asks.

"No."

Bex giggles.

"Well I guess that was a first for the beach," I smile at her and plant a kiss on her mouth.

"That was a first for me full stop," she says.

"What do you mean?"

"That was just a first. I've never done that before."

"What on a beach?"

"No, ever. Well not with someone else." Bex gives a nervous sounding giggle with her words.

I start to grin and pull her tight into my arms. I know I need to go and wash off in the sea, but I also need to lie quietly on the sand with the girl made of sun locked in my arms, from which I never want to let her go.

SIX DAYS TO GO

Bridge Cottage
St Agnes
Cornwall

21st August 2013

Dear E,

I told him. I told him all about those girl and what they did to Emily and in turn what I did to them.

He didn't look shocked, he didn't look disgusted, he looked sad. Then he kissed me and it felt like he was trying to kiss the real me. The girl who's made mistakes, the girl who never meant to do the things she did but lives with them every day.

I wanted to tell him about you. I wanted to tell him that one night you and I went out but only one of us came back. I couldn't though. I wasn't sure if he would be still able to accept me if he knew that I lost you in the way that I did.

I'm not ready to lose him yet.

Miss you as always

Gone

B.xx

Rebecca

Breakfast

The first thing I notice when I wake up is the absence of Joshua's arms. Last night after our day out he parked Daisy on the curb and kissed me goodnight. I came in eager to go to bed after the exhausting day of revealing secrets and dry-humping on the beach.

At half two I glanced at the clock by the side of the bed when I felt his arms wrap tight around my waist. He smelt strongly of turps or whatever it is that painters use with oil paints. I breathed in his smell of mint, sea, paint and chemicals until I fell back asleep. Just as I was slipping into a dream I felt him move forward, his lips low to my ear and he opened his mouth to whisper something.

"Don't say it, Joshua," I said.

So he didn't. He just hugged me tighter instead.

The second thing I notice is the smell of bacon creeping up through the floorboards. Crispy bacon. My stomach gives an almighty grumble as it registers the aroma. It's official, a girl can't survive on sausage rolls, Cornish pasties and snogging alone. I am down the stairs in three minutes trooping into the kitchen where the Munch Bunch are all sitting scoffing bacon.

"You could have called me for breakfast," I grumble as I pull out my seat. Mum is standing at the cooker but I see her glance up at the clock on the kitchen wall. I squint my eyes at it a little. That can't be right can it?

"It's seven fifteen." Dad confirms lowering his daily paper.

Well that's a bit of a shocker. I am up before nine for no reason whatsoever.

"Shit."

"Language," Dad crinkles his forehead ever so slightly in my direction, now this is the family time I am used to.

"So, Rebecca, what are you doing today?"

I take my eyes from the plate of crispy bacon mum has slid onto the table in front of me to answer her question. "I thought we were going shopping for stuff?" This was the plan we made yesterday when mum gently reminded me that I needed to interrupt my two weeks paradise with Joshua to get stuff for Uni.

"Sure, are you not seeing Joshua though?"

"S'don't know," I say with a mouthful of bacon. "Where can we go shopping?"

"Truro?" Mum suggests.

I groan automatically. "I went there yesterday."

"You know they have a University there." It's Emily that speaks but she does not glance at me with her words. She keeps her eyes studiously intent on her toast which she is covering with marmite.

I stare at her until she raises her eyes to mine, her blonde hair shining like a halo in the light from the kitchen door.

"It's not happening."

"Why?"

"You know why?"

"It could be different here?"

"Em, you know it won't, drop it okay?"

"Rebecca," Mum reaches a hand for me and it hovers between us, just the same way it has for months. "Your sister is just trying to say she would like you to stay. In truth we all would."

I turn and find Dad. "Does Dad want me to stay too?"

Dad gives a sigh and slides his hand along the fold in his paper. "Rebecca it's not about wanting or not wanting. It's about trying to make you happy. You haven't been happy for months."

I stare at him open eyed. "Are you kidding me? You know why I can't be happy."

"No, Rebecca, we know why you think you should be unhappy. That's a completely different thing."

"No," I shout as loud as I can. "Unhappy is what I make all of you, and it's all I deserve."

I get up from the table, scraping my chair back along the tiles. I can feel this really annoying lump in my throat and I hate it. I want to pull it out. All this sea air is making me weak. What happened to the girl who stomped about in big boots and inappropriate outfits? I march my way out of the kitchen and head back up the stairs to my room, the room that I never thought I would call mine, determined to find her again.

I can hear them muttering as I walk up the stairs. Mum is saying something about, "A step in the right direction."

I can tell them there is only one direction I am taking and it is away from here.

An hour later I have a classic Rebecca Walters outfit on. I'm not sure why but it feels all wrong, constraining, confining, the exact opposite of free. I march back down the stairs making sure to allow my boots echo on very step.

I can hear Mum flip-flop her way out of the kitchen just as I reach the bottom step. "Are you ready to go shopping?"

"Nah, I've changed my mind."

"Why?"

"I'll just make do, and I don't want to owe you and Dad for anything else."

"Rebecca, for goodness sake don't be so dramatic."

I turn and give her one of my smiles, the smile that I know she never knows how to read. "I'm not being dramatic, I am just being me." And with that I swing out of the front door and down the path. I know she will be standing there watching me, wondering what has happened and the truth is I feel like a bitch. I am starting to resent myself for being the way I am with people. It's not normal is it? But at the same time I know that I can't be normal, at least not until I am away from my family and all the memories that come with them. I want to switch off this new humanity streak that is coursing through me. I don't want to feel bad for leaving my mum standing in the hallway with her mouth hanging open. I want to feel the same way I have for months. I want to feel dead on the inside so that I simply don't feel anything anymore. As I pace away from the cottage I can hear my bangles jingling, it's the first time in days I have been aware of them. The bangles have almost faded into insignificance like I have forgotten why they are there in the first place, but I know I can't forget and whilst I know I can't forget about them I know I need to stay away from the person who is stopping me from concentrating on my sins.

Joshua.

I need to stay away from Josh if I have any chance of leaving this town like I always intended.

Six days to go.

Joshua

Blank Canvases

It's so damn annoying. I just feel this burn all the time in my limbs pulling me back to Bex. Last night I was just going to drop her off and go back to Aunt May's to sleep. Sleep, I can't even remember what that is. When I am with her I am watching her or touching her, memorizing her so that I won't ever be able to forget. When I am not with her I am just engulfed in fire, wanting to be next to her.

Last night I ended up in the studio, which I paced like I was trapped in a cage, until I turned on the painting of Bex still on the easel in the centre of the room and ripped it to shreds. Then I started to paint again, a different view, a different interpretation, a different Bex but still Bex all the same.

This Bex is as pure as the snow, with no taint on her soul. The Bex that I see, but she doesn't believe exists.

I kept thinking of all the secrets that she spilt to me on the beach and it made me feel this deep desire to tell her some of mine. I wish I could. I wish I could find the words.

After three hours of covering the canvas in swathes of white and silver with the faintest tint of the gold of a setting sun I knew I was not going to be able to stay away from her. So I didn't. I ran all the way up the lane until I reached the drain pipe next to her window which I scaled until I was in her room and sliding myself alongside her. Her body fit tight into mine and as I wrapped my arms around her in a grip which I never would have thought I could release, I wanted to tell her. I wanted to tell her how I felt in that very moment, and that even though I never thought I would feel anything like it again, because of her I feel alive. I wanted to give her a little bit of myself, tell her just a fraction of the loss that I feel on the inside, so she knows she is not the only one to lose something. Difference being she lost herself.

"Don't say it, Joshua," she whispered. I didn't. I held it tight inside me until I felt like my lungs were going to burst with the strain of holding it in, like my arms were burning with holding her so damn tight.

When the morning rays started to lighten the furthest corners of her attic room I snuck back out forcing myself not to look back at her. I came straight back to the studio where I have been staring at my new work of art ever since.

I am just working on spreading the lightest bronze tone I can blend into her hair when the door bangs downstairs. Cursing to myself I take my time to place my paint brush back onto my palette before heading down to open it. The deep knot in the pit of my stomach makes me know that I want it to be the girl made of the sun.

It's not.

Faye is leaning against the door, her dark hair swinging in her eyes and a laugh turning her lips into a smile. "And here I was thinking you were going to ignore me the full two weeks."

"I'm not ignoring you."

"Yeah I know, can I come up?"

I want to say yes but at the same time I don't want to show her the image of Bex. I feel like it will reveal far more of me than it does of the picture's subject.

"Nah, I am all done. Shall we go for a surf?"

"Ah, there is my Joshy Woshy,"

"Fuck, Faye, how many times have I told you not to call me that?"

"At least a million."

"So how many more times are you going to say it?"

"At least a million."

I pull the door closed behind us and nudge my oldest friend hard out of the way so I can double lock the door.

"Have you eaten?" Faye is eyeing me up and down with her critical shit detector.

"Nope."

"Slept?"

"Nope."

"Washed?"

"Nope."

"How delightful, quite frankly, Josh you stink." She crinkles her nose and leans in a little closer to give me a small sniff.

"Well don't stand so damn close then."

"I'm guessing Bex doesn't mind if you stink."

I start to grin. Goddam it I can't stop it. "Guess she doesn't."

"Joshy loves Bexy."

"Do not."

"You keep telling yourself that, loser."

I nudge her hard in the ribs which makes her give an "Ouch." In response. "You know," she continues, "I was just about to tell you how nice it is to have my best mate Josh around again, but now you can stick it."

Faye links her arm through mine and we turn around the back of the building where there is a small outdoor space where I park Daisy. It doesn't take us long to unload the boards and walk our way down to the lane to the beach. The sun is so hot and intense I can feel it burning on the back of my neck as we negotiate the sands and head towards the rock by the sea. At first I think there is a holiday maker sat there on the rock, as still as a statue, but the gleam of red gives away the stranger's identity and I feel my steps falter a little bit, my board wobbling unbalanced beneath my arm. I keep thinking of the words I wanted to say to her last night and how she wouldn't let me say them and I don't really know what to do with that.

"You alright, Joshy?" Faye crinkles her eyebrows a little as she watches me hesitate on the sand.

"Yeah, sure, whatever."

My feet walk along the warm sand towards the

rock, and I watch as Bex's shoulders stiffen as she spies our shadows stretch out on the sand beneath her.

"Hey," I greet. My hand automatically stretches out to graze my fingertips along the sun warmed skin of her shoulder.

"Hey." She doesn't take her eyes off the surf so Faye leans forward and shoves her face right into Bex's.

"Hey, Rebecca, fancy a swim with Josh and I?" Faye asks.

Almost in slow motion Bex turns her gaze on us and I feel my mouth drop open. It's Bex alright but not the girl I wrapped my arms tight around all night. This is the Bex I first saw stomping on the beach and along the high street. The make-up is back, as are the boots and the attitude.

I know Faye is standing right next to us but it feels in an instant like she has faded away and it is just Bex and I. The entire rest of the universe has dissolved around us.

"That make-up is going to run." I state.

"Pardon?" Bex looks me up and down, and the ambers instead of looking like warm honey I want to swim in, are rock hard and unflinching.

It makes me want to fight her. It makes me want to get right into her space and lay my hands flat on her skin. It makes me want to move my body until her skin is meshed with mine and I can own her lips and make her knees give way with the intensity of just how much I want to do everything to her. All of it, everything, now.

"I said your make up is going to run in the water," I cast my eyes down at her boots. "I hope that they are waterproof." I incline my head towards her inappropriate footwear and wait for her reaction.

Bex grinds her boot into the sand, her fingers gripping the rock. Her shoulders are high and I can see the rise and fall of her chest through the transparent gauze of her shirt.

"It would be unchivalrous for you to dump me in the sea again," she states, her eyes not making contact with mine.

"Yes, and we know I am all about being gentlemanly." I take a step toward her so my bare leg is pushed up against her thigh, then I lower myself down and kneel on the sand in front of her. "Look at me." I place one hand on her knee sliding it ever so slightly up the smooth curve of her leg.

She does not react she just stares over my shoulder, her eyes still intent on the waves.

"Look at me," I say again.

Bex slowly shifts her gaze to mine and for a moment we are both rock still. The liquid amber is back and I can feel it seep into my being.

"What's wrong?" My voice is lowering of its own accord.

"Nothing."

"Liar."

To this Bex just shrugs offhandedly.

"Is this because of last night?"

"No." But her eyes dart over my face quickly and

now I know she is lying.

"Is it because I was gone this morning?"

"No."

"Is it because I am here with Faye."

"No." More forceful this time.

"What is it then?" I settle back onto my heels and clasp my hands over my knees waiting for her to say something, anything.

Finally after an age she reaches a hand forward and slides one of my dreads back over my shoulder, her fingers lingering just momentarily. "It's because you make me want to be someone I'm not."

I allow the breath I have been holding to exhale out of my mouth. "I don't want you to be anyone other than who you are." And this is the truth. Secrets out, worst bits whispered into my ear, I still only want her to be herself.

Bex leans forward and slides a finger along my jaw. "You make me want to be the sort of girl who can stay in a town like this, but I know I'm not, and you know I'm not."

I laugh a little, I don't mean to, it just escapes before I can hold it in. "Why you being so serious, for God's sake, Bex just stay and have a surf with us then we can go and grab some breakfast or something?"

At the word "Us" Bex's eyes flick over to Faye who is hovering nearby pretending not to listen.

"Forgive me, Josh, but I don't really want to spend the morning hanging with you and your ex-girlfriend." Her words make Faye's head spin around. "And, Josh, I don't think we should see each other again for the next few days. It's just, it's just, making everything too, complicated." With her words she is up off the rock and striding her way back to the car park. I watch her long legs the whole way willing myself to chase after her.

I want to chase after her, but her words are echoing in my head, *"Complicated."* .The irony is apparent to me at once. Bex, who has complicated my life and woken me up with her meddling, stomping attitude and fiery resistance thinks I have complicated her life too much. Instead of chasing my toes dip further into the sand.

"You need to tell her the truth, Josh."

I turn and examine Faye who's watching me closely. "I think telling her the truth will be the very worst thing I could do."

"You're going to lose her if you don't."

I scrutinize Faye, trying to read her expression. "What am I supposed to say?" I throw my hands up in the air with my words, like some profound answer to the problem I face may fall into my open arms.

"Just the simple truth."

A flash of hot anger courses through me. "What, like my girlfriend is dead and it's all my fault?"

The moment the words are out I have an enormous wave of emotion wash over me. Stronger than the waves in the sea, it nearly knocks me off my feet. I can just about register Faye's gasp at my outburst but only just because the rest of my hearing is dominated by a loud pounding in my ears.

"I'm sorry." I say.

Faye takes a step towards me and links her fingers through mine. Normally I would pull away from her touch, but today I don't. I stand there ready to face anything she wants to dish at me.

"I've been waiting six months, two weeks and four days for you to say that."

I said it.

I allow a deep breath fill my lungs and then push it back out into the salty air.

"My girlfriend is dead and it's all my fault."

Faye takes another step in and slides her hands around my waist.

"Josh, it's not your fault."

"Whatever."

My heart is squeezing and my throat tightening. I'm not going to allow the emotion to take over.

"Josh. Look at me."

I lower my glance to hers.

"I don't think she is your girlfriend anymore. Bex is."

I shake my head vehemently at her words. "No."

"I bet you've wanted to tell Bex you are in love with her, that's who you are. You love with all of your being. It's your biggest gift."

"No."

"It's true, Josh."

"I've only known her a week, don't be crazy."

"Well maybe love is crazy."

I glare down at her. "Don't use that word."

Faye pulls away a little. "Fine. Don't use that word, whatever." She mimics my earlier shrug. "But now you're talking about it, you need to talk to *her* about it."

"What about you?"

"Josh you need to say goodbye."

"What if I can't?"

"Well, then you're going to lose Bex as well."

I look into her deep dark eyes and think over her words. "Faye." I slide her hair behind her ear, the most familiar motion. "I lost her the day she walked into town." And with my words I can't stop my eyes from following the trail Bex left indented in the sand.

Rebecca

The Burn

As I walk along the sand I feel the burn that I am so familiar with. Anger, anxiety and destruction lick flames along my insides. I am angry with myself. I can feel anxiety edging up my throat and the need to destruct everything around me that ties the whole package together.

I am destruction, it's what I do.

I destroy the things I want and the people I love.

Fists clenched I walk to the car park and glance about. There is no one here, so I come to a halt and allow my hitched ragged breathing to come under control. I hate myself even more because I know that the reason I have stopped in the car park is to see if he comes after me. He doesn't. Turning my head slightly I look back at the beach. He is pushing his board out into the sea, the sun glinting off his shoulders, with Faye at his side. The bile rises again and I start my march home. There isn't anywhere else to go, I don't know anyone here, I have no friends here, and I know that as angry as I am I can't open the door to the destructive path I took the other night with the vodka. Home and the naughty corner in the attic is the only option I have.

It's okay. It's just six days to go and then I can leave this new nightmare of my life behind and go find another one.

The whole way home I can't get the image of Joshua's shocked face when I said he *complicated* things for me. It was both alarmed and hurt.

I am destruction.

The cottage is deserted. I call out but no one answers so I quickly take the stairs two at a time and enter the room that annoyingly is starting to feel more like home.

I glance at the brilliant white walls and it makes the acid of anxiety rise again.

I wish I painted because then I could do them myself. I don't even have any paints. . . I don't have paints. . . but I do have rather a lot of make-up. I march with a new determination and glance in my box of tricks there is only one colour I want to find. Silver. Silver like the moon reflected on the sea. I find one of my dark eye shadow sets and dip my finger onto the silky powder before starting to apply it to the wall in a small circular motion.

All the silver is gone and I have created a moon the size of a dinner plate when I hear a voice from the direction of the window.

"What are you doing?" The tone is part amused part bemused.

"Decorating."

"With eye shadow."

"Yep."

"What is it?"

"The moon."

"I thought it was a dinner plate."

"Sod off."

I don't turn around but continue to dab silver sparkles on the wall as I wait for his reply. When none comes and I can't feel him move next to me I finally spin on the spot and see that he is not there, which makes me wonder if he was ever there in the first place.

I dig deep through my supply of eye shadow until I find another silver that almost matches. I start my circle creating exercise again and have doubled the moon to almost twice the size when I hear his feet land on the floorboards and feel him move alongside me. I don't want to look at him, I don't want to see any judgement in his eyes at my words on the beach. *Complicated.*

"Try this?" Josh hands me a metallic tube. I take it from his fingers taking extra care not to touch his skin and unscrew the cap. It's a perfect silver with an iridescent sheen.

"Thanks." *And I am sorry.*

"So what you planning on painting?"

"The moon and the sea."

"I was going to paint the sun and sand."

I can't help myself. I lift my eyes to look at him and find him staring at my eye shadow moon, "Maybe we could make them meet somehow," he finally says. His fingers link through mine and slowly he turns me around and I find his gaze on my face. "I'm sorry if I complicate things for you, Bex." I feel a stab in my stomach at the tone lacing his voice. "I never wanted to make things harder for you."

I look him all over. Fresh from the shower, his T-shirt is still damp from where he must have pulled it straight on his wet skin. The thought makes that low stab in the pit of my stomach flare, and my legs get that unique heaviness I've only ever had with him.

He looks to earnest and trustworthy. All the things I desperately want.

I breathe a slow breath out my nose. "I'm sorry, Joshua. It wasn't really what I meant to say, it's just, when I am with you I forget who I am, and I guess I like it a little bit too much." *I like it far too much.*

Joshua breathes in sharply and then using my hand still linked in his he moves me towards him. His free hand comes up and slides into my hair, entwining and pulling on the strands as he lowers his mouth to mine. I don't know what kiss I am expecting, something discreet and safe after the nasty words I have thrown at him today but instead it is hot and hungry and it makes my stomach clench and the burning sensation get stronger. With a kiss like that it is hard to remember who I am or even where I am. His hands fall to my waist and he lifts me up. I wrap my legs tight around him and he walks me back against the wall I have been trying to decorate using cosmetics.

I tug on his dreads, and let them fall through my fingers as I lower my hands to his firm shoulders, sliding them down along his back as he pushes me further into the wall pinning me in place with his body.

"Now do I have your attention?" He breaks his lips away to ask. His green eyes are burning in my direction and I am trapped to the spot.

"That would be a yes."

"Good. Now, Rebecca Walters, I know you are leaving, I understand why you want to leave and I will never, no matter how much I may want to, ask you to stay. But, I won't stand for the not seeing each other talk, that's just not viable. Okay?"

My mouth has gone very dry and my tongue does not seem to be cooperating. "Okay."

"Okay, so we are going to paint your room. We are going to do a lot more of this," with his words he grinds himself into me further still, "Tomorrow we are going to spend time with Faye, who by the way could not be further from my ex-girlfriend if she tried, and then maybe the day after that we will go out to Newquay for some fun, and then finally in six day's time I will watch you get on that train back to London and ultimately know that you have given me the best two weeks holiday I've ever had. One of the flaws of living in a seaside town is that holidays don't happen to us."

This is probably the most Joshua has said in one

breath before and the intensity of his green gaze settles deep inside me making my stomach knot uncomfortably.

"Okay." I start to smile.

"Okay. So no more stropping about, because quite frankly it just makes me want to spank you."

"Now if you'd said earlier about spanking." I don't get to finish because he crushes his lips back down to mine, his hands firmly grasping my thighs.

"Time for painting?" He moves his mouth fractionally to speak but I can still feel his warm breath mingling with mine.

"I'm kind of enjoying this." I kiss him back just to prove how much.

"We've got all night." His voice is noticeably lower and I bite my bottom lip in response which makes him groan slightly before kissing me again.

"All night?" I say against his mouth.

"All night."

FIVE DAYS TO GO

Bridge Cottage
St Agnes
Cornwall

22nd August 2013

Dear E

I feel like I am torn in two. I'm a girl split straight down the middle. Half of me knows I still have to leave. I need to leave. I'm still sure that people here will soon find out about you, and once that comes out it will all begin again.

I need to remember Emily and the fact that I don't want that to happen again.

But, the other half of me wants to stay. I want to be the girl who can stay in a town like this and have a guy like Josh-u-a as a boyfriend. But I am not a girl like that am I? I want to be the girl who can have conversations with her parents and decorate her room with them.

I want to be the girl who isn't scared to commit, isn't scared to show someone the gentle side that wants to trust. I want to be the girl who holds hands walking down the street, who gets kissed goodnight, the girl who gets to make love.

Do you think I could be that girl? Or should I keep running? Part of me wants to stay and hold my head up high. Yeah I've made mistakes but they are not all I am.

I wonder what Josh-u-a would say if he knew about you? Would he understand? Or would that be it? Would it be a final goodbye for me and him?

Do you remember when I said I never understood the big thing about sex? Surely sex was just that. A random act between two people. Every time he is near me now I want to find out. I want him to show me what it is about.

I wish I could talk to you.
Miss you as always
B.
xx

Rebecca

Breakfast

"They know," I screech and crash through the door. Joshua is sitting up in bed grinning.

"It was the sanding wasn't it."

"I told you that was a bad idea." And I did. Repeatedly. Joshua decided that he wanted to sand down the back of the bedroom door because he wants to have the inside of the door the same iridescent silver as the moon he created over my eye shadow blob. The other side of the door is going to be a golden yellow, "Just like you," he'd said.

So in a nutshell the door is going to represent the two of us, but on separate sides. Much the same as us – two people who should never really have met and liked each other. Two people who can't really be together. Two people who can't stay away from each other despite the fact they are so ridiculously different.

To be honest I'm glad that it was only the DIY that my parents heard during the night. At some point after the decorating and giggling I managed to wrestle Joshua out of the majority of his clothes, and it's a miracle my eyes did not just burn in their sockets from the sheer beauty that Joshua simply is. I wanted to see the tattoo again but he seemed almost shy when I finally managed to get past his shorts and locate the small item of art work that is constantly playing on my mind. He shivered involuntarily when I placed my lips to it. I was keen to explore further and whilst I could see and feel he was not opposed to it, he showed enormous resources of self-control and lifted my chin with his finger-tips and brought me back up alongside him. I wanted to ask him why he was so shy, especially about the tattoo but then when it was time for my clothes to be removed, which was so ridiculously erotic I nearly combusted. I also got bitten by the reserved bug and dashed under the duvet. It's silly because I know he has seen me in many states of undress but it feels the closer we get, and the more we know each other, the more I feel I show him when I bare my flesh in front of him.

Last night as I counted off my bangles I had my eyes screwed shut and the atmosphere between us was charged with something I could not name, electricity, desire, respect, need, want. It felt like every emotion I had ever tried to stop myself from feeling was zapping around in the air.

I shake off the thoughts of what could have been last night and clamber back onto the bed. Before I get the chance to settle, Joshua springs forward and pins me down on the mattress.

The greens bore into mine and I can't move my gaze away. "What?" I ask.

"Thank you."

"What for?"

"For waking me up."

"You were awake earlier."

He gives a low groan. "I'm trying to be romantic. Work with me here, Bex."

I start to laugh but try to hold it. "Please proceed to be romantic."

Joshua leans down catching hold of my mouth in a deep kiss which quickly stops me laughing. "Thank you for waking me up. You've made me feel like I can breathe, and live again."

I want to sit up and ask him what he is talking about, but I have a feeling that whatever it is he is trying to say is important. Instinctively I keep myself still, waiting for him to say something.

Joshua just stares at me for the longest moment. "I don't do goodbyes very well. But, but you are helping me to learn, and that's the most amazing thing anyone ever did for me."

I have no idea what to say to that. *What does it even mean?*

So I don't say anything. I just link my fingers around the back of his neck and pull him down towards me.

After a couple of minutes he leans up a frown flickering across his face and he makes a low tutting sound.

"What?"

"You're wearing pyjamas. That is not the way you left the room a few short minutes ago."

I giggle "Well. You know, it's funny but I find walking around family breakfast time practically naked does not work too well."

Joshua flashes me one of his wide grins and kisses around my lips.

"I think that would work for me." He lowers his lips and teases a sweet kiss along the edges of my mouth.

"Yep. Mum and Dad offered you a coffee, or tea, that was all."

"What, not this?" In a quick movement he lowers himself slightly and gently lifts the edge of my pyjama top and traces his deft fingers and his lips along my midriff.

"Nope, I think the invite was for tea and toast." Although I am liking Joshua's breakfast plan better. It's strange, with daylight streaming through the windows, the playful unconcerned side of Joshua's personality is back in control. Last night his lips were trailing the same pattern as they are now but the intent was entirely different. Last night for the first time in my life I wanted someone to read me, body and soul and still want me.

"Well I guess a slice of toast wouldn't go amiss." Joshua raises his head and smiles at me slowly. The last thing I have on my mind is toast, or tea for that matter. "Can I have a shower?" he asks pulling my top down with a disappointing ping.

"Sure, you know where it is."

With a gracefulness his large, athletically firm frame disguises he moves away from the bed and heads for the bathroom next door. The whole time he is in the shower I can hear him singing tunelessly and it makes me grin. Grin like a stupid thirteen year old suffering her first crush.

With a big sigh I sit up and look in the mirror across the room. That girl is back again, the girl that I don't recognise, but am beginning to understand might fit into this sea side town with its sleepy atmosphere, surfers who paint, and cars with names.

Then I realise with a shock just what thought I have allowed to creep into my subconscious.

I've never fit in anywhere. How can I be sure the girl with the freckles on show and the crazy un-straightened hair and the tendency to giggle and wrestle boys out of their clothes is me at all?

Five days to go.

Joshua

Moving On

My phone rings but I studiously ignore it. I know it is under Bex's bed which is where it slid to last night after what I will call 'The Battle of the Board shorts.' It wasn't a battle I was that sad to lose but I knew it would make it harder for me to keep up my paper thin self-control. I wanted Bex so bad last night. The whole time she counted off those damn bangles, all fifty-three of them, it felt like it was pouring over me. An intense need to find her, and I know the only way I am ever going to find the real Rebecca Walters is when I make her my own. I don't think she is ready yet, she is still battling herself and whatever demons she has locked inside. More than that I know I also have to deal with my shit as well. I've got to say that goodbye. It's coming I can feel it. Suddenly the words don't seem as hard to say as I thought they always would.

I lied to Bex when I said that my time with her was going to be the best two weeks holiday ever and then I would watch her leave.

The truth is that I will watch her leave, but at the

same time I will always be watching for her to come back again. Waiting for her to wake me up again. My ear will always be partially tuned to the sound of jingling bangles. Last night after we finished the painting and sanding she was attempting to locate the tattoo on my hip. I felt so self-conscious because I knew that if she asked me where my home was I would ultimately say 'wherever you are,' because in truth that is what she is starting to feel to me. I used to think my home lay on a different path, with someone else, but now Bex has arrived and changed the direction I was ever headed in.

"Is that your phone?" She listens to the ring, her head cocked to one side.

"Nope."

"Yes it is, and more importantly why don't I have your number?" Her face crinkles into a frown, but I can't quite tell if it is serious or not.

"I'm not answering it, and you never asked."

"Shall I answer for you?" Her frown wasn't real. She flashes me an evil smile and makes a dive towards the bed and my phone. I leap after her snagging it out of her hand first. It could be Dan and I don't want him talking to her again, ever.

It's not Dan, it's so much worse. It's Aunt May who wants to know when and if I plan to ever enter the shop and serve those annoying people called customers again.

I try not to sound too sulky or distracted as I negotiate some hours with her. Cradling the phone under my ear, I walk over to Bex's dresser and grab an eyeliner, I then scrawl my number along her mirror. I can see her smiling in the reflection and it makes me smile too.

"This afternoon then?" I confirm to my Aunt before swiftly hanging up and turning to face Bex giving her all of my attention.

I have spent the last couple of hours creating the mural onto the wall. Bex has been telling me where I have missed bits. Emily was up here but she said all the kissing going on was destroying her artistic vision.

"The bad news is I have got to go to work." I say. Bex tries not to drop her bottom lip but fails and I move towards her and kiss her on it, giving a gentle tug with my teeth which makes her close her eyes and part her mouth beneath mine.

"And the good news?" she eventually pulls away to ask.

"Is that you get to come with me." I grin. A flicker of something I can't read crosses her amber gaze but before I can pin it down she turns her head and looks at the wall I have been working on.

"I am worried we may not get this done in five days." Bex offers a shrug with her words but I notice the slight catch in her tone and it goes hand in hand with the weird tightening sensation filling my chest area.

"We could call in back up?"

"You know a troop of artists all ready to work for free?"

"Nope, but I know some friends who are handy with a decorating brush."

"Really?"

"No harm in asking." I grab my phone and send some one-handed text messages as my other hand slides into the back pocket of her teeny tiny cut off shorts. The slight splodge on one of the trees on the wall was caused by the slip of my brush when she walked in a while back wearing just them and her bra towel drying her hair.

We have already been downstairs for what Bex called a 'hearty breakfast of awkward silence and over cooked eggs.' To be honest it wasn't that bad. Bex's parents seem to be completely accepting of the fact that I am here every day, which is a good thing considering I don't plan to be anywhere else for the next five days. Emily most of all seems pleased that I am around and that so far today Bex hasn't shouted at anyone or stomped about in her boots. Nope, definitely no boots. Just shit hot sexy legs and bare feet.

Speaking of little silver flower fairies, Emily walks back in and I swiftly remove my hand from Bex's back pocket which causes her to scrunch her face.

"Here, I did this for you." Emily hands me a small flat parcel wrapped in brown paper and tied with string.

Bex holds her hand out expectantly, "And mine?"

"You can share." Emily grins at us and bounces a little bit on the spot before waltzing straight back out of the bedroom door.

I don't waste any time. I quickly unloop the string and slide off the wrapping. Inside is a piece of mounted vellum on which Emily has drawn an exquisite pencil sketch of me and Bex at the castle. That days seems ages ago. How many days ago was that? Five? Four? It feels like a lifetime.

"Wow," Bex whispers.

"Wow."

There was something special about that day and you can see it in the closeness of the image on the picture, the way our bodies are just ever so slightly turned towards each other, the tilt of Bex's chin as she looks up at me, the incline of my own in response.

What was it about that day? I can't even remember now.

Oh yes I can.

That was the day that Bex told me about her dad finding her at that party. My fingers tighten on the frame as I recall her words and the way it made me feel the first time Rebecca Walters let me into her little cupboard of dark secrets where she hides all the stuff about herself. I remember how her story made me feel, the rage, the jealousy and the deep intense need that I wanted her all for my own. It's fair to say that feeling has not diminished over the last week.

"Your sister is very talented."

There is a heartbeat of silence before Bex responds, "Yeah she is." Her voice is low and I turn a little to look down at her. Tears are lining her eyes and the bottom lip is back.

"Why are you upset?"

"I'm not." Bex straightens her shoulders and

shakes out her hair.

"Yes you are, I can see it." I lift a finger to her face and trace along the outline of her eyes swimming in pools of unreleased water.

"I'm not upset. I'm scared."

"What of?" I move myself in towards her a little feeling the friction in the air move between us.

"I'm scared what's going to happen to her in a few weeks at her new school. I'm scared that I won't be here to help her, but most of all I am scared of what impact it would have if I stayed."

It feels like the moment and her words are weighted in something. Does she want to stay? I always thought that was never a viable option.

"Rebecca," I start but my words stop as her mum calls up the stairs.

"Joshua, Rebecca, your friends are here!"

Bex shakes off whatever it is she is feeling and raises an eyebrow at me. "Well it must be your friends, because I don't have any."

"Yes you do."

"Who?"

"Me."

"Are we bestest friends forever now?"

"Maybe."

She is staring at me, the ambers burning. I know she is trying to think of something to say. "Stuck?" I prompt as she continues to fish around for some clever comeback. I start to smile a cocky grin which makes her bite her bottom lip a little bit. I wish she would stop doing that. It's crazy sexy.

"Don't mind us." Faye bashes into the room closely followed by Andrew. Painting and matchmaking, now who says I am not the perfect friend to have?

Rebecca

Frescoes and Easels

"Joshua, do you think you are fucking Michelangelo?" Faye has marched into the room and is staring at the wall in front of her, her dark shiny perfect hair falling in a wave down her back. I feel that familiar little pinch of jealousy enter my head and heart but I bolt it out, slamming all my mental doors in its face.

I turn to Joshua laughing at the idea of him assuming Michelangelo characteristics and hanging off ceilings painting upside down but Joshua isn't laughing. He is watching Faye with caution and worry etched across his face. I flick my eyes towards the guy who walked in with Faye and find that he is watching her the same way. It doesn't feel like anyone is breathing in the room apart from me. I am taking in huge lungful's of air as I try and decipher the look on Joshua's face.

That's weird. Isn't it?

"It's true I prefer an easel." Josh shrugs, his eyes still steady on her.

"Ya, I know," Faye glances around the rest of the

room her hands on her slender hips, "It's much better than the roses."

I'm sorry what?

"It's true, the roses were terrible." The guy I have not properly been introduced to muses and turns towards me. "Hi I'm Andrew, we sort of met at the beach the other week." He holds his hand out to me and I reach for it in mine and give it a firm shake. It's my sole aim in life to never have a limp handshake no matter what the circumstances.

"So did you used to climb in the window too?" I ask him.

Andrew laughs, a deep sound that reverberates off the walls. "Uh no, I'm not that agile at shimmying drain pipes, although I hear that our Josh has developed quite a skill for it."

"Apparently so." I sound stroppy, and yet I can't quite stop it. "So did you used to live in this room?" I turn my attention to Faye without missing a single beat. Whatever the answer, surely it's not going to hurtle me over the edge of rational behavior? Apparently they have been friends since they were five. I guess girls and boys sit in their rooms just like girlfriends would. Trouble is, I don't really know what friends do when they hang out. In truth, I only had one close friend my entire life. One person who could handle Naughty Rebecca Walters. I jingle my bangles and centre myself around them.

Faye holds Joshua's eye for just a fraction too long and then lets out a laugh of her own. "There is no way I could have lived with those roses. I had the room down below."

I gasp a little. I mean I think I'd guessed, but the confirmation tightens my chest.

"Anyway," Faye says linking her arm through mine. "It was a long time ago." She looks me over and smiles at what she sees, I can't think why. My hair is all over the place and I am covered in paint. It's my face she is reading, not my outfit. "It was a long time ago, at least it feels like it to me," she adds.

"Whatever, that's cool," I say for complete lack of knowing what else to say. She must think I am a complete bitch. I haven't managed one normal conversation with her yet.

"What shall we paint then?" Andrew asks grabbing a brush and walking towards the wall and waving it around.

"Ooh, no. Thank you, Andrew, I'll take that." Josh laughs as he takes away the brush and replaces it with a sandpaper and block. "You can sand the other side of the door."

"Shouldn't you have sanded it all before you started painting?"

"Shouldn't you shut your face?"

Andrew takes the sandpaper heading for the door and I watch Faye's gaze follow him as he moves.

Ah.

Josh offers me a small smile and a wink nudging his head slightly towards Andrew and Faye.

"Shut it, Josh," Faye says when she spies his movement. "I know way too many secrets about you, don't tempt me to spill."

"What?" Josh raises his hands in an innocent gesture which makes me giggle. His green T-shirt is streaked with silver paint and there is also a dab on the end of one of his dreads.

Reaching my hand out I run it through my fingers feeling the familiar sensation register deep inside me. "You're gonna have to shave them off."

Andrew and Faye both make funny snorting noises and Josh places his hands on his hips, "Now, Rebecca Walters I have told you these beauties are a lifestyle choice and I will never lose them." He raises an eyebrow at me, "Do I need to remind you?"

I put my hands on my own hips to replicate his combative stance. "And how exactly do you plan to do that, Joshua Adams?"

"Death by tickling."

Faye snorts again. "Are you ticklish, Bex?"

"No of course not, I am eighteen years old, not eight."

"Prepare to want to die," she laughs.

Turning to ask her what she means I miss Joshua leap forward and reach his fingers for my rib cage. I can't quite make out what else she is saying, something about farting, and laughing because I am screaming in part agony part complete hysteria as Joshua somehow manages to wiggle his deft firm fingers into the gaps between my ribs. I land on the floor with a bang but he doesn't stop, he straddles me and carries on with the torturous tickling as I make noises I never knew I was capable off and tears of laughter escape out of my eyes.

Fuck.
Apparently I do giggle.

Later the giggling is over, and we are packing up and getting ready to head out to the shop. I've had so much fun. Normal fun. Well what I think could be counted as normal fun if I really knew what it was like. Emily has been back with us, safety in numbers she said when she told Faye and Andrew that all Josh and I do is snog.

I grab a cardi just in case it's a late one and we head out the door. Joshua lingers behind and I stop to see what he is doing. He has Emily in a huge hug and is whispering something in her ear. Watching the tender moment between this stranger who is completely dominating my life and my most precious thing makes tears sting again in the back of my eyes. Shit. I can't keep crying all the time until I leave. What would be the point?

"What did you say to her?" I ask as we pace down the stairs to catch up with Faye and Andrew who are already saying goodbye to my mum in the kitchen. Dad has left, I think the crazy giggling was too much for him.

"I told her that I think she is very talented."

"Thank you."

"Why are you thanking me, it wasn't hard to say, she is extraordinarily talented."

"I know." And I also know that the immense sense of pride that colours my tone speaks volumes.

Once out the house we stand in the sunlit street

and say goodbye to Josh's friends. Faye leans in and hugs me, taking me by surprise. "Fancy coming out tomorrow?"

I glance at Joshua who nods his head at me. "Sure why not."

Faye looks very pleased and starts to walk down the lane with Andrew, an uncomfortable distance between their steps. I watch them with a frown on my face.

"Don't, it's a lost cause," Josh says his lips close to my ear.

"Does she love him?"

"Yes."

"Does he love her?"

"Yes."

"Well that's a bit dumb then isn't it?" I look up into Joshua's face and find his green gaze settled on me, something about his expression makes my stomach do a weird flippy floppy thing.

"Yeah that would be really dumb."

"Good, glad we agree." Then I turn my feet away from whatever disastrous conversation that could have been and walk towards the town with Joshua an uncomfortable step behind me.

Joshua

Paintings on a Wall

At the shop Bex's entire body language changes. Aunt May is clearly not here. The door was locked and there was a stroppy note stuck on the glass saying the shop was closed due to unreliable staff. I left the note in the window after scrawling a smiley face on it. I then firmly shut the door again, despite the heat, in the hope that we don't get disturbed by annoying tourists buying pencils and the awful postcards Aunt May decided to buy last year in the hope of bringing in some trade.

"So what do we do?" Bex asks. She is leaning against the counter, her long legs crossed at the ankle.

"We listen to music, drink some tea, generally bum about until it is time to lock the door at which point I am planning on taking you out on another date." I offer with a wink. "Assuming that is okay with you?"

I don't add the rest of my plan which is taking form in the back of my mind for later tonight. The extended plan involves removing most of her clothing with as much dexterity and reserve as I can combine and then trying to read every bit of her skin. Every mark, every blemish, every curve that I don't already know.

I am stepping towards her to demonstrate just a little bit of my plan when the bloody annoying doorbell that I hate jangles the arrival of a customer.

What are the chances?

My head falls onto her shoulder as I let out a groan of disappointment. Bex starts to laugh but the sound quickly falters and I feel her stiffen under my touch.

"Can I help you?" I spin and ask. It's not a customer, it's Dan. He has his habitual smirk smeared across his face. Instinctively I edge closer to Bex. Dan narrows his eyes as he registers the movement.

"Josh and the holiday maker!" Dan shouts the word like he is addressing a vast audience not the two of us.

"Hm." Bex and I both state at the same time which makes me smile. *She is no holiday maker.*

"Josh, it's been days!"

Possibly not enough days for my liking.

"Hey, Dan, I've been busy sorry, mate, how are you?"

I haven't seen him since he upset Bex in the pub. And it's not because I have been too busy. I don't know what it is but there is something in his eyes when he looks at Bex which sets me on edge. I haven't felt this uncomfortable around him in a long while. He is always pulling some holiday maker when we are out but I have never until the last few days noticed how blatantly territorial he is around women. But then maybe it's me that is being territorial. Maybe Dan has always walked around stripping off a girl's clothes with his eyes. I just never read it for what it was before. Now it makes me uncomfortable. I am starting to wonder what else I may have missed.

"Oh, Josh, you know what it's like. Out in Newquay, a different girl every night, you remember that don't you."

I grimace in response. I can't lie outright and say no. Because I am still trying to forget that one summer when I decided to act out of character, it seems Dan is not going to let me forget.

"Nice." I nod eventually.

Bex is standing there, her arms folded tight across her chest, completely unmoving. She is reading him too, and I think she agrees with my current summation of my friend's personality.

"How's St Agnes? No more strops in pubs, Bex? I heard you caused quite a scene the other day offering Josh here a blow job in front of all the old grannies."

I flush hot with anger straight away. "That's uncalled for." I glare at him.

"Just saying. Everyone knows about it." Dan does not make eye contact with me. He keeps his attention directed at Bex.

I expect her to flip or go to that place inside herself where she hides the other Bex.

"It's Rebecca."

I suppress a smile but Dan just grins and changes tact. "So are you love birds coming out with us tomorrow?"

Jesus! That's the quickest word has ever spread in St Agnes.

"Yep." I interrupt, making him look at me instead

of her, but Bex just smiles at me and straightens herself up a little further.

"So you going to show me the sights, Dan?" Bex smiles at him and hoists herself up onto the till counter, re-crossing her legs as she does so. Even I am wide-eyed. Dan is gob smacked.

"Uh, yeah I guess."

"I bet you know how to have a good time hey?" she smiles.

"Yep, I know all the sound spots." He is looking a little wary, as he probably quite rightly should.

"Excellent, I can't wait. Josh, that sounds so much fun, it will be great to go out and meet everyone else." Bex tugs at my T-shirt sleeve and leads me over to her perch on the counter where she then wraps her arms tight around me, resting her chin on my shoulder so she is still looking at Dan. "What time shall we meet?"

"Uh about eight."

"Excellent," she says. And with that he is dismissed. He stares at us for a moment longer but Bex just ignores him and turns my face gently with her fingertips around to hers, kissing me on the lips and swiftly shifting herself up closer to me so I can move between her knees. Bex has completely disarmed him by not fighting him.

The door opens and the tension I hold inside me when he is around releases. I think he is gone but I have not waited long enough. "Josh mate, bad form to leave those pictures up there what with your *new* girlfriend sitting right underneath them.

And with that parting shot Dan has the last word, as per always.

She does not say anything, in fact she just keeps kissing me with a steady enthusiasm, her mouth moving against mine, her fingers gripping my shoulders and her legs moving further apart so I can get as close to her as possible.

A few minutes later she pulls away. The ambers are dark and hazy as she watches me, a faint smile lingering on her lips. "Want to have sex with me now?"

I smile against her cheek, "What makes you think that?"

She shifts slightly against me creating the perfect pressure point, "Nothing."

"Most guys walk around with hard-ons."

"And are you most guys, Joshua?" Ah, there it is again her sing-song way my name trips off her tongue.

"Well no," I start but she chuckles against me.

"That's good." She pushes against me and I see a flash of fire in her eyes which makes me believe she has been purposely misleading me. "Because your friend Dan is one of the biggest twats I have ever met and believe me I have met a few."

I sigh a little and slide my hands along her bare legs pushing myself away from her so I can look at her properly.

God damn it, she has just completely trapped me into making a ridiculously sexist comment about hard-ons after my friend told her that I spent some time putting it about one summer season. What he didn't tell her was that it made me feel gross and that I don't think I learnt anything that summer apart from how to close my mind off to what I was doing, which has never been an easy task for me.

"It wasn't like that," I say as I reach a finger and slide it along her eyebrow.

"Dan seemed to think it was."

Part of me doesn't really want to explain, but I also know Bex has told me stuff about herself, the secrets behind why she is the way she is now. I feel it's only fair for me to share a part of my past with her. Desperately I flip through the images in my mind choosing which part of myself to give to her. "It was stupid childish stuff, Bex."

She leans towards me and kisses me as I start to speak. "I said you could keep your secrets."

I stare into the ambers. "Yeah, but maybe I shouldn't anymore." I kiss her again and then take a breath. "So, uh," Okay this is making me feel all wishy washy. I have spent months pushing all of these memories to the furthest corners of my mind.

"Josh, please. I actually don't think I want to know."

Okay now I feel like a prat because I have made this sound worse than it actually is. It was never that bad, it's just I don't like to think about it anymore.

"Bex, it was nothing bad. When we were growing up there was a whole gang of us, and we were all really tight. Dan and I were the closest for a while and then it started to become obvious that we both liked the same girl, and well that's a bit of a problem between mates."

Bex gives a nod of her head like she may understand this.

"So we kind of got into this ridiculous situation where we were vying for the same girl. Apart from which I thought I was the one who should win because I was actually in love with her. It never occurred to me that he might be in love with her too."

Bex is watching me carefully, her lips clamped together as if she is trying to stop herself from speaking. Her hands are jammed under her thighs so she can't touch me while I tell my tale.

I wish she would.

"So anyway I played the sensitive game giving her all these paintings, and I used to write gay little poems for her and all sorts of crap. Dan went for a different approach. He shagged everything that moved. I knew that I would win her because of that. I knew she would hate that sort of behaviour."

I take another breath, this story seems too long now.

"Anyway about two and a half years ago we were all out for one of our gang nights out. I went to go and get some drinks at the bar, and I found them kissing. He had her in a corner seat at the club we were in. It made me see red. There I'd been for all these months, years even, trying to win by playing the *nice boy* game and I had lost. She liked her boys bad after all. I went a bit off the rails, did some things I regret. I ignored her and Dan for weeks until one evening she walked down a back alley in Newquay and found me shagging a girl against a wall. She went mad, like hysterically mad and I finally took her home where she told me she had always been in love with me but as I'd never made a clear move, she thought I was just being friendly. Then she told me that Dan had pushed himself on her that night, it hadn't got far, but the kiss that I had witnessed wasn't one that she had wanted to give away."

I take a deep breath and watch for Bex's reaction. She is staring off into space, mulling over my words.

"So what happened then?"

"Well then she was mine and Dan's behaviour became even worse, to be honest, Bex I try and ignore the way he is, but seeing him look at you that way he does, with the words he says, I should have taught him respect a long time ago. It makes me think that perhaps she didn't tell me the whole story about what happened that night I found them kissing."

Bex glances down and runs a finger along her bangles. They chink against each other as they reposition against the skin of her wrist. "So I'm not the only one to be caught doing things down alleyways?"

Her words make me feel sick, her joke in the pub days ago wasn't a joke at all. It was a bitter barb at herself.

"I guess not." I literally can't stop the next words out of my mouth. I wish I could. "What did you do down alleyways, Bex?"

She raises an eyebrow at me but a faint blush illuminates the skin under her freckles. "Let's put it this way, I am known for doing stupid things when I've had a drink."

I know she is. I have a very clear visual image of her passed out on the sand inches from the night tide. At the same moment I recall the faceless girl I got caught with in Newquay and I know I will never judge her.

"That makes two of us then."

"And the girl you were in love with," her eyes briefly glance at the paintings, "Where is she now?"

"She is gone, Bex. Just gone." As I say it the weight on my chest lifts, but underneath it I can feel a well of emotion bubbling to the surface. Gently Bex slides her arms around my waist and places her ear just above my heart which is thumping in an erratic manner.

"Can I ask where?"

My heart starts to race even more as I chase words around my brain trying to think of the right ones to say.

For the longest moment I just stand there suspended in time. Eventually I let out a sigh and push myself away. Raising her head she looks at me questioningly. This is it, time to let the moment go, time to let the past go.

I'm just about to. I cast my eyes around the shop and take in the paintings on the wall. They draw me back in and it makes the words form in a lump in my throat.

"I want to tell you, Bex," I start and the ambers watch me, waiting for me to explain. "I'm going to try and tell you but I need to sort some things first, can you wait?"

Bex has an emotion flash across her face, at first I can't read it but as she silently slides her arms back around my waist I realise what it is. Hurt. Bex has told me everything and yet I can't do the same.

Joshua Adams hurts everyone again, and the kicker is that by hurting Bex I am ultimately hurting myself too. I hold my arms around her as tight as I possibly can in the hope that my embrace will speak the words that at the moment I still can't. As I grip onto her like a life raft I look up at the paintings one more time and I know it's finally time. She does not say anything, what can she say? Her arms cling around me though, and I hold her for everything that she and I are worth.

Later as the afternoon slowly ticks to a close I take down all the paintings, and as Bex minds the shop I walk them out the front door and up to the studio. Thirty paintings, thirty pieces of my past and thirty reasons why I still need to say goodbye. As I walk back into the shop and catch sight of Bex dancing to a tune, twirling around the stand of oil paints I am sure that my time to say goodbye has arrived.

It's time to go and see Faye. I need to leave all the past behind me. It's time to move on.

I find Faye emptying ash-trays in the pub garden. "I didn't know you were working here now," I say as

I walk towards her and perch myself onto the edge of a spare picnic bench.

Faye laughs. "There are so many things you don't know about me anymore."

I raise an eyebrow. "Yeah like what?"

She thinks hard for a moment, her face scrunched in concentration. "I have realised that having an artist as a best friend sucks, because you always end up helping them and having this happen to your hair." She pulls forward her ponytail from over her shoulder and waves the end at me which is covered in specks of paint.

"Me too." I groan comparing one of my paint spattered dreads with her glossy dark locks. The two don't really compare at all.

"What you doing here anyway? Shouldn't you be off spending every last moment of time with Bex before she leaves?"

I blanch a little bit at her words.

"Yeah that's why I am here. I need your help."

"I'm sorry, what? Can I have that in writing please?"

"Faye, come on, I'm trying to be serious." And I am.

Faye sits on the opposite bench and waits for me to get my words together. They blurt out of my mouth. "I want to move things on with, Bex," I start to flush. "You know. But I'm worried."

Faye sniggers a little. "What are you worried about exactly?"

"All of it." I wave my hands in the air. "Worried

I've forgotten how, worried it will be too different. Worried that I am cheating. Worried that it will confuse Bex even more."

"Okay, just to be clear, we are talking about sex here?"

"You're not helping at all."

"Okay. Honest best friend opinion. No you're not cheating, it's natural and right, and it's about time you let it all go and moved your life forward. I don't know if you even recognise this but you and Bex are something else entirely together, you can't even compare it with anything you knew before. When I see you together, I see two planets that are orbing around each other. You have never been like that before not even with…" Her voice hesitates and cracks. "Not even before."

I take a step towards Faye and put my arms around her. I whisper the words so low I don't think she can even hear them. "Will you speak to your mum and dad for me?"

Faye's shoulders heave high and then shudder back down. Pulling away from my embrace she looks up at me. "Yeah. Lets get this sorted so you don't end up saying goodbye to the wrong girl."

The wrong girl.

"I need to go and find Bex."

Faye offers me a broad wink. "Don't do anything I wouldn't do."

I roll my own eyes in response. That leaves me a whole list of stuff to do.

Rebecca

I've been staring at the unturned page of my book with my earphones jammed in when I see a foot land on the window sill.

I breathe out the breath I didn't even know I'd been holding since Joshua and I parted outside the door to the shop. He told me he had to go and sort something out and that he would see me later. I had to battle down the disappointment at being separated from him for even a few moments.

My eyes watch in the half light as he walks towards me. He's holding his body all wrong, not the usual easy relaxed gait that he walks with.

"Josh?"

Holding a hand out he cuts off any further question I may ask. "Rebecca," he kneels on the bed and grasps my hand in his. I sit up straighter in response. He is completely freaking me out.

Opening my mouth I go for another question, but the words die before they've even been formed as he lowers his mouth to mine and grazes my lips with his own. One hand slides around the back of my neck and his thumb traces along the edge of my jaw. Tilting my head back I open my eyes and watch him kiss me. His own eyes are gently closed and I can feel a smile against my mouth.

"What?" I try again.

"No, Bex. I'm going to do the talking." Josh moves away from me and settles on the bed in front of me. "I realised today, that you've told me so much about yourself, all the secrets that hurt you in here." He touches his fingers to the place where my heart is beating fast. "But I never told you anything, about me."

"Yeah you have, you've told me about your parents and stuff."

He nods his head in assent and I reach a hand to smooth along the eyebrow and ring.

"Yeah, but I never told you the things I'm scared of. And I know when you were telling me about Emily and what happened that day at the school you were really telling me that your biggest fear for Em is that she will be like you, or having you around will ruin her life."

It's my turn to nod my head, any words would get stuck in my tightening throat.

"I understand that, I do." He hesitates, clearly unsure what to say next.

"But."

"My thing, is, that I can't really do goodbyes. I hate them. That's one of the small reasons why I never interact with holidaymakers. I can never see the point in getting to know someone if eventually you just have to say goodbye to them."

Okay, I'm not sure this is good. I'm leaving in a couple of days and a goodbye is imminent.

"But," I start again.

"Wait, Bex, wait." He chuckles a little and leans in placing his lips against mine. Just a quick short tender kiss the type that I can't really imagine not having on a daily basis anymore. And for a girl who never used to kiss before and when she did, didn't enjoy it, that's a huge statement to make.

"Before you came here I was just existing, every day the same. I didn't spend time with my friends, I didn't go anywhere, and I definitely didn't paint. And then you came and I started wanting to do everything."

I raise an eyebrow. "Well, Joshua, that's rather rude."

A blush burns along his cheeks which I don't think I've seen happen before.

"I'm trying to be serious here, Bex, work with me."

"Sorry, please proceed with being serious."

Joshua lunges forwards pushing me back onto the bed, pinning me down with his body. "You are so difficult."

"I know, that's why it's good I'm leaving, so you can live in peace again."

Leaning back, Joshua stares at me, the greens dark and intense. "Rebecca, I don't want to live in peace without you. I want to be challenged by you every day. That's why I don't want to say goodbye to you."

"Josh," I sigh.

"Wait." He smiles again. "I feel enough for you that I'm willing to learn to try and say goodbye. I want to say goodbye to everything so that I can try to keep you."

I don't really know what he is talking about. The words sound like a riddle but the look of determination in his eyes makes me believe him. For the first time in my life I realise that someone actually wants to keep me, to have me for their own.

"Even with all the things I've told you?"

"Nothing you have told me has made me want you any less."

Our eyes lock and my heart starts that erratic beating again. "How much do you want me, Joshua?"

"I want all of you, Bex, every single bit of you."

A fracture of a pause makes time spin around us like an endless moment, and then slowly because I want to be the one to initiate whatever happens next, I place my lips against his. "I want you too, Josh."

With a low groan he lowers his body so he fits against every contour that I have. His hand moves from my hair and down the length of my body. Rocking himself away from me slightly he gives his touch space to slide along my thigh, and along my belly which quivers under his firm fingers. Slowly he carries his determined hand all the way up to the top of my halter neck tie. Arching my neck so he can grasp the bow and pull it undone I hold my breath as he trails his lips along my throat. The sensation of the softest butterfly kisses landing on my sensitive skin makes my break out in goose-bumps everywhere.

"I'm not going to be able to stop this time Bex." His voice is low and by my ear which makes the goose-bumps intensify.

"I don't want you to Josh. I want this, I want you."

With a firm tug the bow unravels and with gentle fingers Josh pulls the top down until I am free of clothes on my top half. Pressing himself into me he lowers his body back into mine and it feels amazing. The stab of longing in the pit of my stomach flares at the sensation of my bare skin pressed against him. Wrapping my arms around him as tight as I can, I kiss him and try to express every emotion I have in the movement of my lips and the flick of my tongue.

"You do bad things to me, Rebecca Walters."

He laughs against me and the motion rocks us together.

"Well I am a very bad girl."

For the first time in my life I don't feel like a bad girl at all, well not in the way I used to. I feel like a good girl about to come right.

I shift to roll us over, and he watches me with dark green pools as I sit up and slide off the top no longer doing what it was designed for.

Pulling him up I straddle his lap and yank his T-Shirt up and over his head. Grasping my arse he anchors me close to him and I can feel his desire for me as our naked skin meshes together.

Gently I push him back against the pillows and work at untying the tie of his shorts. I can't stop my damn fingers from shaking though so after a few fumbled attempts Josh's own fingers take over. Undone I lever the shorts over his slim hips and try not to look too alarmed or scared as I see him fully naked for the first time.

Tentatively I reach my fingers for him and trail them along the length of him hearing him sigh with my touch. Leaning forward I softly follow my fingers with my lips and the sigh turns into something else, a groan tangled with a gasp. I kiss my way along his flat stomach until I reach the tattoo that hides on his hip. It seems like an age ago that we were in his studio and I first placed my lips against it. I repeat the motion again now as my hand grasps him firmly and starts to move up and down.

Surprising me with a sudden moment Joshua rolls us back over and smiles as he leans down and kisses me. I keep the motion of my hand steady as he undoes my shorts and dips his fingers under the waistband. My entire body holds itself tight as I wait for his fingers to go to the place I most want them. I'm not disappointed, as his fingers slide between my legs creating a sensation I've never felt before. My own hand stops it's motion as I concentrate on Josh's long slim fingers delving deep inside me.

Desire washes over me and I writhe against his fingers willing them to probe deeper.

I still want more though and I know there is only one way I'm going to get it. Lifting my hips off the mattress as Joshua's fingers keep up their quick dance I wriggle out of my shorts. Pulling him gently by the shoulder I slide my legs either side of him as I wait for him to replace his fingers and work his way inside my body the way he has worked his way into my head, heart and soul.

"I should put something on." His voice is so low I

can barely hear it over the wild thudding of my heart.

"It's okay, I've got it."

And I have with the small white pill that my parents insisted I start taking after my Dad found me at that party.

I block the nasty memories from my mind and concentrate on the here and now which is how it should be. Now, not the past. Good, not bad.

"So it's just us then, Bex."

I nod my head and open myself up to him as he guides himself inside me and it feels all at once like I'm going to explode. Instinctively we start to create a natural rhythm unique just to us, and as I concentrate on the feel of him pushing deeper and deeper with each movement he makes, a molten hot lava starts to spread from the pit of my stomach and around the whole of my body.

I grip my legs and arms around him as tight as I can and push my body up higher towards him. A gasp escapes me as the pace increases and Josh looks at me quickly reading my face with his green gaze.

I can't even concentrate on his face as I climb higher and higher on what feels like a roller coaster with every movement of our hips. I clutch at his shoulders and dip my face into the crook of his neck trying to hide my emotions which must be all over my face. The steady climb doesn't lessen, it just grows and grows and I rake my fingers along his back as I try and cling on.

I can hear him whispering something in my ear but it is deafened by the whimpering noise I am making with every movement he makes inside me. In and out, either way, every motion creates a physical response in me.

"Look at me." Josh moves himself away from me a little and the roller coaster starts to crash back to land with his movement.

Oh god, it feels like I am going to die.

"Look at me, Bex. Don't hide from me anymore."

And I do, I force my eyes to remain on him as he begins the whimper inducing rhythm again. Faster and deeper, higher and higher until finally I know I am at the top and I start to panic. It's too soon, it's not supposed to be this soon.

My entire body goes rigid as he reads me like a book and starts driving even deeper and I spin out from what feels like the very top of the sky, my entire being lost in space as waves of pleasure roll out of me. I cling tighter and tighter onto him as I feel him stiffen and pause for one moment before driving himself home one final time.

Minutes tick by and we lay still and together neither of us moving as we wait for the moment to pass. Then slowly Joshua pulls himself away from me, kissing me all over my face until he reaches my lips.

"I'm going to say this once. And once only." He voice is deep and low. Content and satisfied.

"What?" I croak back.

Smoothing a piece of hair away from my face he scans me over like he is reading something there. "I don't want you to go."

I laugh, a chuckle of hope and optimism brimming

to the surface. "Really? You want me stropping around the place making everyone stare at me, and you, and specifically at the two of us together?"

Right in this very moment I don't want to go. Could I stay? What if I stopped running and faced up to who I was and what I'd done? What if I showed people who I really am, not the labels that other people had put on me. What if I should show people the person Joshua has helped me find? Maybe I could stay with my family after all, stay with Josh.

"Well you know, I think we've given the locals something to talk about for a while, it should keep them busy until you come back." He chuckles and I move with him the motion making me grip my arms tighter around him like I am clinging onto a life raft,

"Do you want me to come back, Josh?" I peer up at him with my question.

"I'm counting on it."

FOUR DAYS TO GO

Bridge Cottage
St Agnes
Cornwall

23rd August 2013

Dear E,

Do you know what I am feeling today more than anything else? Guilt. Overloads of it, beating down on my heart and on my soul.

Why? Because it kills me that you will never experience what I did last night. You will never feel your legs get that heavy dead sensation, the tingling in your toes, the sheer pleasure of losing yourself in a moment and sharing it with someone else.

You my best friend deserve that, it should have been yours. We could have giggled down the phone and told each other what it felt like. But I can't do that with you and I know it is my fault why not. You will never get to be like that with someone. I took that away from you.

Gone

What would you say if I told you I thought I'd fallen in love with Josh-u-a? That somehow he's melted every concern, every worry that I ever held inside. That I don't want to leave him. Last night he told me he didn't want me to go.

He says he is counting on my coming back to see him.

I'm going to come back and see them all in the strange village that is starting to feel like home.

I wish you were here with me. I miss you. Today I miss you more than ever before.

B.xx

Rebecca

Breakfast

"So this feels a bit different?"
It's definitely different.
I roll onto my side and face him. I'm smiling, I'm not even going to bother trying to hide it. "Good different or bad different."
"Good, very very good."
"Good." My smile ratchets up into a grin.
"Good."
Giggling I reach up and linger my lips against his. His hand slides down the length of my spine coming to rest on my right butt cheek.
"Do we have any plans for today?" he asks.
I can think of a plan for today and it involves replaying last night over and over again, until I fall back into an exhausted but satisfied sleep.
"Hello, Rebecca!?" Josh waves his hand in front of my face with his words.
"Sorry." I stretch a little, I ache all over. The stretch works well because it slides Josh's hand around to the front of my body. I stretch a little more, directing his hand downwards with my movement.

The greens darken as he watches my reaction.

Reaching down to kiss me he teases his tongue against mine. "I can't imagine not being with you now, Bex. I hope you know that." I shut my eyes as his fingers stroke in feather light caresses along my skin. It feels damn good.

"Rebecca, open your eyes and look at me."

I do. His hand stops its teasing patterns which is a little disappointing.

"I've still got a lot to tell you, I know that. And I am going to, I will tell you everything. I just hope you don't think I've rushed anything with you. It wasn't my intention, it's just when I'm with you all I want is you. It was too exhausting fighting it anymore."

Tears sting my eyes. This is the first time in my life anyone has told me that they wanted me.

"What have I said?" Josh looks alarmed.

"Nothing." I brush away a stray tear. "It's just no one had ever said they wanted me before."

"I wanted you pretty much the first day I saw you." He thinks for a moment. "Actually make that the third. I thought you were really rude the first time I met you."

This makes me laugh loudly. "Me? Oh my god, you were so rude!"

"Well you know only my best customer service for the holiday maker." He offers me a broad wink. It's the first time in days I've forgotten his initial hatred of holidaymakers. Aren't I still technically a holiday maker if I leave in two days?

I don't get a chance to ask.

Mum interrupts any questioning with a shout from the bottom of the stairs, "Rebecca, Josh do you want breakfast?"

"Rumbled," he breathes into my ear. A delicious shiver spreads down my arm.

"You may as well come in using the front door." I slide out from under him and head to the dresser where I push my bangles on, counting them on in rough handfuls not individually.

"Now where would be the fun in that?" he laughs.

I glance at him in the mirror and notice his gaze on my bangles and wrists. "Quite right where would be the fun in that?" The dark green gaze meets mine in the reflection and he grins, and I grin back completely aware of just how crazy demented happy I look.

We are heading down the stairs when I ask the question burning my tongue. "Will you come and visit me, Joshua?"

"Only if you come and visit me?" He grins with his answer.

"Yes."

"And that's a yes from me too."

"That's good." I smile again. Ugh, too much smiling.

It's good though, because I know I have got to start to pack today. I think the thought that he may follow me to London at some point will make the painful prospect of packing a little easier to bear.

"One thing Rebecca," he says at the front door his eyes glinting in the morning sunshine. "I know this was only supposed to be a fling, but I hope you know that it isn't."

"What is it then?"

Josh starts walking down the path turning to raise his arms up at the heavens. "I have no idea, but I am kind of liking it."

After I have slammed the door shut I screech full speed into the kitchen. "It's not a fling." I shout at the top of my voice.

Emily sprays her orange juice all over the table while Dad does the whole newspaper rustling thing, lowering it to look at me. "What is it then?" Dad's eyes are dancing with humour and it feels like I've never not been his happy daughter grinning across the kitchen at him.

"Who knows?" I throw my arms in the air just like Joshua did.

"That's nice." Dad confirms with a heavy lace of sarcasm. "That's good though." He does that throat clearing thing so I know he is about to say something serious. Or, I am about to be told off for something.

My laughter dies on my lips and my stomach squeezes. I don't know why I have but I have a strong feeling something bad has happened. Maybe this was all too good to be true. I glance at Emily, my concern instantly going to her. She is grinning though.

"Sit down Rebecca. We want to talk to you about something." Dad speaks but Mum, who has been silent until now pats the kitchen chair next to her.

I walk to the seat my feet leaden.

"What? What have I done?"

"Nothing at all." Dad assures me. "We just want to talk to you about something."

"Yeah what's that?"

"We want you to stay and we are wondering if you would consider discussing it with us. As a family."

My jaw hits the ground as I register his words and I look around the table at the expectant gazes of my family who I was sure wanted to get rid of me just as much as I wanted to escape.

Joshua

Packing and Painting

I swing down the street towards the shop like a different man. And I don't mean it in some pervy just wants sex way. What I mean is that I feel totally alive. And I am sure this is all going to work out. Ever since I've known Bex I've always known she is fiercely guarded. I knew it even that first day when she wouldn't tell me her name. Then finally when she told me about that night at the party and what happened with Emily I started to understand. It made me want her more. Last night she finally let down her defenses and just let me see her for who she is. It was as I always thought it would be, by getting lost inside her, I was able to find myself again.

For the first time in a long time I feel just like me again. The Josh who used to live in this town. I want to ring Faye and see if she wants to do the goodbye we talked about yesterday today. But I don't want to rush her, that wouldn't be fair on her.

At the last possible moment I change my direction and head instead to the headstone in the church courtyard, the one I used to visit every day, until Bex came along and woke me up, filling my days with sunshine. The opposite of words chiseled in stone.

Today for the first time ever instead of hovering on the edge I kneel down and smooth my hand over the cool stone and speak. "It's nearly time." I whisper the words. They don't feel like they are going to break me like I always thought they would, instead they strengthen me. Standing from my crouch I stride from the cemetery ready to fill my day with painting and time wasting until it's time to pick Bex up for our night out in Newquay. My first visit to Newquay since my life changed its course there six months before.

At half seven I am knocking on her door. For the first time in months I am wearing a button down shirt with my jeans, and I feel like a complete dork. I've kept the flip flops on out of principle. Emily opens the door and leads me in twirling around in front of me in excitement. "How did the painting go today?" I ask.

"Great, how about yours?"

"How do you know I was painting?" I smile and ruffle her hair.

"I can smell it," she informs me with a serious nod of the head. Well that's crap, I showered for bloody ages.

After Emily has turned away I give myself a discreet sniff. All I can smell is shower gel.

Bex's dad walks over from the lounge and shakes my hand. After a bit of general chit chat he seems to be loitering in an uncomfortable way. "Don't tell her I said this," he says.

"Said what?" I shove my hands in my pockets. I feel like a school boy picking up his first date.

"Please keep an eye on her. Bex likes to party hard. She's been better since, uh, well since we have been here but just watch what she drinks. I don't want to nag her right now we are trying to show we trust her."

"You should trust her."

"Yeah," he takes a deep breath. "Trust isn't something that comes that easily in this house, but it's something we are trying to work on."

"You are going to pay for her fees aren't you?"

He laughs, "Of course I am, I just wanted her to get a grip of herself before I managed to let her go and do her own thing."

"I think she is going to be fine."

"Well, you never know, everything may change yet." He says cryptically and I can't really tell what he is getting at.

"She'll be back." I assure him.

"Do you think so?"

"I know so."

"And what if she doesn't?"

He seems to be finding my level of determination quite amusing. I straighten my shoulders and try to look manly.

"Then me and Daisy will go and get her."

He crinkles his forehead at me. "Who the hell is Daisy?"

"His car," shouts Bex from the top of the stairs. I watch as she walks down barefoot, long slim legs encased in super skinny black jeans. I thrust my hands deeper into my pockets as the rest of her comes into view. It's not the green top, but it's the same style. This time instead of dazzling like emeralds it is shimmering like a flash of liquid gold. As she gets closer I can see a pattern is marked out in a contrasting bronze, it's like the top was created to merge perfectly with her skin.

"It's not the green top," she confirms when she notices the speechless mouth open pose I am holding.

I snap my mouth shut. "No it's not."

"So, Josh, drive carefully," her dad begins the parental goodbye.

"I always do."

"And make sure you both have fun." He gives me a nod here which I know means make sure we have fun, but just not too much.

"Yes Daaaad." Bex rolls her eyes.

"And lastly, Josh, please come in the front door when you get home, we won't be waiting up."

I flush crimson when I realise her dad has always been more than well aware of my pipe scaling abilities.

"Uh thanks." And then before he can impart any more advice along the lines of using condoms or anything equally embarrassing I grab Bex's hand and yank her towards Daisy.

Once we are in the car I turn to her, making my voice stern as I reach around her and trail a finger up her exposed back. "Rebecca Walters. Now you are my girlfriend, and especially as you are wearing this goddamn top, you are under no circumstances allowed out of my sight this evening."

Bex looks shocked at my use of the word girlfriend. Probably not as shocked as I look but then she slowly grins at me, "That shouldn't be a problem." She pats my leg with excitement. "Come on, Joshua, lets go and have some fun together."

Laughing I start the car and manage to restrain myself from saying that I will have fun, but not as much as I plan to have when we get home later and I walk through the front door to her house, follow her up the stairs and spend the night making the girl made of the sun mine again.

Rebecca

Shots of Pain

The club, which is really just an oversized bar, is jammed to the rafters. "Wow, the Cornish start early," I shout to Josh over the music. The bar is dark and there are clusters of tables lined all around the edge. Music pounds at a deafening level.

Turning to me he pulls me by our joined hands tight into his side. "There are about five Cornish people in here, everyone else is a tourist." He speaks right into my ear and a wave of goose-bumps spread along my hairline. Josh slides his arm around my back and his fingers graze over the exposed skin revealed by the slash in the gold silk as he weaves us around clusters of tables until he gets to the table he is looking for. "Hey losers," he shouts when his feet come to a stop.

Andrew and Faye are leaning over the table together, heads tilted towards one another. There is no sign of Dan for which I breathe an enormous sigh of relief. Whilst I was all bravado in the art shop yesterday, I was only trying to get him to back off. I never had any desire to sit making small talk with him all night.

I want tonight to be fun.

Faye glances up and smiles at Josh jumping out of her chair and throwing her arms around his neck. She squeezes him so tight and for a couple of moments he releases his firm grasp on me and wraps her in his arms whispering something in her ear. I could have felt excluded but before the emotion has any time to settle over me Faye flings her arms around me as well. "So glad you came out. We need to party!"

I laugh as I squeeze her back. "Why are we having a party?"

"Well lookie what we have here," A voice booms loudly over the music behind us. I don't need to turn to see who it is, I recognise the tone immediately and feel Joshua's shoulders stiffen as his fingers instantly reach out and entwine with mine binding us together. "The prodigal son returns!" Josh turns to face Dan and plasters a smile on his face. It's not his natural cheek splitting grin. It's fake and forced.

"Hey, Dan, good to see you." Josh says. I offer him a smile and a small wave.

"Well it's good to have you back?" Dan says with a squeeze on Joshua's arm.

Joshua looks around the bar, his fingers still grasping mine tightly. "Do you know what, Dan, it's great to be back as well."

"Shots!" Dan shouts as another track with a thumping base cranks louder than the tune blaring out before.

"Your round." Josh laughs, the sound of his

laughter far louder than the music and he drops his long legs into a low seat pulling me down to sit on his lap. I giggle again, this giggling business is getting ridiculous, and lean myself back against him.

"You're happy," I turn and say into his ear.

"Yeah I am," he says with his lips close to my earlobe. I lean myself back against him tighter still and his arms wrap around my waist.

"I don't like these jeans," I say nodding my head towards Joshua's choice of outfit.

"Why on earth wouldn't you like my jeans?"

I give a little wiggle of my bum to make my point.

"Oh, that's dirty, Rebecca."

"Bex."

"Rebecca."

"Very funny."

A shot glass is thrust under my nose which I take in my hand. Everyone else takes a glass except Joshua. I turn to him with a quizzical glance and he motions driving a car at me.

"Are you washing the dishes?"

"Funny and cute. You're too good to be true."

I knock my shot back, letting the sharp liquid line my mouth before swallowing it down. "Look she's a pro," Dan shouts. "Bex, you forgot your lemon and salt."

I glance at the tray that has wedges of lemon and a shaker of salt on it and offer a shrug. I twizzle myself on Joshua's lap so my lips can find his mouth and kiss him with a tequila fuelled smacker. His hands slide along my jean clad legs until they reach my arse and hips which he anchors down towards his lap. "I'm liking your jeans," he says mouth against mine.

"Yeah why's that?" I'm completely losing focus on the crowd around us. All I can feel is his hands on me and the beat of his heart thumping through his chest against my own.

He rocks my hips slightly and I laugh.

"Joshua!"

He leans forward so his words are only for me. "I can't wait to take them off later." Even just his words make a lance of fire settle deep in the pit of my stomach.

"Is that so?"

"That's so."

Another shot glass is thrust between us. "You may as well have Josh's," Dan says. I keep my eyes on Josh as I knock the fluid back.

"Take it easy, I made a promise to your dad." Josh speaks straight into my ear so the others can't hear.

For a moment I feel the old Rebecca struggle to come out of her box. I hate being told to behave or conform but Josh is grinning at me and I can easily clamp her back down.

"I'll take it easy," I lean in and tell him. "But because you just made me a promise, not because you made my dad one." And with that I get up from his lap and turn to Faye. "Will you help me find the loo, and then I need to dance, and I am guessing Mr. Sober isn't going to be doing any dancing."

Faye laughs and starts to get up linking her arm through mine, "Josh always dances no matter the alcohol level." I raise an eyebrow at this piece of information which makes Joshua smile wider.

"I have many talents." He shouts as we walk away.

"You better." I wink without missing a beat. But the truth is I know he does already, and I am not just talking about the painting or the surfing.

Faye and I are staring at ourselves in the bathroom mirror being jostled by a whole bunch of girls, some older than others and many of whom have a serious amount of sunburn. For once in my life I'm grateful for the freckles and the need to wear factor fifty even during the winter months.

"You know," Faye says as she wipes at a smudge of eyeliner. "I've never seen Josh the way he is with you before."

"What? Ever?"

"No not really, even before, when we used to come here all the time, but he would never have sat snogging anyone in a bar like that! Never!" She giggles like Josh's new PDA's are highly amusing to her.

"How long has it been since he last came out?" I ask.

"About six months."

"Can I ask what stopped him coming?"

Faye turns to me and sweeps a lock of my straightened hair away from my face. "I don't think he wants to keep secrets from you, Rebecca, it's just for a very long time he hasn't been able to admit what happened to himself. I think the moment he tells you will be when he closes his door on the past. I hope so anyway."

I ponder her words in silence for a moment. I want to probe more but then I have a strong feeling I need to respect Joshua's need for space. I have to remember this was only supposed to be a fling and there is still lots of stuff I never planned to tell him. Still haven't told him.

"I wish you would stay. I like the Josh who skinny dips and snogs in bars!"

"How did you know about that?" I shout.

"Josh and I have been friends for a very long time, there is no chance he would do anything that exciting and not tell me."

"Oh god does that mean he told you about last night?"

"What?!" It's her turn to shout. "What happened last night?"

"Nothing at all." I laugh and flush at the same time.

"Wow." She muses turning to face the mirror.

"Wow what?"

"Well, uh, that's a big thing. He must be desperate for you to stay."

"It's just a fling." I say although I don't really mean it. I no longer believe this was ever just a fling.

"Can't you stop running and stay?" she asks, her face suddenly serious.

No one, not even Joshua knows about my conversation with my parent's earlier, nor the fact they have offered to pay for my fees at the local Uni. And no one knows about the fact I am almost decided to stay.

It's definitely not a fling.

I register her words which confuses me for a moment. "How do you know I am running?"

"Because you were running when you came into town, don't think I don't know how quick the house sale went through. I know that my parents let yours move into the cottage before the sale was completed, and I know that you will still be running when you leave."

I turn back and look at myself in the mirror. Somehow during our words she has managed to twist me towards her. "What if I am walking when I leave and walking when I come back?"

Faye grins at me. "What if you stay here and walk around with Josh, and walk to the local college, and walk back home again and hang with us, because things are better when you are here. Much better."

"How about we let what happens happen and just go and dance. I haven't danced in months and now I really feel like it."

Faye grabs my hand. "That I can do."

We push out onto the dance-floor and although I purposely keep my face turned away from Joshua out of the corner of my eye I can see him watching me. I turn my back and close my eyes, allowing the music and the base to flood through my body, and then finally for the first time in what feels like an age I start to dance. It comes back easier than I expected and before I really know what I am doing I am lost in the music.

The tune changes and I feel hands on my hips. I have my eyes closed and my hands above my head as I move to the beat, the hands gently turn me around and as I open my eyes I gaze straight into Joshua's greens. "Now I see what your talent is."

His words make me feel something. Pride. Time to let one more secret go.

"It's what I used to do." I speak directly into his ear and his arms slide around my body tucking me in tight as he slows my pace down.

"What is?"

"Dance."

"What made you stop?"

"Everything."

"When."

"Two years ago."

Josh unravels one arm from around my waist and lifts his fingers to my face which he cups gently in his palm. Such an intimate act for a packed dance-floor filled with people making out. My heart starts to thud its own pounding rhythm against the music.

"You should never stop doing what you love," he says. We are standing dead still, no movement from either of us as his dark green eyes sweep over my face reading every inch of it. My heart starts to pound quicker and quicker. It's pounding for him. Beating through me with a rhythm of its own.

"Didn't you? With your painting?" My voice feels tight in my throat.

"Yes, but because of you I have found it again." His lips hover down and kiss me with the gentlest kiss

I have ever experienced. He moves in towards me so our bodies are flush and no space exists between us and as he does my head spins with words that I want to say. That it's crazy because I have known him one and a half weeks but I think I may be in love with him. That I don't ever want to walk away from him, and that I want him, not his friend to ask me to stay. That I want him to promise me that he will help me battle the old Rebecca until the end of time, or until the end of my days. That every day from here on in he can fill my world with the calm essence of the moon that only he can provide. And that more than all the other things I want him to be the one who stops me running. The one who holds me still. The one to prove to me that bad stuff does not always happen to me. That sometimes a girl like me deserves something else.

I pull my mouth away ready to say something, anything. Ready to tell him that I am going to stay. That I am no longer going to run from who I am or what I've done. "Josh."

My words are stopped by another shot glass being thrust between us.

"Okay break it up, guys." Dan smiles with his words.

"You've always had impeccable timing." Josh smiles too, the good feelings seem to be extending to everyone.

"Here you go Rebecca," Dan says. He passes me the shot glass and gives me a wink which I try and ignore.

"Thanks." I knock it back and scrunch my face, "What is that?" The liquid had a bitter edge that is lingering on my tongue.

"Just Vodka." He assures me

"No drink for the driver then?" Josh asks.

"Nah, mate, you know my rule."

Josh stiffens a little. "Yeah I remember." He turns to me, "You okay dancing? I'm going to go and grab a coke."

"I'll come with you," I offer.

"Nah, stay and dance with me." Dan links his fingers through mine and prevents me from following Joshua off the floor.

"Sure," I say. I turn away from Joshua's retreating figure and start to move myself to the tune again. Dan doesn't try and get too close so after a few minutes I start to relax and just let the music take me to the happy place it gives me. As the track changes for the third time I realise that my head is starting to feel very fuzzy. I'm not overly surprised. My alcohol consumption has been way below average the last two weeks, it's probably a shock to the system.

"I'm gonna find Josh," I say to Dan who is still making his crazy dance moves by my side.

"Sure, I'll come with you." He takes my elbow in his hand guiding me in the opposite direction of the bar.

"The bar's that way." I point in the right direction.

"Oh he would have got his drink ages ago," he speaks into my ear and I can smell the beer on his breath. "I know where he will be."

We walk among the tables, with every step my head feels foggier and foggier, my stomach starts to roll, and I am not sure whether I should make my way to the toilet. Dan grips my fingers and steps into my side, "You okay, Bex?"

"Rebecca." But I can't even put any conviction into my voice. "I need the bathroom." I spin trying to locate it but can't work out where it is.

"Sure," Dan confirms pulling me in towards a corner. I recognise the steel lined door of the ladies straight away.

"Oh look there's, Josh," Dan says. He points at a low sofa with his finger and I follow its direction.

Josh is sat on the sofa his head bent towards the dark head of Faye, he is whispering something in her ear. I just stand and stare. Wasn't he supposed to be coming to find me on the dance-floor?

"You know," Dan leans into me. "He is still in love with someone else. You are really just a holiday for him." His words don't really register at first then they seep into my consciousness like poison.

"I'm going to be sick," I announce to no one in particular.

Dan pulls me towards a fire exit and pushes through. The fresh air hits me but does nothing to clear my head. I follow Dan down a path which really bizarrely leads to a beach. I didn't see that on the way in. I look back and forth between the beach and the club. Now I am outside I feel I should go back in and find Joshua. It's doesn't feel right to walk away, that's something the old Rebecca would do. Although my head is spinning and I can't see very well I am aware that it is only me present in my mind. The old me is still caged. I want to tell Joshua that I've kept her at bay all by myself but then I recall him sitting whispering to Faye and I doubt whether he would even want to know. My stomach rolls and this time I gag.

On the sand I lean down with my hands on my knees. Dan's hand rubs up and down my back like he is helping me to be sick like my mum used to when I was little. I pull myself under control and stand up straight. "Thanks," I say. "That's a bit embarrassing."

"That's okay." Dan smiles his hand still on the bare skin on my lower back. I edge away slightly hoping to break the contact. He moves with me. "Don't be shy, Bex."

"Rebecca."

Dan laughs and steps closer. "Come on, you can't let Josh have all the fun."

I take a clear step away, he matches me.

"Dan, you are making me uncomfortable," I say the words but my tongue feels fat and useless. The shots make my words come out slurred.

"Now, Rebecca." He makes my name sound dirty as he trails a finger up my arm to the tie of my top around my neck.

Fear grips my stomach, a cold fist of it squeezes at my insides. Clarity comes to my eyesight either too late or too soon as Dan grabs hold of a handful of my hair and smacks his lips against mine forcing his tongue into my mouth. I pull away but he yanks my hair tighter at my protest which makes me gasp. My exclamation makes me mouth open automatically and Dan makes full use of the extra room. I start to gag but he ignores me and carries on. The hand that isn't gripping my chin and holding my face to his grabs at my arse, pulling me in closer to him so I can feel his erection straining against my stomach.

Like a flash of white lightning I realise what is going to happen.

I shove as hard as I can, the motion makes his fingers pull painfully at my hair but I don't care. I just want to end the nightmare and I will take any pain for that.

I scream and twist out of his grip hoping someone will hear me or see me. I manage to break free and I run across the sand my feet sinking with every step I take. I just have to get back to Joshua. It's the only thought I have. I don't know what direction I am running in, I am so busy trying not to trip on the sand, glancing up to check my surroundings and realise to my horror that I have run into darkness. There is nothing around me at all. Just sand and sea.

Dan grabs my shoulder and I give another shriek as his fingers find purchase and twist me around. "Where do you think you are going? Come on, Bex, it's only fair to share."

"You can't share me, you sick bastard."

Dan smacks his hands into my chest and I lose my balance onto the sand landing backwards, I try to scurry back, my legs kicking into the sand. It's no good. He grabs my ankle, easily pulling me back in.

"I don't plan to share. I'm just going to have you."

He breathes into my face as he grips my arms into the sand. The pressure is so extreme, but I still squirm against his hold. His places his foul mouth back against mine and I clamp my teeth shut. He moves back slightly and I gasp a lungful of air, I don't even see the stinging slap before it hits my right cheek.

Pulling at my top he tears it easily, and his fingers scrape painfully across my skin. "Only a slut would wear a top like this." His words are nothing more than a hiss as his mouth comes back down on mine and his hand squeezes my right breast so hard it makes me scream.

"I've been finding things out about you Rebecca Walters, very interesting things. I wonder what Josh would say if he knew."

I try and kick free again, but it's no good, the weight he has on me is immense and crushing. "He knows everything about me."

"Does he? Does he know you are the very thing he hates most in the world?"

"I'm not a holidaymaker." I spit the words with as much force as I can muster but it just makes him laugh.

"Not that. A drunk, a person who causes car accidents, who kills people." His words along with his breath on my face makes bile claw up my throat. I swallow it back down.

As his hand reaches for the waistband of my jeans, I start to realise that with all the bad things that I may or may not have done this will undoubtedly be the worst. And with that thought I understand that there is no chance of me ever winning my fight against the past.

Joshua

The End of Times

I laugh as I pat Faye on the head and get up from the table. She has been telling me about the conversation she had with Bex in the toilet. It's convinced me that I am making the right choices with the decisions I have made the last couple of days. I've been keeping them to myself but it has involved resolving my past and starting my future all at the same time. It's time. And right now I am going to find Bex and see if she fancies ditching this place so I can take her home and spend time getting to know her just like I did last night. Slowly, gently, and thoroughly.

I can't find her on the dance-floor. Searching amongst the crowds I look for a flash of hot gold that will show me where the girl made of the sun is. My eyes start to feel dim the longer it takes me to find it.

"Have you seen, Bex?" I ask Andrew who is also circling the dance-floor undoubtedly looking for Faye.

"Yeah she was with Dan, they went that way." He points towards the sofas where Faye and I were sat. I would have seen her surely?

I pace across the floor pushing people out of my way, there is still no sign of her and an unsettled feeling starts to grip my stomach, my chest feels tighter with every second that I can't lay my eyes on her.

I get to the sofas and stare about wildly. Nothing.

"Have you seen a redhead in a gold top?" I ask a group of guys loitering near the chairs.

"Yeah we saw her," one smirks. "She was really hot until she nearly threw up everywhere."

"Where did she go?" My voice is rising.

"Out the door with her boyfriend."

What? She can't have. I'm her boyfriend aren't I?

Dan.

I push through the doors and down the path to the beach. The sick feeling I had walking across the dance-floor intensifies as I search the scene in front of me and see numerous couples making out in the sand but no girl in gold.

My heart is thudding fast and I am not even sure why, apart from this feeling I have in my gut which tells me I need to find Bex. I ditch my flip flops and start to run across the sand. I shout at people as I run past. "Have you seen the girl in gold?" But no one answers.

I am about to stop running and turn back in the opposite direction when a flash of something catches my eye. Gold.

Running as fast as my legs and the sand will allow I chase towards the flash of light. As I get closer my brain can't take in the scene around me. The girl dressed in gold is sprawled on the sand, her legs bent at strange angles with a guy straddling across her lap. She does not seem to be fighting so I almost stop running. It's just another couple making use of the dark but the girl turns towards me and my entire world stops spinning. It's Bex and she has her eyes screwed tightly shut. Just like she does when she counts on her bangles. Apart from right now she is not counting on an overload of jewelry.

I am over the sand in five easy paces. I drag Dan off her landing a sharp kick to his ribs to get him as far away as I can manage. I give her a quick glance up and down. Her jeans are undone but still up, although her top is ripped off her shoulder and one breast exposed with an angry red mark streaked across it. She opens her eyes and stares at me, no expression on her face. I would have thought she was dead if I hadn't just seen her eyes flutter open. *Shock*.

"Oh what a surprise, Josh Adams saves the day again." Dan snarls rounding on me. He does not stand a blinding chance. I lift two years worth of innuendo and punch him with it.

"You'd better run because I am going to fucking kill you." The words rip out of my chest.

He does, he doesn't miss a beat but slides his feet across the sand and I spin from watching his retreating form and fall to the ground next to my girl made of the sun.

"Bex, my angel." Sobs start to rack my chest as I lift her onto my lap. "Bex, look at me."

Her eyes raise and she offers me a small smile. "I

always knew you would be the one to save me, Joshua."

"Always. That's what I met you for." I try and shift her torn top over her exposed body as I lift her into my lap, wrapping my arms around her.

"Josh?"

"Yes." I whisper into her hair which is knotted and matted.

"You can't save me. I can't be saved." And with those words she throws up on the sand and starts to sob and I start to sob with her, my chest rising and falling in time with hers as I try and deal with the horror of just what could have happened if I'd arrived another two minutes later.

After a while I sit her up on the sand so I can unbutton my shirt. "I need to get you home."

She starts to cry louder and harder. "I can't go home. I can't see my dad. He will know."

"Bex this is not your fault."

"It is. It is." She is almost wailing now. "It's always my fault. Everything I do ends in tragedy."

I ignore her words and start to slide my shirt onto her, buttoning it up with shaking hands.

"I'm going to take you home with me."

"Where?" she whispers against my neck as I pick her up in my arms.

"Just home, Bex."

And with that I march across the sand leaving the horror of what could have been indented on the sand behind us.

First I have to get her safe and then I have to kill

Dan. They are the only two things I have left to do tonight.

Rebecca

Saving Grace

Josh pushes Daisy faster than I ever thought she could go to the studio, screeching the van to a halt, and carrying me up the stairs with neither of us saying a word. I have my lips clamped shut to stop them shaking or letting out the scream that I am containing. Once inside the studio Josh lights a lamp in one of the furthest corners of the room before placing me on the sofa. Moving back towards me with calm even steps he lowers himself onto the floor at my feet then silently with a million unspoken words racing between us he unbuttons half of his shirt that I am wearing. The gasp he allows to escape when he catches sight of the gash along my chest is the only sound he makes. Slowly he dips his face to the mark as I hold my breath waiting to see what he is going to do. I think for a moment he is going to kiss it. I almost want him too as perverse as that may sound. But he unwillingly drags his eyes away from the mark and finds mine. Then he breaks the silence between us forever more.

"Bex, you need to go to the police, right now while they still may be able to find DNA or something."

With his words every shred of self-resolve I am managing to maintain shatters into a million pieces. The scream that rips from my lips is one of the most horrific noise I've ever made. I scoot away from him but his gaze and his touch are gentle as he slowly grabs hold of my hand and brings it up to his lips. The words that follow are steely and determined. "You've got to report him. He could have done that so many times before. He could–"

I stop his words with a firm shake of my head still unable to find my tongue.

"Bex, my angel." Joshua moves himself closer, sliding his hands around my shell-shocked body.

"I can't."

The greens watch me intently. His hand brushes my hair and smooth's down the section Dan pulled at so hard. "Why?"

"Because they will think it was my fault."

His hand maintains its smoothing glide. "That's crazy they won't."

"They will. It will drag up what happened in London, everyone will know I am the girl who causes trouble and then my family will be branded again."

"That's not true. Is this because of what those people called you on Facebook after that party?"

"No, it's about everything I've ever been called. They will find out everything I've ever done." My voice has risen to the point of shattering.

"This is ridiculous, you must be in shock. You've got to go to the police."

I give my head another firm shake. "No. He didn't

even hurt me tonight, not really." I know I am not being truthful. I just don't want to go to the police. If I go to the police then everyone will find out about me and then I know I will never be able to stay in this town. And I know I will not be able to stay with Josh. Not ever.

"You're telling me he didn't hurt you tonight?" He slides the shirt off my shoulder exposing the long red welt.

"It could have been worse."

In a flash he is up off the couch. "It could have been worse? That's all you have to say? For fucks sake, Rebecca, he could have raped you. Another few minutes and it would have been done. It could have been so much worse."

"He didn't touch me, Josh." My mouth can't form his full name. The letters have got stuck on their way out of mouth.

"Of course he did, Bex. Your bloody jeans were undone."

Objectively I make myself scan back through those moments on the sand. It feels like I am watching them on a movie screen. Shaking my head I reach for Joshua. "He didn't touch me, I promise, you stopped him." It feels strange that I am assuring him and making him promises but he looks like he is being devoured from the inside out.

Joshua starts to pace the room, his frustration seething, and his torment painfully clear. I feel a strange detachment from the situation. With a humourless laugh I realise why I'm not feeling it. The sad truth is that I expect nothing less for myself, trouble follows me everywhere, which makes me realise that it is not technically following me but rather that I am the trouble itself.

Oblivious to my inner epiphany Josh turns on me, his body rigid as he fights with himself. "Do you know what the worst bit is?"

"There is a worse bit?"

Joshua's green eyes storm like the sea as he holds himself in check. "The worst bit is, I still want you, even now. Even though I've seen that happen to you, I still want you. I still want every bit of you to belong to me."

Hot fast tears start to slide down his cheek as he hangs his head in shame.

Slowly ignoring the pain in my aching legs and stiff arms I get up from the sofa and walk towards him. "Josh look at me." He does, his face wet and flushed. With tentative fingers I reach for him and press my body against his. "Will you help me wash it away, like you did the sand that one day?"

His face crinkles into a frown.

"If you wash it away then they won't be able to prove anything."

"Just help me get rid of it." And with that I start to unbutton the rest of the shirt. Once it has dropped to the floor Josh sweeps his eyes over me as he takes in the bruises over my body. Lifting me up into his arms and carrying me to the shower he flicks on scalding hot water, strips off his own clothes and we stand together under the steaming jets. Desperately I cling onto my saving grace, until at last I begin to feel real again.

THREE DAYS TO GO

Bridge Cottage
St Agnes
Cornwall

24th August 2013

Dear E,

Was I being naïve? Stupid? Was I fooling myself into thinking that I could belong anywhere? I can't stay here now can I?

Josh must know that I can't stay. My parents will soon know that our conversation we had yesterday where I tried to convince them that I could be a different girl, and they begged me to stay and be happy was just make-believe.

I've never wanted to talk to you more than I do this morning. I will never regret more than I do right now that you are no longer here with me.

It's my fault that you aren't here. It's my fault that your family have to miss you every day. Dan may be a beast but his words were right, I am a killer. As soon as Josh finds out I will lose him forever just like I lost you. Maybe that's all I deserve.

Gone

Every day I wish I could turn back the clock. Wherever you are, do you wish it too?
Always missing you.
B.xx

Rebecca

Breakfast

I wake and glance at the form next to me. It's not Josh. Josh walked me in the front door just like he promised my dad he would. He walked me up the stairs, pulled back the cover on the bed and then tucked me in.

"Stay with me." I begged as he edged the duvet under my aching body.

"I can't. I've got to do something. I will be back okay, get some sleep." With his words he kissed me on the lips and walked away towards the door, determination set in his shoulder but his feet dragging against the floor.

"Joshua, don't do anything. Please." I pleaded with him to stay. I didn't want Josh to get hurt because of me. Enough people have been hurt over me. Everyone I know gets hurt one way or the other.

He turned and smiled at me. "I'll be back before you wake up, my angel." I watched the door swing shut behind him a smile on my lips as sleep over took me and I went under wondering why he had suddenly started calling me angel.

Gone

I woke two hours later screaming the place down as all thoughts of angels had left me and all I could remember was darkness, vile hands on me and the words "A person who kills people." As cold sweat clung to my skin, and my heart crashed in my chest a small body crept into my bed. Emily. Smoothing my hair like Josh did hours earlier she wrapped her tiny arms around me and I went to sleep comforted by the presence of my baby sister holding me tight.

"You're awake," she says, blue eyes sharp and alert.

"Yep." I try and stretch but there is not a single part of my body that does not scream out in resentful agony. I wince with the movement and Emily watches my face.

"What happened?"

"What do you mean?"

"Bex you are covered in bruises. Josh isn't here, and you cried in your sleep the whole night."

"It wasn't Josh." I blurt the words, completely ruining any further lie I could have told. Still no harm in trying. "I fell over on the dance floor."

Emily raises an eyebrow and moves Joshua's shirt which I am still wearing out of the way. The red mark is still there, still vibrant and still an angry reminder of what nearly happened.

"I'm going to get Mum." She starts to move and I grab her back.

"Please don't."

"You need Mum."

"What for?" I hear mum's voice as she walks into the room. "There you are. I've been looking for you.

It's been years since you two slept in the same room."

It's been a year and a half. A year and a half since my counsellor said my parents should stop it because that way I may break the protective bond I felt for Emily.

Mum's smile falters as she sees me. "What happened to you?" Her mouth is open and her hands automatically shake as she takes in my appearance. Her colour fades to a strange shade of pale.

"Nothing, Mum, it's nothing."

She shakes her head in response. Moving towards my dressing table she grabs a small mirror and brings it over to me. "Nothing?"

I almost don't want to look but with more bravery then I feel on the inside I take the mirror in my hand and glance at myself. My lips are doubled in size, my eyes and right cheek are stained black, and there is a red streak along my neck where I guess my halter neck top was yanked. I don't know what to say, or feel, or do. I continue to watch my deformed face in the mirror as I wait for someone else to take control for me.

"Emily, go and get dressed then find your father and tell him we need milk, bread and something for lunch from the shops. Preferably shops far away."

"But?" Emily looks at me, fear written across her face. It kills me to see it there when I always promised she would never feel fear again.

I nod my head at her encouragingly. "It's okay, Em, take Dad out, Mum is going to look after me."

Emily listens to me like she always does and moves

swiftly from under the cover on the bed where she has been keeping me warm all night. I feel the absence of her warmth straight away and a shiver runs along my skin.

"Well done, Em," Mum calls after her. "But you should have called me in the night. I am Bex's Mum."

Emily gives a small nod of her head and walks out the door allowing it to close softly behind her.

Mum walks towards me her colour coming back and then some. "What happened and don't lie. I want to know the truth."

I open my mouth ready to construct a lie, but search as I might, I can't find one in my soul. "There was a guy." I stop. Already the images are barraging inside my mind, the objectivity I felt last night is long gone and this time I don't have Joshua to hide behind. I don't even know where he is, he never came back like he said he would. *Where is he?*

Mum's voice pulls me away from this new line of thought. "Yes Rebecca."

My full name on her lips sounds strange. "Can you call me Bex, I don't think I like Rebecca anymore."

There is a single beat of silence as she registers my request.

"Why's that, Bex?"

"Because bad things happen to her." Then, finally, the tidal wave hits me and I can't fight the tears I couldn't find last night in Joshua's studio.

Two hours later the front door slams and I lift my head from my mums lap. "That's Dad."

"Yeah probably."

"Are you going to tell him?"

"I think *we* should." She smiles at me encouragingly.

"I can't. I can't do that to him again."

"Reb-, Bex. Why are you always so keen to protect everyone else but never yourself?" This isn't the first time she has said this over the last couple of hours. Mum was furious when I told her that I had showered off any evidence that my body may have contained. I told her that despite Joshua's insistence, I didn't think that without Dan actually completing his task there would have been any DNA, and in the grand scheme of things I'd rather go without the DNA than live through the full ordeal.

"I don't understand how on the one hand you can break a porcelain sink with a girls head because she hurt your sister but you can't stand up for yourself," she continues.

"Mum I already told you, he was too strong." I have been through every gory detail with my mum until she was satisfied I was not hiding something darker from her. I know that I got off very lightly and I know it's thanks to Joshua searching for me across the beach that this is the case.

"No but you could have protected your honour, told everyone what he had done to you. This is what we should have made you do the other week when those people were spreading lies about you."

"Mum." I stop speaking because the door to my room opens and Faye walks in.

"Sorry to interrupt," she starts to say but stops when she sees me. I seem to be having that effect a lot. "Oh my god, Bex." Faye starts to cry which also seems to be happening a lot.

"Faye, don't." I hold my hand up to stop her.

"Shit." She brushes her hands quickly across her face trying to remove the tears.

"Where is Josh, Faye? He said he would come back?"

"That's why I am here," she wipes her hand along her nose. "He was arrested this morning. Aggravated assault, or some crap like that."

"On?" I don't really need to ask.

"Dan."

Oh shit, what have I done? Dan should be the one with the police not Joshua. If I had done what he asked and gone to the police then Dan would have been arrested and Joshua would not have taken the law into his own hands.

Not only have I been unable to protect myself, I have failed at protecting Joshua as well.

"They need you to corroborate his story otherwise the charge is going to stick." Fays adds.

"I can't. I washed it all away."

"At least just tell them, they will only have to see you to know."

"I can't."

"Why, Bex? What are you so scared of?"

I bite my lip as I think of all the very many things I am scared of. Leaving, loving, wanting, needing, failing.

"I'm scared of everyone knowing the person I am." My breathing starts to hitch. "I'm scared of Joshua knowing what sort of person I am." A sob wrenches from my chest. "But more than that I am scared of being the person I think I am."

Mum leaps forward and grabs my face in her hands. "You are not. Stop saying things like that."

"Mum you don't even know half of the stuff I have done."

"What, that you were in a tragic accident which thank God you managed to walk away from." I flinch at her words but she continues without pausing for air. "That once you protected your sister and scared everyone with the level of the love you feel for her. That once you got drunk at a party and did something stupid."

Faye looks at me puzzled.

Mum's words tip me over the edge, I don't want anyone trying to rationalize or excuse the things I have done. "Mum not everyone gets caught giving a stranger a blow job at a party by their dad. That's not normal!" My voice rises as I think back to my dad's face when he walked into that party a few weeks back.

"Oh my god, Bex," Mum splutters. "All girls do bad things, it's part of being young, don't you think I used to do stuff before I met your dad. That's what youth is about."

Faye nods her head. "I snog a different guy every weekend whilst trying to get the guy I am in love with to give me a go."

"I'm not talking about snogging, Faye."

"So. Look at you. No girl deserves that. No one regardless of what she has done before."

I glance into the mirror still on the bed, my resolve strengthening when I see my reflection. "Give me a minute to get dressed and I will go to the police station."

And I will. I will go to the police station. I will help give Joshua his freedom, but then I will finish my packing and be ready to go. I will be gone before the rumours start. It's time to start running. Again.

Joshua

The Price of Freedom

I have my belt back, so that's a good thing. They took it from me at the front desk, like they thought this was going to be the moment when Joshua Adams was finally going to top himself.

Everyone has been on suicide watch for months. It's quite funny that the time it's the furthest thing from my mind is the night they take measures to stop me.

Fools. I don't want to top myself I want to kill Dan which is what I almost managed to do last night until a well concerned neighbour decided to call the police.

Since I've met Bex I have felt such a tangle of emotion so rare to me, most of it has been hard to name or recognise. Not last night. That was plain white hot fury. Not just at him though, also at myself. I should have done something about it two years ago when I first got an inkling of his character, instead I ignored it. I am disgusted at myself and probably always will be. Of course he denied everything that I told the police. My freedom walking out of the police station tells me that Bex must have come forward after all. I know it will destroy her, and I know that because of it she won't stay here with me, which is what I was going to ask her last night before our evening went so horribly wrong.

In doing so it is going to destroy me too.

Aunt May is waiting outside the Newquay police station, her face is set with worry. Next to her is Emily. I'm surprised because as far as I know they've never met. As I get closer Emily dashes forward and throws her little arms around me.

"Hey, Midge. Are you my glory parade?"

"No, you bloody idiot, I am here to smack you around the head." And she does hard, reaching onto tippitoes and using a bit of a jump. "What were you thinking, Josh, now Bex has another reason to leave. She thinks she has ruined your life as well as all of ours and her own."

I stare at the angry flower fairy in front of me. "Sorry."

"Sorry, Joshua. Sorry?" Aunt May turns her death stare on me. "Dan is your oldest friend, why would you do that to him." She is challenging me with a look I don't understand. It works.

The white hot rage flares inside of me again. I move Emily out of my path and edge in front of my only living relative.

"My oldest friend is a sick pervert who prays on young women, my only regret is that I didn't finish the job." I flex my fingers, my knuckles split again with the movement and warm blood trickles down my skin.

May evaluates me carefully and then shocks me by leaning forward and grabbing me into a hug. "At last you've woken up my boy."

"What?"

"I've been watching you drift for too long, but now it's time to become a man and chase your dreams." She smiles at me and tugs a dreadlock hanging on my shoulder. "And if I ever see that Daniel boy again he will be getting a right hook from me."

I slide my arm around her and grab Emily's hand. "So how do you guys know each other?" I ask as we get close to May's car.

Emily looks at me like I am stupid. "Your Aunt owns the only art shop in town, of course we know each other."

"Your sister is a brave girl," May tells Em and Emily's little face lights with pride.

"I know, she is the bravest person I know, always has been and always will be."

And with that my two oddest fan's and I, make our way back to St Agnes and all the demons that I have to put to rest.

***

Bex is lying on her bed staring at the ceiling when I walk in through the door. "No drain pipes and windows today?" She does not turn to face me but continues to stare at a specific spot above her.

"I think we may be past that now." I sit on the bed and she resolutely keeps her gaze turned away. "You okay?" I ask, but I know it is probably going to be the most ridiculous question I ever ask someone.

Slowly she turns to face me and I hold in the pathetic sound that wants to whimper from my lips. The lower half of her face is swollen. Last night it wasn't so obvious a little red and swollen yes, but now it's horrific, big black eyes and lips that look like they may never deflate again. No wonder the police were so quick to release me.

I'm so distracted by the sight of her mouth, her beautiful mouth so perfect for kissing that I don't even notice the leaking, fast tears. "Josh, what did you do?" She brings herself to her knees next to me and gingerly slides tentative fingers along my face. I haven't looked at it. What would be the point, I know Dan got in a few punches of his own. It seems my old friend has been holding a lot of resentment towards me for the last couple of years, resentment that he took out on my Bex just because he could. I feel the white hot fury rush through my veins again but I lock it back down.

"You didn't need to do that," Bex whispers. Her head lowers with shame and my heart does this strange squeeze. My desire for her has not diminished at all but it is veiled beneath something else more precious. Love and respect.

I use careful fingers to lift her face back to mine and ever so slowly brush my thumb over her lips. The ambers hold mine as we try and read each other's thoughts. "Bex I would do anything for you." I say after an ocean of silence has swept between us.

Bex leans forward, closing her eyes as she does, and places her lips against mine. She doesn't wince or hesitate, she just applies the lightest of pressures like a kiss made of feathers. Finished she rocks back and looks at me hard again.

"I know you would do anything for me." My chest tightens more with her low words. "That's why you have to let me leave. The truth is, Josh, I don't deserve it. I don't want to bring you down, and I will. The whole town will know soon all about me and I don't want you living with that. You're too innocent to be tainted by the things I've done."

Her words make no sense to me. What is she talking about?

"What do you mean innocent? You don't even know the stuff I've done because *I've* never been brave enough to tell you."

I wish I had been. I should have told her about my heartbreak right at the beginning. Instead I've let it become this huge secret sitting between us, effectively destroying us.

Bex offers herself a sarcastic sounding chuckle. Her fingers wrap tight around the bangles on her wrist, the bangles I hardly notice jingle anymore.

"Maybe if I shared some of myself with you, you'd understand why I'm not perfect." I add. Too little too late.

The tear-lined ambers sweep up and look deep into me. It feels like they are searching my soul.

"Bex." I try and continue but she places a finger against my lips.

"It's crazy really. Just before Dan twisted everything, I was going to tell you that despite all the crazy and the shit I have going on, there was a part of me that felt like I should be here with you."

I try and interrupt again but she won't move her finger from my lips and I know I won't make her. I won't ever make the girl of sun do anything ever again, not if she doesn't want to.

"But the thing is, now I know I need to go. Not just because I need to run away for myself but because I need to run for your sake too. I've caused too much hurt to the people that I love, and I don't want you to be hurt anymore, you deserve more than that."

My eyes widen. Did she just say she loved me?

I am considering how to remove her finger from my mouth without using force when the door opens and Bex's Dad storms in, his face like thunder. He marches right into my space, his face a mask of rage. "I thought I told you to look after her."

For a moment I'm completely speechless, his words bring it home to me. I did promise to look after her. Just like months before I promised to look after another girl and I failed her too. The wind knocks out of my lungs.

"Dad," Bex screams and leaps herself forward getting in between us. And still she is trying to protect another. Protecting me.

When I was young I used to think it would be cool to be a dad. As I never had one I thought it would be a great adventure in the unknown. Watching his face as he looks at Bex I know I probably won't ever go down that road.

He holds a hand out to Bex but lets it drop. "Bex?"

"Daddy," her voice is so small my stomach actually pinches at the sound. "Don't be angry."

He leans down and with tender hands grasps her in his arms. "Baby, I am never going to be cross with you. This wasn't your fault, mum and Josh's Aunt have filled me in."

"I'm sorry, Mr. Walters, I promised to bring her home safe, and I didn't." What an understatement.

He kisses Bex on the top of her head and turns to me. He gives his head a slow shake like he is trying to order the thoughts in his brain. I know how he feels. I have been trying to do the same since I lifted Bex off the sand in Newquay. I don't expect his forgiveness.

He turns his attention back to Bex. "Baby, I am going out and won't be back until tomorrow. I am sure Josh will stay with you and your mum and sister are right here too."

"Where are you going?"

"I am going to go and put a few things right. I'll see you tomorrow okay?"

"No," her voice is at the pitch of breaking and it makes my eyes swim with stinging tears.

Bex's dad lets out a chuckle. "Don't panic, there has been enough fisty cuffs for today, I am just going to see an old friend. I'm sorry I have to go today."

Bex links her fingers through mine, running her finger along the new scabs forming over my knuckles, every time I flex my hands the buggers re-split.

Bex gives her dad a small nod. "Okay."

"Okay."

We watch him walk away. As he gets to the door he turns and his gaze finds mine. "You did bring her home safe, Josh. Thank you." His words make a massive lump of emotion well in my chest.

After the door has closed Bex turns to me. "I'm so tired, Josh."

"Me too."

"Will you stay?"

"You wouldn't be able to make me leave."

Rebecca

Only in the Night

This time when I wake in a panic and the scream starts to build I feel Joshua's arms link around me pulling me back into his embrace. After Dad left on his mystery adventure I had been knocked by a wave of tiredness. It had been all I could do to lay down without falling asleep first.

Now I can feel Joshua, my beautiful boy made out of the moon and sea, sleeping next to me, his breath fluttering over my skin, and I know that I need to tell him everything. I want to feel like for the first time in my life one person knows every single bit of me. He knows so many of my dark secrets, my regrets. He knows my body like no one probably ever will again and as I feel his chest rise steadily next to mine I know I want to bare my soul to him. I want to tell him everything.

"Josh?" I nudge him and edge over, kissing my lips against the soft spot of skin below his ear.

Automatically his arms tighten around me. "Are you okay?"

"Josh, I need to tell you something." I tug his hand

so he sits up next to me. He rubs the sleep off his face with the palm of the other hand.

He doesn't say anything. He just sits there silently and expectantly.

"You know how you think I've told you all my darkest secrets, all the stuff about Emily and about that party,"

"Yes." He reaches a finger to trace along the edge of my collarbone. His touch is as light as a feather and despite the events of last night it makes me want him to hold me firmer and tighter. I don't move towards him though.

"I never knew how to tell the one secret that really defines me."

"Bex," he interrupts. "I haven't told you everything either."

"I know." I entwine my fingers with his. "But I can't hold mine inside any longer." And then I open my mouth and my terrible truth, my terrible past starts to blurt out of my lips and there is no way I will be able to stop and hold it in again. "Remember you asked me if I had a friend to stand by me during the trouble after Emily was bullied, and I told you I did but I pushed her too far."

"Yes." Josh's thumb circles a pattern on the palm of my hand.

"When I say I pushed her to far, what I really meant." A massive solid lump blocks my throat like a lump of dry clay. "What I really meant was that she died. And she died because of me."

The circling stops on my palm and Josh's spine

straightens a little. He does not say a word, so I bumble to fill the space.

"It's the one label I was given that I've never been able to deny, because the truth is I can't remember what happened the night of the accident. The only thing I remember is her shouting at me and screaming at me. "Will you just learn to behave, Rebecca, and get in the damn car.""

"What?" Josh's voice is nothing more than a low whisper.

"We were out, and I was well, behaving like my normal self. I'd drunk too much, smoked too much and then, well then I don't really remember. The next thing I knew was that I woke up in the car, but there was something not right with it, the glass was bending, there was this terrible screeching noise and then just a huge bang." I take a deep breath as I remember the terrible noise and the way it echoed in my mind for weeks after.

"It was the counsellor my parents took me to who explained that the noise I could hear but couldn't forget was the sound of my own scream."

Josh is as still as an unmoving rock and it feels like a palpable silence is deepening between us.

Again I try and fill the emptiness between us with words. Useless words.

"I couldn't remember anything about the accident, I still can't, but everyone blamed me. I guess it wasn't hard to blame the girl who was known for being dangerous. Rumours spread that I must have tried to get out of the car, I must have grabbed the wheel, a lot of whispers and a lot of people calling me a killer."

A gasp escapes Joshua's lips. "Are you, Bex? Is that what you think you are?"

That's the question of my existence. Am I a killer, or am I a girl in the wrong place at the wrong time. I know what my head tells me and it isn't what my heart wants to hear.

"I don't know. I just started to believe it, I was drunk, and I was out of control. I must have really pissed her off if she was shouting at me like that. If I couldn't recall that small fragment then maybe I would believe my innocence but the truth is I don't know."

"What happened then?"

"Nothing. Everyone made stuff up about me, and I sat in my room hiding from the world. The only thing the police could tell me was that the car was travelling at fifty three miles an hour."

Joshua's fingers reach for the bangles and run over them one by one. "Fifty three?"

I hang my head low and let tears run down my face. In six months I've never talked about that night. Even during the counselling sessions I just sat silent ready to bear the prison sentence I served on myself for being in some way to blame for my friends death.

"So I never forget." The words creep out of my soul along with tears of anguish.

Slowly Joshua leans over the bed and slides his arms around me. Then he gently pulls me onto his lap, smoothing my hair and planting kisses on my damp cheek.

My crying gets harder and harder until it feels like I am going to swim away in sea water.

"You've just got to let it go, Bex." He whispers into my ear, and with his words he gently lays me down on the bed and fits himself around me, cocooning me in the safety of his arms.

TWO DAYS TO GO

Bridge Cottage
St Agnes
Cornwall

25th August 2013

Dear Ellie,

There I've said your name. All these months, and those four short letters have been so hard to say. Ellie, my friend.
Last night I told Josh all about you. For the first time ever I told someone about that night, but I still couldn't get my words to express just what I feel at losing you.
I wish you could tell me what happened. I wish you could tell me what made you/us get in the car?

Josh was gone when I woke up, but do you know what? It didn't hurt that bad because I think now I have finally acknowledged losing you, anyone else leaving me is just a fraction of the pain I felt over you.
My final truth was too much for Josh. I always knew it would be. The whole village will know about me soon enough,

but it's okay. It's time for me to move on. Just me and you. I will never leave you behind.

Still missing you.
B.
xx

Rebecca

Breakfast

Josh is gone when I wake.

I knew he would be. I never expected it to be anything else. No one wants to find out the girl they have spent two weeks with could have caused the death of another.

It's okay. I'm going to start packing and then I will be gone.

Another chapter in my life to leave behind me.

The Day to End Days

As I step out of the shower I can hear the chattering of loud voices. Whatever is going on down there my mum sounds very over excited. I catch a note of another voice which I don't recognise through the floor boards. For a split second fear grips hold of me and I wonder if it is the police coming to talk about the other night. I don't know what else they would want me to say, I told them every detail I could remember yesterday.

I quickly rough dry my hair and run a comb through it before counting on my bangles and pulling on a pair of cotton shorts along with a vest-top and flip-flops. The bangles don't feel as heavy as they did yesterday, nor the day before that, nor the day before that.

As I head out the door I notice a fold of paper dropped in the corner of the room. Scooping it up and unfolding it I stare as a mammoth lump fills my throat, this lump aches like my heart. It's a piece of paper with the local police constabulary's header on it. On the paper Joshua has drawn a field of sunflowers with their faces turning towards a sun that you can't see. In a scrawl at the bottom he has written, 'It's time to say goodbye.'

Shit. That's it. He's saying goodbye to me. A deep twist of pain settles somewhere in my chest. . With heavy feet I walk down the stairs ready to tell my parents and Emily that as they have probably guessed I will be leaving. As I swing into the kitchen I plan to tell them that I will leave tomorrow. I don't want to stay here any longer than I need to.

My feet screech to a halt. Sitting at the table is someone who I never expected to see again. I glance at my mum who is bright red in the face and my dad who is running a rueful hand through his hair.

"What is *he* doing here?" My voice is so loud it reverberates off the kitchen cupboards. I can't keep it down. I want to be sick. It's too much. I want to reach for Joshua but he left me and told me goodbye.

Sitting at the kitchen table is Drew my Dads former

bosses son. The guy who four weeks ago ruined what little semblance of a life I had. I appreciate now it wasn't that much to ruin, not compared to what I have here, but he did it all the same. Not just what happened that night at the party, but also with all the shit on Facebook afterwards.

Drew looks so out of place in this kitchen it is almost laughable. His designer clothes and spiky hair could not be more wrong. Drew in turn flicks his eyes over me, first taking in the red marks I have on show under my vest-top and then the bangles I have lining my wrist. "Hi Rebecca." He shifts uncomfortably.

"Dad what have you done?" I demand.

Dad looks at me his gaze defiant. "Rebecca, I won't have my daughter thinking that she deserves to be treated a certain way, the wrong way. And I won't have her thinking that things are her fault when they're not." He coughs a bit. "I hope you can forgive your old man for trying to do the right thing and save his daughter."

I stare at my dad for a long moment while his words swim around my brain. "Save his daughter." He was trying to save me? My parents were trying to save me when they dragged me away to the back of beyond?

"You were trying to save me? I thought you were trying to save Emily?" My heart thuds in my chest as the understanding makes the last two weeks take on a very different meaning.

Dad laughs, one short sharp burst. "Why would we need to save Emily when she has an older sister who kicks the shit out of anyone who comes near her?"

I never thought about it like that.

"Well that's true." I shrug offhandedly, not wanting anyone to see just how much my dad's words mean to me. Specifically not wanting Drew to see. I can show my parents later. I *will* show my parents later. When I leave I will make sure they know I am trying to *save* them, not run away from them.

"Bex. Let Drew speak. He might be able to help you get some closure."

I turn to Drew. I can't even bring myself to make eye contact.

"Want to take a walk?" He asks scraping the chair back across the kitchen tiles and standing.

No not really but I walk towards and through the kitchen door without a glance in his direction.

"Pretty town," he acknowledges as he sparks up a cigarette. The smell makes my stomach roll. I never realised how much I hated it before.

"Yeah it is."

"It looks like it agrees with you, you look amazing. Well, apart from the bruises." His eyes flick over me quickly, but then slide away again.

We are heading into towards the town and I start to feel nervous that we may bump into Joshua or, well, anyone. "Yeah, well I am learning the hard way to be very careful about who to trust." I stop my feet and turn to face him. "What are you doing here, Drew? Did my Dad come and get you?"

He blows a lungful of smoke away.

"Yeah, he turned up yesterday and told me that

something bad had happened to you, and he was hoping I could help you. Thing is, I have been trying to contact you for ages, I just didn't know how. I know you have changed your number and as you are not on Facebook anymore I didn't know how to get hold of you."

"Funny that, me not being on Facebook," I say.

He reaches his hand out, the one not holding a cigarette, and holds my fingers. It feels wrong. So wrong. I pull my fingers away and jam them into the pocket of my shorts.

"So are you Bex now?"

I stop and stare.

"No, I am Rebecca to you."

"Guess I deserve that."

Silence clings to the air around us. What was my Dad thinking? A feeling of anger starts to burn in my chest. This is the guy that made my family move two hundred and fifty miles and now he is standing in front of me pretending that he's been trying to contact me, smoking a cigarette that stinks, in a town that I now consider to be home?

The burn of anger flares into a full out rage. Not the rage of London Bex, but a new rage, one that I can control.

"I don't know why you are here, and I don't know why my dad bought you here."

"I wanted to apologise about what happened at my party."

I can't speak. It's all too much.

"And I wanted to apologise about what happened

afterwards, on Facebook and with your dad losing his job. I should have stood up for him and told everyone what really happened. That he was just trying to protect you."

"Why didn't you?" I don't even have the energy to shout. I just keep remembering my Dad's face when he marched in and saw me there.

"The truth is I kind of always wanted to mean more to you than some guy you would get drunk with and do silly things with. I took advantage of you, I know that. It's not something I'm proud of."

"I fucking hate you."

"I know. I deserve it. I hated the fact that you only got close to me when you were drunk." I cringe with his words. "I always knew the only time you considered me was when you went to that destructive place you always held inside." The switch. He means my switch.

"What so you didn't want anyone knowing that the only way you could get a girl to go down on you was when they were paralytic." My words are cruel but I don't care. Drew doesn't flinch though. He takes my anger.

"I just didn't want anyone thinking I may have forced you to do worse than what your dad saw."

I think back to the wet sand the other night and what someone did nearly force on me. I hate Drew for what he did but I know he is not a depraved pervert.

"Okay. Are we done now, I've got some packing to do."

"No, I need to tell you something else." My stomach pinches with his words. I can think of nothing he can tell me that will make any of this better.

"I know you always believe what people say about you. And I know after Ellie died you just believed what people said. That it was your fault."

"What are you talking about?"

"It wasn't your fault Rebecca."

"You don't even know what you are talking about." Now my voice starts to rise. It gets louder and louder with every word I say. "It's the only thing that I can remember, that it was my fault. She screamed it at me. "Can't you just learn to behave, Rebecca and get in the damn car."

A slow tear slides its way down Drew's face. "No Rebecca, that's not what she said at all. She said." He hesitates but then takes a large intake of air. "She said. "Can't I just behave? Rebecca get in the damn car. We've got to go."

My head spins with his words.

"You're wrong."

"No Rebecca. I heard as clear as day because she was shouting about me. Ellie had been begging me to give her a line of coke."

My shock at his words knows no bounds. Ellie hated drugs. "What?"

Drew holds his hand up to stop me. "Wait let me finish. I think she was trying to impress me. I knew it wasn't her scene and I thought she would regret it so instead I gave her a crushed up tranquilizer. I didn't expect it to effect her. But it did. Half an hour later she was crazy. You didn't see any of this because you were off dancing across the room. Ellie tried to make a move on me, she was all over me but I kept trying to push her away. I didn't want to hurt her feelings."

"But?" I can't believe I am hearing any of this.

"I think she saw me glance over at you. You were dancing with some guy that I hated and I wanted to come and interrupt but I couldn't get to you. Ellie saw me look at you and put two and two together. That was it, she went crazy. That's when she shouted at you. "Why can't I just learn to behave? Get in the damn car Rebecca." You didn't do anything Rebecca. It was never your fault. I never expected her to drive that fast or flip her car on a roundabout. I don't know what I expected but her dying and you suffering was never it."

My breath comes out in ragged drags of air, each one stings my throat as I gasp for oxygen. My mind freefalls as I absorb the things I have heard.

The truth. My truth.

"I am so sorry Rebecca," he says as he leans back and looks at me through his red tear filled eyes.

I take a deep breath and focus my stinging eyes on the past standing in front of me.

"So am I sorry, Drew. I need you to go now and you need to know that when I come back to London I won't want to see you. I need to leave everything behind me. I can't walk around with it hanging over my heart anymore."

"I know." He stands an awkward distance away

from me.

"I am sorry you have come so far." My voice cracks a little.

"It's okay, I would have gone further just to tell you the truth. I'm going to go to the police as well. I should have done it months ago. I know I didn't give her anything illegal but I should own up to what I did, for her families sake more than anything else."

I don't have anything else to say, I don't really know what to begin to think. I want to get home and write Ellie a strongly worded letter that she is crazy, and silly and just dumb but then at the same time I wish I could hug her so tight in my arms I would never have to let her go.

Walking away from Drew I head back to the cottage no longer sure what I am doing.

I slam back through the front door and look about the deserted cottage. That's strange? They must be hiding from the wrath of Bex.

"Guys, you can come out of hiding now!" I call and then stand waiting for them to appear. I know they will not be far.

Mum comes through first and bursts straight into tears the moment she sees me, "Bex, Bex," she croons as she puts her arms around me, "My baby." She sobs some more.

I can see Emily hovering by the door.

"Come here, Midge," I call motioning for her to join us before I start to cry again.

The relief of Drew's words wash over me.

I didn't make my friend drive a car because she was

angry, or because I was getting into trouble as always.

Over and over again I think the words.

I am not a label.

"I'm so sorry," I snivel into mum's neck.

"Shh, baby. I'm sorry too. Sorry you've gone through so much and we haven't been able to help at all." She steps back wiping snot up her wrist.

"Where's Dad?" I ask when he does not follow them into the kitchen.

"He's gone for a walk, he needed to clear his head," Mum tells me.

"I'm going to go and find him," I say stepping back and pushing my clammy wet hair out of my face.

"No need, Bex, I am here." He walks into the kitchen and towards me. As he gets close he stops short and hands me an envelope.

"What's this?"

"Your leaving present."

I rip the seal and glance inside. There is a train ticket and a very fat wad of bank notes. I slip the ticket out and glance at the destination. London Paddington.

"What?" I start to ask but I don't get to finish. Dad steps towards me and grabs me into a vice tight hug. He squeezes and squeezes until I am not sure if I can hold my breath any longer.

Placing his hands firmly on my shoulders he stoops so he can look me directly in the eye.

"I want you to go back and I want you to show those fuckers that you've done nothing wrong and then I want you to live the life that you want and not the one we want you to have."

Okay firstly my dad just said the F'word. Secondly *what*? He wants me to move back to London? I thought they wanted me to stay here.

"What?"

He stares at me long and hard.

"The worst lesson your mum and I could ever have taught you was that running away was the best option. We should have taught you to stand your ground and fight instead."

"I don't know what to say." And I don't. I really really don't.

"Sleep on it. The ticket is for the day after tomorrow. Figured we could have two last days together before you leave home for good."

"What makes you sure I will go, what if I want to stay and fight here?"

"Maybe, I guess that depends on what you are still running from."

"I need to sleep on it." I turn and face Emily. "What do you think?"

"I think if you leave you will still be running, and that you may never stop."

I look at her for a long moment. I can't say she is wrong.

"If I stay, can I live here with you?"

Dad looks at Mum before turning back to me. "We charge thirty quid a week rent."

I laugh, a crazy sound.

"I need to go and tell Joshua the real truth."

"Go get him," they shout as I dash back out of the

kitchen door. As I pace down the lane towards the village I hope I am not too late.

Joshua

The Good Bye

I left Bex before the dawn light had started to creep into her room. All night I held her trying to make sense of what she had told me and what it meant for me and for us.

She thought I was going to hate her for the final secret she revealed. She could not have been more wrong. It made me feel something I was never expecting. It made me feel relief.

Finally I am strong enough to say my goodbye.

It was just starting to get light when I got to the grave yard. I walked straight up to it and lay on the cool stone the picture I have been keeping in my wallet for six months. The last picture I drew before Bex woke me up and helped me start living again.

Then I started to shout, filling the dawn air with my repressed anger. Six months I've been blaming myself for my girlfriends death, all because she wanted to go home one night and I refused to drive her. Six months of internal hatred all because my girlfriend couldn't wait half an hour for me, and instead got into a car with some drunk holiday makers. Six months of hating all visitors coming to my home town.

It wasn't me.

It wasn't even them.

It was her choice.

I stood there laughing in the end as the weight lifted from my chest.

Bex did that. She freed me. By sharing her darkest deepest moment she set me free from the dark prison holding me in place.

Finally, finished with my ranting and emotionally battered I went to the beach. I have been sitting here ever since watching the sun come up waiting for Faye. She will meet me when she is ready.

As soon as Faye sits down next to me on the sand I can see she has been crying. In complete silence we watch the surf roll in and out for what feels like hours. I hold her hand in mine and she rests her head on my shoulder as we both take our time to focus on what I need to do.

"You are going to forgive me for letting her go aren't you?" I ask her when I can bear the silence no more. I tighten my fingers around hers and stare at the back of her hand that is so similar to the one that I used to know. For months it hurt seeing the similarity between them, the straight edge of their noses, the curve of their shoulders. Now I worry that if I don't see Faye I may forget, or that the brightness of the sun that is Bex will erase all memory.

Faye reads my thoughts. "You're not going to forget, Josh, you've just got to forgive yourself. That night was not your fault. You know Mum and Dad never blamed you. I never blamed you. You are the only one who has ever felt that you were at fault." Faye leans into me and rests her head against my shoulder. "We've all been waiting for you, Josh, we all want you to be happy again."

I squint out to sea and think over her words.

"I know I wasn't to blame." I say finally.

Faye makes a strange sobbing noise. "No. It was my dumb assed sister being a stubborn cow. Come on Josh, no one could ever stop Aimee from doing anything, even you. She would have got in that car regardless."

I chuckle a little bit, my shoulder brushing against Faye's. "She really was very stubborn."

I smile as good memories crash into my mind. Memories I haven't allowed myself to think of for the longest time.

Silence falls between us as we both sit with our personal thoughts.

"Did you bring it?" I ask eventually.

"Yeah." She motions to her bag.

"And your mum and dad they were okay?"

"Josh, this goodbye is yours. Mum and Dad have said theirs, and so have I." she looks up at me and gives me a small watery smile. "I spoke to them this morning, they are relieved you are finally ready and they're going to be thinking about you." She glances at her watch. "Right about now."

I give a sigh and lean forward reaching into her bag. I pull out the box which is much smaller than I remember.

"We're going for a last swim together," I tell Faye motioning towards the box in my hand.

She doesn't answer and glancing down I see that she has her fists over her eyes and her shoulders are heaving. I don't stop to comfort her. I grab my board and stride for the sea. I can't look back and I won't.

I paddle out, as far as I can until the sea is dark, cold and smooth beneath me. The waves are still crashing on the shore but I am far enough out that I am not even rocked by their movement. The sun glimmers off the water's reflection and I wait for something. I am not sure what. A sign maybe.

My throat tightens and I know I am just waiting to say the word. The only word I have left to say. Loosening the lid on the box I sprinkle the contents onto the water. Swirling my hand in the water I watch the murky mixture as it floats away from me. I try to catch some back, panic taking hold of me as the words burn in my throat and I fail to keep any of the dusty water close to me.

"Bye." Is all I manage and my chest makes an almighty heave. I throw the box in after the ash and it sinks straight down. I watch the ripples increase until they wave under my board. The sun burns into my shoulders and I absorb some of its strength.

It's my final goodbye and now it's done it feels good. The last six months of having the words in my head but unable to express them evaporates. As I turn my board towards the beach I know that it's the best goodbye I will probably ever have.

Back on the shore I leave the board and walk

towards Faye who is standing with her toes in the water. She slides her hands around my waist and leans her head on my shoulder and I pull her in close.

"Better?" she asks.

I lean down and look her in the eyes before kissing the tip of her nose.

"Better." I confirm. "I think I need to go home." I tell her.

She looks at me. "Where is home, Josh?"

I smile. "It's not where, it's whom!" I laugh and it feels good. It feels like months and months of hurt have been lifted from my chest.

"You go tiger," she smiles. "Love you, Josh."

"Love you, Faye."

I am just turning back around to get my board when I catch a glimpse of sunshine up by the top of the beach. It's not the sun in the sky it is my sun and she is watching me with a look of confusion on her face.

"Bex wait," I call but she doesn't. She starts to run and for some stupid unforgivable reason my feet don't run after her, they root in the sand instead.

ONE DAY TO GO

Bridge Cottage
St Agnes
Cornwall

26th August 2013

Dear Ellie,
You daft, dappy ridiculously dead, mare! WHAT WERE YOU THINKING? That's me shouting by the way.
Ellie what were you thinking? My stupid, crazy, beautiful best friend who stuck by my through everything. What were you thinking? Drugs? Driving under the influence? Even me, Dangerous Rebecca Walters would never do that! And now I am living without you. You're not here to tell me what the hell to do.
You've broken my heart. All these months and I've been blaming myself for the way I feel and for losing you.
I want to be cross with you, but really I just want to hold you and laugh with you one last time.
I want to stay so bad but I don't think I should. Not because of me, not because of Em or my family. But because of Josh. It's ironic really when I thought he was going to be my reason to stay.

Gone

Yesterday I saw him at the beach, hugging Faye. He looked ripped apart. I stood for ages watching them before he knew I was there. I think he thought about chasing me, but he didn't.

I didn't want to come home either so I went for a wander around town, trying to sort out a new plan of action. I found my way to the local church, I'd never been there before.

I kept thinking of you, and your service and how I wished I'd gone but didn't because I was too scared of what people would say. Supposedly everyone wore pink to your funeral. Did you know that? I laughed when they told me. Okay, okay, I was on anti-depressants. I just thought you would have found it funny because you hated pink with a vengeance. You always said it made you want to puke. Maybe I was the only person who knew that.

Anyway, I saw lots of purple flowers on a grave so I wandered over there. It was for a young woman not much older than us. "Beloved daughter, twin and friend." I thought it was so sad and it made me think of you so badly it hurt to breathe. I know you were never a twin, but you were like a sister to me and sometimes that's stronger than blood.

I was turning to leave when I saw a square of paper on the ground. I shouldn't have picked it up, it's rude I know. I just thought maybe it had fluttered down from somewhere and I could return it to its rightful location.

It was a picture of Faye. Well at first I thought it was a picture of Faye. Then I saw the writing on the bottom, "Goodbye," written in Josh's hand. Suddenly it clicked, the pictures in the art shop, the pictures that Josh took down just the other day. The other day when we had sex for the first and only time. The pictures that looked like Faye but wasn't her. Her twin. The girl that Josh was in love with. The girl who died six months ago. The girl who he has never told me about because he must be so in love with her he can't even talk about it.

The reason why Dan told me on the sand the other night that Josh would hate me.

The reason Josh left me and told me goodbye.

Aimee. That was the name on the grave. It cut into my heart, not with jealousy, rather with pain at her loss. Loss for Josh and Faye. Loss for her family.

It made me feel my loss of you all over again.

I've got to leave Ellie. I'm going this afternoon.

Will you come with me? I'm scared to go by myself.

B.xx

Rebecca

Packing

Yesterday I came home from trying to find Josh and all the truths I found instead, and I told my family that I was still going to leave. I said I was going to leave today instead of tomorrow, then I came upstairs, finished my packing, before sitting on my bed waiting for Josh to turn up and tell me I had read the situation all wrong.

He didn't.

Eventually I went downstairs, sat on the sofa with my family and enjoyed our first family evening in a long time. Shame it had to be our last one for a while,

Now I am waiting for the time to tick past. That's all I have left to do.

Joshua

Breakfast

I left her by herself last night. In truth I didn't know what to say. I know why she ran. I completely get it. She almost can't help herself. But I knew that if I turned up I would end up telling her everything and it felt too raw, especially after what Faye and I did yesterday.

I'm going to go and find her now. Tell her to stop bloody running, or if she has to run maybe she could just slow down to a jog so I can keep up with her. I'm going to tell her everything, and in doing so I hope that she will finally trust me and tell me everything too. It's the only way we can be together. I'm just hoping she still wants to be with me.

"Hey mate." It's Andrew, I haven't seen him since the disastrous night out. He's tried to call but I dodged it. "Shit you look terrible."

"Yeah, Dan looked worse."

"He left, have you heard?"

I give a heartless chuckle. "Yeah I thought he would."

"Was what Faye told me true, did he attack Bex?"

"Does Faye ever lie? Well to you?"

"What do you mean?"

"Oh, Andrew, give it up. Go and ask her bloody out, it's stupid you guys messing about all these years."

"I don't know what you are talking about?" He laughs though and so do I.

"So will you?"

"Maybe. Where are you going anyway?"

"I'm going to find Bex. I need to tell her she is an idiot as well."

Andrew shifts a bit. "That's why I was trying to find you."

"What?" For a moment I think that she has left without saying anything.

"I saw her in town with some guy. She was crying, then he was crying, then he kissed her on the cheek and then he walked away."

"Jesus are you the neighbourhood watch?"

"No. I just thought you should know. They looked close, you know."

"What time was this?"

"I don't know, about eleven maybe, definitely before lunch."

This was before she saw me at the beach. "Okay, mate, thanks."

Instead of walking up the lane to the cottage I head to the shop instead. Aunt May is there with her classical music blaring. "I told you this crap frightens away customers." I shout over the din.

"No it doesn't." She points behind me and I turn

to find Emily standing there.

"What's up, midge?"

"You." She pokes a finger in my chest and glares at me.

"What did I do?"

"Where the hell were you yesterday? Bex had the most profound moment ever and you weren't bloody there. Yesterday she told us she was going to stay and asked Mum and Dad if she could live with us. Today she has her bags by the door. What the hell are you doing?"

I process her words quickly. Well I pick out. Profound. Staying. Leaving.

"Why is she leaving?"

"I think she is trying to prove a point."

"What bloody point?"

"That she is not going to run anymore."

"But isn't she?"

"Well duh." An angry flower fairy is a scary thing. "Fix it, Josh. Before you lose her forever and we do too."

She marches out of the shop the bell trilling behind her.

Aunt May is watching. "How are you going to fix it, Josh?"

"I don't know. What if she resents me for not being brave enough, what if she wants to forget everything that's happened here?"

"I have no idea what you are talking about, you sound like a lunatic. Fix it!"

Dashing straight out the door I chase after Em.

"Wait." I grab at her arm to make her stop. "Help me?"

Emily tilts her head thoughtfully to the side. "Maybe."

"Please."

"She's on the one o clock train. Is that something you can work with?"

"I can try."

"Try."

I will. Even if it means telling every secret I have ever kept hidden.

Rebecca

The Pain of Goodbye

It's been one of those days. One of those no breathing days.

This morning Em came and sat on my bed. I was wrapping all my letters to Ellie in an elastic band.

"You know you're going to be okay." I assured her.

She laughed. "You know you're going to be okay."

"Josh will watch out for you, so will Faye. You will be better off without me here. Everyone will be talking about what happened with Dan. It's best that I'm not here for a while."

Em shrugged a little. "I'll just tell them to fuck off. Just like my sister would."

I clutched my hands to my ears, "Oh my God, my poor baby sister has a potty mouth."

"Well you know, hang around someone long enough." She trailed off and giggled. All I could think was *Please don't let her be like me.*

As if she was reading my mind she grabbed my hand. "Bex, you are the bravest most inspiring person I know."

"What because I'm running away?"

"No. What you did back then, to those girls. They'd been tormenting me for months, every day beating me down. You faced off to them in one afternoon. That will inspire me forever."

Her words made tears sting behind my eyes.

"Okay just don't ever break someone's head against a sink."

"I will try very hard not to."

Now we are at the station and mum is fidgeting and dad is hugging me and straightening my outfit up. My outfit is one to be proud of. Jeans – normal ones. A T-shirt. And a hoodie. Who'd have thought it?

"Okay guys, leave it off." I shrug away from them all. "I'll see you guys at Christmas. Try not to make my room into an office."

Mum bursts into tears. Dad grimaces his lips wobbling. Emily jumps up and down. "It's going to be my art studio mum's already promised me.

"Fu..." I start.

"Rebecca!" Dad warns.

"Okay I'm going." And with that I swing myself up onto the carriage and make my way down the aisle.

I've timed it just right. The conductor's whistle blows as soon as I am in my seat. No long painful moments waving out of the window for this girl.

Out of the station I start to relax. I didn't say goodbye to Joshua but I did leave a note for him at home just in case he turned up looking for me. In it I said I was sorry. Sorry for not being able to share my secrets sooner. And thank you. Just thank you for liking me, loving me maybe, despite everything that I am.

"Sorry." A voice calls above me.

Shit. A massive canvas bag hits the back of my head as some tall guy with a skin head lifts it into the overhead compartment.

"Watch it." I grouch slumping back down into my seat.

To my complete horror the dude with the lethal bag sits in the seat next to mine. Way too close for comfort. I move myself even closer to the window. I am now firmly wedged.

"Long trip to London."

For the love of God.

"Mm."

"I've got a great story about the girl that I'm in love with, if you're interested."

I glance up into the window and see the reflection of the stranger sitting next to me.

"What happened to the dreadlocks?" I can see myself grinning in the window.

"Well they were always a lifestyle choice."

I chuckle as Josh repeats one of the first things he ever said to me.

Josh stretches his legs onto the seat in front of him. "Now about that girl I'm in love with. It's a bit of a messy story. Are you ready?"

I take a deep breath. "Are you talking about Aimee?"

Josh looks into me, the greens swimming with an emotion I don't yet understand. "No, Bex. I'm talking about you."

Swiftly he swoops forward his lips catching hold of mine, and I smile against his mouth.

It's just as well this is a long train journey this is a story I want to hear.

I settle down in the seat and rest my head against Joshua's shoulder. Ready to hear his story.

My story.

Our story.

GONE

It's ironic really that I finish telling Bex my story, the story of us, on the beach where I first caught sight of her.

As we sat together on the train I told her everything. Everything. I told her all about Aimee the girl who broke my heart and left me stranded for six months. And then she told me everything she knew. It would never have made a difference to me what she found out from that guy from London. But it helps her and that matters. I always knew I was in love with her. I knew it that first day at Crantock beach when she came up from the bottom of the ocean clutching her nose and covered in wet sand. I knew it a couple of nights ago when I rescued her on a different beach from something far worse than cleared sinuses.

Bex. It's just her. She makes me live, and she makes me breathe. She makes me want to be something.

We climbed off the train at Paddington and looked at each other before Bex started laughing.

"What?" I asked.

"I don't know what I'm doing here?" she said doubling up as giggles racked her frame.

"What do you mean, you don't know what you are doing here? I followed you?"

"I just want to go home." Her laughter quickly turned to tears.

"Where is home Bex."

"It's not where. It's who."

And that was it. The moment I finally knew.

Home.

We got on the next train home, turning up tired, and travel worn but happy at six this morning.

Bex's mum burst into tears the moment she saw us enter the kitchen. Walking into Bridge Cottage it felt like I was coming home too.

Home with her.

Finally settled back into the place where we belong we wander down to the beach, our hands entwined tightly like neither of us ever plan to let go.

I've helped her dig a huge hole in the sand, right down by the tide. Slowly together we have dropped her bangles deep in the ground, Bex counting them off with her eyes shut as she always has, but with each one landing on the sand we know she will never wear them again. As we cover them Bex looks up at me, her ambers bright with tears but a smile across her lips.

"The past is gone Josh."

After we have sealed the past in its sandy grave I pick up a splinter of driftwood and doodle my last picture in the sand.

Butterflies with one word etched into the ground next to them.

"Gone."

The girl who was meant to be gone is staying by my side. The only place I ever want her to be.

~The End~

ABOUT THE AUTHOR

Anna Bloom is a contemporary romance writer who likes to write about life and how it actually happens. Whilst working on The Uni Files and other projects, she is a wife and mother, and also spends time working in a local school where she reads books to the children whether they like it or not.

Contact the Author @;
annabloomwrites@gmail.com
On twitter @annabloombooks
Or visit the website www.annabloomwrites.com for updates on the series and other projects.

Also from Anna Bloom:
The Uni Files: Book I
THE ART OF LETTING GO

For Lilah McCannon, life has taken a bit of a wrong turn. Engaged to a guy she is not in love with and stuck in a job with her tyrannical father as her boss, life has definitely not turned out the way she expected.

At twenty-five years old, Lilah knows that she has a

simple choice: live the life she has created or change it.

Enrolling on a course at the local University, Lilah sets out with some clear rules to ensure her success at being a grown-up. No alcohol, no cigarettes, no boys, and no going home. But the last thing she anticipates is meeting Ben Chambers, the lead singer of a local band. With Ben, it's instant, it's hot, and it's deep, but when Ben is offered the opportunity of a lifetime and it looks like his future lies on a different path to hers, Lilah has some heart-rending decisions to make.

With the academic year slipping by too quickly, Lilah faces a barrage of new challenges. Will she ever make it up the library stairs without having a heart attack? Can she handle a day on campus without drinking vodka? Will she ever manage to read a history book without falling asleep? Most of all, will she be able to make the ultimate sacrifice and learn The Art of Letting Go?

Available now from Amazon

The Uni Files: Book Two
THE ART OF KEEPING FAITH

Lilah and Ben. They are meant to be a thing.

Well, they were. The best thing ever. That was until Lilah decided to teach herself a lesson and let go of Ben since she's learned The Art of Letting Go.

Now it's a new academic year, and Lilah has it all to play for and it all to lose as she battles scary lecturers, evil PR girls, and her own inability to make the right decision at the right time.

Life has moved on for Lilah and her friends, and life off campus is more complicated than any of them would have guessed. As the reality of being second-year students sets in and the study starts to build up, cracks begin to appear in the very fabric of their friendships. There is a chance that none of them are going to complete Year Two in one piece.

Facing down her worst enemy, herself, Lilah has to try and change her own past mistakes when she realizes that the only way she is going to get the future she wants is if she manages to learn The Art of Keeping Faith in herself.

The Art of Keeping Faith is the second year in The Uni File Series and continues Lilah McCannon's diary as she searches for love, tries to find and earn trust, and ultimately discovers who she is really meant to be.

Sometimes the only way to meet your future is to face your past.

Available now on Amazon

Made in the USA
Charleston, SC
12 May 2016